STU JONES

THROUGH THE FURY
TO THE DAWN

Through the Fury to the Dawn

Copyright © 2011 by Stu Jones

ISBN:1-4637-2402-0

ISBN-13: 978-1-4637-2402-3

LCCN: 2011912403

CreateSpace, North Charleston, SC

To my son Macsen:

May you honor the Lord your God with every breath,

and may you always stand against the plans of the wicked.

I love you.

NEVER. GIVE. UP.

PREFACE

I'd like to start by saying that I fully understand this novel is a bastard child of sorts. The simple nature of its duality will likely render it impotent in the scope of any sort of marketing. Many who will accept the rough nature of the book will be turned off by the Christian themes; conversely, those inspired by the Christian themes will be turned away by the rough and uncompromising depictions of real life—especially life after the death of society.

There are many great Christian writers out there, but as I read their books over the years I found that only the smallest few dared to depict the realities of sin in their stories. To my dismay, much of the more difficult subject matter was always candy-coated and processed into something that just never felt real. Not that I desired to wallow in evil, but I felt it necessary to experience it to truly understand the desperate nature of the situation. With each encounter with the candy-coated version of sin, evil, and conflict, I found that the subsequent triumph of the protagonist was often so terribly muted that the entire gravity of the situation was lost.

To these writers' credit, I understand that some of this is also the fault of the Christian publishing industry, which largely believes that Christian themes and elements that depict gruesome violence, sex, or harsh language cannot be married to each other. Writers who would try to mix the two would never make it to publication.

Regardless of what I personally believe as a Christian, the world is still drowned in sin and the evil of human nature. We can see it all around us. Reality does not cease to be reality just because of what we believe; violence and oppression do not cease to be horrific and brutal just because of an individual's beliefs or inability to accept it as real. It is for this reason that I have included these elements in my story.

Because of this, it is likely that many who disagree with me will put this book down after reading this preface. But I promise you this: you will not be taken to dark places without being shown the light at the end of the tunnel, for the light is so much more beautiful after you have experienced true darkness. After all, this is a story of faith, conviction, and redemption.

This is my challenge to you, Christian or not: take heart and begin this journey. There are some things that are worth the desperate path one must tread to get there.

iv

ACKNOWLEDGMENTS

First and foremost, I want to thank God for everything that He has so generously blessed me with, for His ultimate sacrifice, and His patience and love for me as a most imperfect man.

My most amazing, loving, supportive wife, who has been my greatest cheerleader over the last five years; she is more than I deserve. Without her suggestions and corrections, this work would have never been completed.

My parents, who dared me to dream and never told me what my dreams should be.

My father and my brother-in-law, David, for their necessary and thoughtful criticism. The changes that were made have enhanced this work beyond measure.

Authors Douglas Preston and Lincoln Child, whose tireless devotion to the art of excellent fiction inspired me to read for pleasure. Their masterful style and endless creativity imprinted upon me in more ways than one and inspired me to write. They are truly two of the best writers in publication today.

Christian author James Byron Huggins, who showed me through his work that it's not wrong for Christian fiction to be dark, gritty, and sometimes quite violent. He was kind enough to offer his help and guidance through some of the writing and publication process. He, too, is a master of his craft.

Also, I would be remiss if I did not extend a heartfelt thank you to my editor Karen Harris. Her expertise and knowledge was indispensible, and her additions and suggestions on how to improve the work and bring it all together were absolutely invaluable.

Thank you to all of my family, friends, and others who have contributed to this work in numerous ways, either by support or guidance. You all are greatly loved and appreciated.

APRIL 16, 2012.

ST. MICHAEL'S HOSPITAL
KNOXVILLE, TENNESSEE

Kane Lorusso sat at a forty-five degree angle in his hospital bed, staring numbly at the small TV in the upper corner of his room. He gazed sleepily at the screen, which hour after hour had shown an endless display of human depravity. They had medicated him heavily. His head felt as if it were the size of a school bus and weighed as much, and he had a strange prickly sensation in the center of his chest.

He watched as a pretty blonde reporter spoke to an overseas correspondent, gesturing dramatically. For the last few months, the big news had been an emerging alliance of the People's Republic of Iraq, Afghanistan, Palestine, Pakistan, Iran, Turkey, and several other Middle Eastern and Eastern European countries. The media stated that the alliance had formed to foster increased commerce, trade, and security in the Middle East—but most of the world knew otherwise.

In addition, an emerging radical Islamic organization calling itself the Sword of Destiny had surpassed al-Qaida and Hezbollah to become the premier terrorist entity—and the most violent in recent history. Supposedly, the Sword had been receiving funding, aid, and support from several of these allied countries and had already claimed responsibility for the rash of suicide and car bombings that had occurred in the United

States and Western Europe over the past year. What they had been most recognized for, however, was their followers' signature "sanctions." In Washington DC, London, Hamburg, and Madrid, during horrific active shooter situations, the terrorists had gunned down innocents in schools, malls, and train stations; they had also taken hostages, promising their release if authorities cooperated. They then waited for the media and emergency responders to arrive to complete the scene, at which time they savagely decapitated their captives, mostly women and children, and tossed the heads out for the media to broadcast before taking their own lives and those of the emergency responders in an explosion of fire and debris.

This is what happens to the infidel.

This odd union had the Western world living in real fear. Everyone but the peppy blonde on the TV in front of him—no fear there, as long as she got her airtime. He wondered if she was really that good-looking in person, or if it was a fabrication just like everything else in the news today.

A young black woman came in and picked up his chart, and he clicked the TV off.

"You can leave it on, it won't bother me," she said, as she made notes on his chart.

"It bothers me," he said with a weak smile. "I was finished anyway."

"Can I get you anything?"

Kane shook his head. The ID badge clipped to the woman's shirt showed the name Monica under her picture, and Kane tried to decide if she looked like a Monica. The nurse had tended to him for the majority of the day, and he had been grateful for her attention to his needs. Some people were just gifted with karmic care.

"Alright, Mr. Lorusso, lie back for me and just rest for a few moments. I've got to check your vitals."

"Okay."

He laid his head back on the pillow and closed his eyes, listening to the symphony of electronics around him. He had been in the hospital since early afternoon and had yet to hear anything definitive from the doctor who had seen him.

It had all started with the government takeover of the health-care industry. It had only been a few years since the invasion of the government into private health care and what had it done? Taken every human being to the same level of care, regardless of what they put into the system. Young and old; rich and poor; hardworking citizen, illegal alien or welfare gobbling, drugged-up scumbag—none of it really mattered anymore. Many doctors' offices had closed down, the hospitals were overwhelmed with patients—overfilled, with beds in every hallway—the insurance companies had capsized, and your average Joe was unable to get the basic care his family needed from the failing system. People were now paying thousands of dollars under the table just to get good primary care. It was a nightmare.

Kane lamented the fact that he was even in the hospital at all. It had taken him two hours just to be admitted as an emergency, priority patient.

An ambulance had brought him in after he had collapsed at the office. It had been a strange, surreal moment, now frozen in his memory. Like every other normal day, he went about his business until suddenly he had been struck so hard by a blast of pain that, as he crumpled to the floor, he had probed his chest with his fingers for a gunshot wound, as if he had just been gunned down by some hidden assassin. The pain had been overwhelming, and a single thought had occupied his mind all the way to the hospital: *Heart attack at thirty-two years old. I can't believe it.*

The blood pressure cuff tightened around his bicep, and he unconsciously flexed his hand. As long as he could remember he had been active and fit, playing sports and running. At 5' 10" and 195 pounds, Kane had a very solid muscular structure—though not without a little extra rubber around the midsection. He had a loving wife, two beautiful children, and a nice place outside the city. At the Green County Sheriff's Office, Kane had applied himself diligently and had recently been assigned to a new multijurisdictional organized crime task force in cooperation with the FBI. Things were going pretty well...until this.

No way, not a heart attack, there's just no way.

He had eaten a lot of junk on duty, and he knew his blood pressure had indicated pre-hypertension for a couple of years now, but this was unbelievable.

"You're holding your breath."

"Bwhaaahtt," Kane said, exhaling.

"Your breath, you were holding it. How are you feeling?"

"Half dead...and the rest is dying," Kane said morosely.

"Well, you look alright to me," Monica said with a warm smile. "Your vitals are stable, if a little weak. I'll go check with Dr. Atwood to see if there are any updates." She winked as she whisked out of the room.

☆ ☆ ☆

Dr. Chip Rosen, the head of surgery, was a handsome man in his mid-forties with dark hair and perfect teeth. He was tall and slim, with an air of athleticism and understated confidence. He stood in the fluorescently lit hallway, staring blankly at the wall. It simply was not looking good for Mrs. Beasley. Dr. Rosen had been in surgery so long that his hands, arms, and shoulders had begun to cramp. She wasn't fixable. "Acute gravity attack" was the morbid slang that had been thrown around by the staff upon bringing her in.

The poor woman had been brought in after a particularly nasty fall from her balcony that resulted in serious blunt trauma to her head, neck, chest, and abdomen when she hit a railing at the end of her descent. They had used all the resources and expertise at their disposal, yet Mrs. Beasley would still die. Quite simply, too much had ruptured upon impact. This happened much more frequently than people liked to believe, and as much as he genuinely cared about the welfare of his patients, some of them just brought about their own demise.

In truth, "accident" was a term used by most people to avoid blame. Although true accidents did occur, many people the hospital saw each day were victims of their own stupidity or carelessness. Even victims of violent crime—shootings, stabbings, and rapes—were frequently in the wrong place at the wrong time or around the wrong people by their own choosing. This woman, fifty years old and healthy as a horse, just stepped off her third-story balcony while watering her geraniums. It was all so unnecessary.

"Dr. Rosen, would you please take a look at this patient for me?"

Rosen shook himself back to reality and focused on the young nurse whose ID badge read "Monica Watkins."

"Uh...what?"

"He was being seen by Dr. Atwood, who took off unexpectedly for unknown reasons. Then we got hammered with patients, and we've been trying to catch up ever since. Somehow, this guy got passed over in all of it," Monica said hesitantly.

"Atwood. Uh huh, yeah...uh, Miss Watkins, I..." he paused. "This is not how this works. I'm the head of surgery, and I'm very busy. I can't be looking into the ER's patients...right? You understand?"

"Yes, Doctor, I understand, but he's been here since late this afternoon for chest pains and is still waiting on some semblance of a concrete diagnosis. There's no one else."

"What about Gibson or Martinez? I've got a woman dying on the table in there," he said with some irritation.

"There *is* no one else, Doctor. Gibson quit last week and Martinez...I don't know where Dr. Martinez is, she's not answering any of her pages."

Rosen sighed heavily, the weight of responsibility showing on his brow. "You're telling me we don't have any available doctors in the ER."

The nurse slowly nodded her head.

What is happening to this country?

Dr. Rosen rolled his shoulders forward and took the file from the young nurse.

"I'll take a stab at it, I guess," he said, opening the file and looking it over for a moment. "Heart attack has been ruled out?"

"Not completely, but it's unlikely," the nurse replied. "He's had a reduced pulse and low heart rate. Dr. Atwood also had put him on alpha-beta blockers for his heart rate and BP, as well as pain meds."

Rosen glanced through the file. Atwood was incompetent, and nobody liked working with him. And why were no other available doctors available? This was seriously unbelievable. Rosen felt like dropping the file on the ground and walking out right now. He glanced up at the double doors to his left; the glowing green exit sign above beckoned him to go, to leave the oppressive, crowded hospital. The desire to just walk out coursed angrily like one too many poisonous cocktails through his blood. He'd had enough. He felt as though with each passing day he was scrambling more and more madly for his job, his identity as it deteriorated under him. He looked again at the young nurse's face and caught a slight glimpse of the same desperation he felt in his own heart. It was a fatal disease, and it had infected almost everyone in the medical sector. Hope lost.

The bloodsucking government.

"Has anyone looked at his labs?" he asked.

"No, not yet; nobody would," she replied.

"Right. Well, have all his x-rays, ultrasound results, and everything else sent up to my office. An angi was ordered?"

"Yeah. It's all done."

"Alright, send that up as well, and I'll take a look at it when I get a moment."

The young nurse reached out and touched the sleeve of his shirt. "Thank you, Doctor," she said flashing a quick smile as she turned and headed back down the corridor. Rosen sighed. Maybe there *was* still hope.

"Dr. Rosen," a young surgeon covered in blood said, sticking his head out the door. "Mrs. Beasley just passed away on the table."

"Alright. I'll go down and talk to her husband," Rosen said.

The poor man had been a wreck, sobbing and carrying on in the lobby only two hours earlier. Rosen looked down at the hands that had failed to save Mrs. Beasley. He hated this part of the job. The helplessness of having to break it to someone that his or her most cherished loved one was gone and never coming back...it was relentless. People reacted in so many different ways—sitting as still as statues in a stone trance, screaming, even thrashing and writing on the floor of the waiting room as the devastating news was delivered.

Third shift was coming on soon and would hopefully bring with it some doctors to help regain control of the chaos. He'd make it quick with Mr. Beasley, take a look at the heart patient, and go home to soak his feet while drinking a double scotch on the rocks with a twist.

✧ ✧ ✧

Kane stirred restlessly in a shallow, dreamless, chemical sleep, his eyes bouncing horizontally as if reading the backs of his eyelids. A petite brunette woman slid quietly into the room, trying to avoid the congregation of electronics and tubes. Slowly, she took a seat to the left of the bed and reached out, running her fingers down the outside of the motionless arm to Kane's hand. Kane's eyes flashed open wide, disoriented, then settled on the woman and relaxed.

"Suz," Kane said weakly and smiled.

"Hey, sweetie. How ya feelin'?" Susan said in a Southern accent, sweet as honey.

"Like a train wreck." He smiled again. "Didn't think your husband would break down on you so soon, did ya?"

"You were broken on day one," she said, smiling back, and then briefly a worried look passed across her face. "The doctor, has he told you what's wrong yet?"

"No, baby, you know how it's been with the health-care system. They're drowning in patients. I think the doctor who saw me even left the hospital for some reason."

"*What?*" Susan exclaimed, standing in irritation. "You can't be serious!" she said, almost shouting.

"Honey, please."

"Kane," she said, lowering her voice. "My *only* husband, the man I love and depend on, is in the hospital for some terrible unknown illness, and you want me to be satisfied with them doing nothing?"

"I'm sure they're working on it." He patted her hand softly. "The nurse has been really nice and accommodating, so please...I'm not supposed to get excited."

Kane watched as those big green eyes that he had looked deeply into so many times began to tear up. After six years of marriage, he still loved this woman more than the air in his lungs.

"I just love you so much!" Susan gasped, choking back a sob. "Your babies and I need you, we need you so much. I'm just so worried, and they won't even tell us what's going on."

"I know, but it'll be okay. Look, if it were that bad, they would have prioritized me higher, right?" He smiled weakly and squeezed her hand. "Speaking of my babies, where are they?"

"I left them at your parents' house."

"Good. Dad and Mom made it home okay?"

"Yeah, your mom was dealing with everything pretty well, considering—"

A handsome doctor, skinny and dark-haired, stepped into the room, interrupting the conversation. "Hello," he said, extending his hand to Susan. "I'm Chip Rosen, head of surgery."

"Surgery?" Susan replied.

"What is it, Doc?" Kane said taking the offered hand. "So how bad is it?"

"Well." Rosen paused. "Let me first apologize for the delay. We have been flooded in the ER today, so I'm very sorry to have kept you waiting."

Susan nodded, her face softening slightly.

"So, about your condition: it's not good, but it's not all bad either," Rosen managed with a tired smile.

Kane shifted uncomfortably.

"Mr. Lorusso," Rosen continued, "you are suffering from a pretty rare occurrence for a man your age. Your heart is failing. The *why* is what we don't know yet. The scans we ran show some sort of deterioration in the wall of the heart muscle itself. The muscle is dying. Somehow the walls of the aortic valve appear to be eroding, but I'm afraid that I can't give you a better explanation until we do some more tests."

Kane's expression remained blank, but his body felt as if it weighed a million tons.

"Is there anything we can do?" Susan asked, her voice trembling.

"Yes, and that is the good news," Rosen said with a genuine smile. "Right now we should be able to temporarily medicate the condition, although it appears that if the heart muscle continues to deteriorate, you will need a transplant."

"Dr. Rosen," Kane spoke weakly, "what does this mean for me?"

Rosen's expression became more serious. "Kane, you don't seem to be the kind of guy who likes surprises, so I'm going to give it to you straight. The walls of your heart have become very thin and weak. Until you get a donor heart, any activity that puts strain on your heart could cause a massive hemorrhage that would result in heart failure—and ultimately death. The real problem is, with the current lack of funding for organ donation and an unbearably long waiting list, finding you a matching donor quickly could be very difficult."

Susan began to cry quietly.

Dr. Rosen, seeing Kane's expression, added quickly, "Look, a friend of mine is a wizard with the heart. His name is Charles Fisk, and he's in Miami. He's in private practice...so...it'll be expensive, and you might need to keep it hush-hush, but he's worth every penny. Most people have to wait months to even get an appointment with him, but if you'd like, I'll arrange for you to meet with him as soon as possible, okay?"

Kane nodded. Susan squeezed his hand.

"Until then, I'm going to put you on some additional medications for the pain, and we're going to do a few more tests. Please understand that this is not my specialty, so I'll speak with Dr. Fisk as soon as possible to get a real professional's opinion." Rosen flashed another genuine smile. "You're going to be alright. I'll have the nurse come in and get you all set up."

"Okay," Kane said. "Thank you."

After a slight bow, Dr. Rosen was gone.

The silence in the room had an eternal depth as the clock slowly ticked away what was left of Kane's life. Susan was staring at him with a penetrating gaze, tears running down her face.

He couldn't look at her. He had failed her, his children, and anyone who had ever needed him or counted on him. Failed. What was left? Just the shallow husk of a dead man. He balled his fists, his shock and dismay turning to anger. God had done this to him; this was God's jab at him for having not been to church since high school.

"Kane?" Susan reached out for his arm, but Kane pulled away, putting his hands to his face and exhaling loudly through clinched teeth.

"Kane, let me pray for you—for us."

"Susan, is that really necessary right now? I'm dying, okay? Can you just let me have some peace so I can deal with this?" Kane said sharply.

Susan withdrew quietly and sat back, her eyes pinched closed in what he knew to be the start of a silent prayer.

That's it. Pray to the God who disabled me.

He sank back and stared at the ceiling. Why even try? They wouldn't find a donor for him. That was a hopeless endeavor, to be sure. People were having a hard time getting basic care. How was he going to find a healthy heart?

He would never play ball with his son, never see his daughter get married, and never again go with his wife on a romantic adventure. Thrown out by his employer, counted as disabled, and incapable of anything, he would be relegated to a life of bed rest, inactivity, and pity.

His life was over, and as he pondered it, the sour feeling of an early death began to creep over him from the inside out.

APRIL 20th, 2012.

THE UNIVERSITY OF TENNESSEE RECREATION CENTER
KNOXVILLE, TENNESSEE

It was different. They had altered it again. Molly Stevens slapped her hands together a few times, creating a small chalky white cloud around her. As she squatted to test the fit and feel of the climbing harness, her chin-length blonde hair scattered across her forehead and nose. It wasn't the harness she normally used and trusted, but it would do. She turned and smiled at Chad, the wall manager.

"What's up, Chad?"

"Hey, Molly. You all set?"

"I think so. Can you check me?"

After a quick visual sweep, followed by a bit of tugging and a check of her carabineer and figure eight, he turned to her and gave her the thumbs up.

"You're good. You going to do the possum today?"

Molly squinted slightly. "Possum?"

"Yeah." Chad stepped to the right and pointed to another face of the climbing wall that showed a ninety-degree overhanging ledge near the top. "It's brutal."

Molly gazed upward at the possum ledge. "Did you make it?"

Chad shook his head slowly and smiled. "Not yet. Like I said, it's brutal."

After a moment, Molly shrugged. "Sure, I'll give it a shot," she said as she moved to the possum climb.

Chad stepped in behind her and clipped into her rope as her safety. "Let's do it then," he said, smiling.

But Molly wasn't smiling. A look of determination began to set in over her features as she approached the wall.

"Belay on. Climb when ready," came Chad's voice from behind her.

"Climbing."

"Climb on."

Molly stepped forward, with her right foot mating the sticky surface of her climbing shoes with the first foothold. Slowly, deliberately, she stepped up and pulled herself onto the wall. Moving carefully, eyes roaming, each fingerhold and toehold precisely planned—this was the reason she loved climbing. Molly was a runner by trade, cross-country long distance to be exact, and it showed in her slim, hard muscular figure. Though she spent most of her exercise time running and training with the cross-country team, climbing was her escape, her opportunity to "exit" for just a little while. Something about the raw physicality of it, the absolute physical focus, allowed her to rest and relax her mind. Sometimes she just needed time to not think.

She moved to the left, scanning as she bumped her right foot to where her left had been on the purchase below her and hugged herself close to the wall made of multiplex board. The idea, she reminded herself, was to keep her hips under her and not hang away from the wall to reduce fatigue as she progressed.

"How we doing?" came Chad's voice just below her.

"Doing good," Molly said, breathing out.

"Right on. Twenty-five feet down, Fifty to go."

As Molly moved—methodical, slothlike in her steady precision—the walls of her mind began to clear, and the cares and worries that had accumulated over the course of the last nineteen years slowly began to evaporate: her credit card bill of school expenses that she couldn't pay; a recent argument with her boyfriend, Eric; that huge biology test tomorrow; and her overprotective grandmother, who called continuously.

This was exactly the type of activity that frightened her grandmother. It was the height and the potential for disaster as she hung there, supported only by a single rope. Her grandmother had treated her like a baby ever since she had known her. This practice had only intensified when she had assumed guardianship over the adventurous girl at a young age. Molly loved her grandmother, but the woman was incessant. Always warning, always behind her, saying that she shouldn't be doing whatever it was she was doing. Much to her grandmother's dismay, Molly had never been one to conduct tea parties or play dress-up. She had been cut from the same fabric as her father—adventurous, driven, focused, willing to take the risks necessary to succeed.

Molly's arms shuddered with just the slightest tremor of weariness as she blew a puff of air from her mouth to get the hair out of her face and began to calculate her next move. She shook her head as if to clear it.

"Not the time to think of grandmother," she mumbled under her breath. "Focus."

"Good job, Molly, keep it up. You're not too far now. You've got some good ones just up and to your right," Chad said as he took the slack out of her rope.

She was in the zone now, moving, melting into the wall. The holds were becoming more and more difficult, but she had already ascended to just under the ninety-degree overhang.

"Okay, you're going have to dyno to get it. It's a tough grab, but if you look back, you'll see the bucket," Chad called from below her.

"Yeah, I'm dialed in," she said, breathing hard, tilting her head back to look at the underside of the ledge. It was smooth except for the solid bulbous hold, or "bucket," just at the bottom of the slope, where the wall jutted back in. It was a good hold, but she was not going to reach it unless she jumped out and back into open space to get it. That was the only way.

Molly dipped her fingers into her chalk bag and rubbed them together as she leaned back ever so slowly, allowing her body to drift away from the wall. She switched hands and chalked the other. Bending her knees and turning her head back to look at the hold, she paused momentarily before launching herself backward and singlehandedly snagging the hold with a grunt.

"Alright, Molly! Nice grab!"

Breathing heavily, she dead hung by her right arm, suspended sixty feet off the ground. She paused for a moment, allowing the ligaments of her arm to absorb the stress and weight.

Never give up. Fall before you give up.

Molly took a deep breath, and with a burst of energy, she pulled up with her arm and kicked her left leg up to another hold on the edge. Straining, her muscles screaming, Molly let out a verbal accompaniment as she pulled and dragged herself up over the forty-five degree slope above the "possum." Snatching a few more holds, she regained her composure, drawing herself back into the wall.

"Awesome!" came the cheer from below her.

Her muscles cramping and shaking from exhaustion, she took the last few holds and slapped the barrier at the top of the wall.

She turned and looked down, flashing a broad, beaming smile that seemed to swallow the rest of her features. She had done it.

Chad pulled her rope tight, allowing her to rest. "Molly, I gotta say, you're the coolest girl I know," he said, smiling back.

"Thanks for the beta, Chad. You're a good morale coach," she said, leaning her weight into the harness. She closed her eyes momentarily and said a quick prayer, thanking God for a body that was healthy and liked to work.

It was going to be a good day after all.

APRIL 20TH, 2012.

GREEN COUNTY, TENNESSEE

Kane's house was nestled in the western end of Green County, about a twenty-mile drive east of Knoxville. It was a beautiful place, 12.7 acres of Bermuda grass, oaks, and pine trees, with the peak of Crenshaw Mountain visible from the front porch. His refurbished country home was two stories tall, not large but still roomy, with a cozy cedar sitting room and stone fireplace. It had belonged to his grandparents, and Kane and his father had worked hard to get it into shape, making some welcome additions. Kane had grown up in Tennessee. What was a state of hillbillies and rednecks to a lot of people was home to him. The people that branded the Southeast this way truly misunderstood it. It was a place of rolling mountains, quiet streams, and humid summer stillness. It spoke to his soul. He had always loved it there.

He lay in his bed, looking out upon the yard as it faded into dusk, a crisp breeze blowing in on him from the cracked window. In a moment of frustration, he had gotten up and left the hospital. Regardless of what they promised, they weren't going to be able to do anything for him anyway. Why did he have to stay and be uncomfortable in that wretched hospital bed if they couldn't help him? So he had gotten up, removed his tubes and IV, shrugged off the coercive nurses, and left.

Forget them, they had nothing for him anyway. They could bill him.

When Susan found out about his little stunt, she had come apart and insisted upon having a nurse at the house to look after him. He had adamantly refused, knowing all the while it would do no good. Susan called it "in-home care," but Kane called it something else, because he knew what it really was. Hospice. The very same thing prescribed to those who were terminal.

The telephone was trilling softly in the kitchen. Kane looked back to the TV and turned it up a few bars to hear the anchor for the nightly news speaking excitedly.

"This just in. I'm getting reports that we now have video of the latest of a string of what the Sword of Destiny is calling their proclamations to the West. The Secretary of Defense in a statement earlier said that they had upgraded the terror alert to orange and that these proclamations were blatant terrorist threats aimed at the United States and her Allies. Here's what The Sword had to say in the most recent video.

The anchor folded his hands as the news cut to a taped address featuring a masked speaker in a dimly lit room holding a machete, which he waved dramatically. The video quality was so bad that Kane squinted to decipher the image.

"We believe that Fate has intervened in the lives of the downtrodden." The man spoke in a strong Middle Eastern accent. "We have allied with our brothers in suffering in other nations to stand against the Jewish and Christian pigs who so arrogantly push their ways upon the rest of the world. We have risen to represent our people and our ways, and to strike fear into the fat hearts of the nonbelievers who dictate. There will be no negotiations; this is your only warning: if you do not agree to submit yourselves to our supremacy and authority, we will strike with terrible force at the core of your nations. Do not believe that we are incapable of this—"

Kane clicked the TV off. How come they always had to come off all tough, videotaping the message from down in a cave in the middle of nowhere, as though the attitude somehow added legitimacy to their message and trumped the fact that they were hiding in a cave? The world was all screwed up, and Kane was beginning to realize that he couldn't care less about the world and its problems.

Kane's father rapped on the door to his room and entered with a slight limp, a memento he retained from the war in Vietnam. At sixty-four years old, he was a tall man with sturdy forearms and a beer belly. As he hobbled in, Kane observed him and was thankful that his father had been around for him for so long. He had stayed with Kane while Susan and the kids were in Florida, arranging a place to stay and communicating with Dr. Fisk.

"Susan should be calling any second." His father said motioning with the cordless phone. "How are ya feeling, buddy?"

"I'm okay, I guess."

"Your sister called all the way from California while you were sleeping. I told her you're recovering well." His dad smiled. "Why the long face?"

"I don't know, I just...I dunno."

"Everything happens for a reason, Kane. If I hadn't been shot in 'Nam..."

"I know, you'd have never met mom in the hospital."

"The love of my life," his father said and smiled.

"Thanks, Dad," Kane said, "For everything."

"No problem. Hey, so you know, I put the stuff you had on that list in the kitchen in the storm bunker."

"Dad, you didn't have to do that;, that list has been sitting out there for weeks."

"Yeah, well, I'd go crazy around here all day with nothing to keep me busy, so it's done."

"Well, I appreciate it, then."

The phone rang.

"You bet. I'll be in the living room if you need me," his father said as he handed Kane the phone and turned toward the door. "Oh, and early tomorrow morning I was going to go fishing for a while. I should be back by lunch."

"Okay, Dad," Kane said, as he raised the phone to his ear and hit the talk button. "Susan?"

"Hey," she said.

"Honey, I'm sorry about the other day at the hospital," Kane blurted out. "I was reeling from the news about my condition, and I was a little harsh with what I said. I'm sorry if it frustrated you—me leaving and all. I just couldn't take it anymore."

"It's okay, baby. I know that you've had a lot on you. I just wanted to help. But thanks anyway for apologizing."

She was being gracious to him, but Kane knew he had wounded her. Her faith as a Christian was very important to her.

"I just wanted you to know..." Kane started.

"Kane, it's alright. Listen, I've got two hungry three-year-olds here, so let me tell you what the deal is. I met with Dr. Fisk today, and he said because Dr. Rosen referred you, he's going to work you in the day after tomorrow. I've arranged for you to be flown down tomorrow afternoon, and your inital surgery to help stabilize you will be the following morning. Your dad has offered to take you and the nurse to the airport."

"Jeez," Kane said. "Is it really necessary for the nurse to accompany me? I'm fine. I'll take it easy."

The nurse, Charlene, was an extremely obese woman in her fifties. Kane was sure that she had good intentions, but she treated him as if there was nothing he was able to do for himself. She had even offered, to the point of insistence, on giving him a sponge bath, which he had defiantly refused.

"She will be along just as a safety precaution during your trip," Susan said.

"Well, that's fantastic. I'm looking forward to being treated like a child some more."

Susan was quiet for a minute. Kane couldn't tell if she was worried, tired, or just preoccupied.

"Just take care of yourself and don't stress getting down here. We'll have it all taken care of." She paused. "I've got two munchkins who want to say hi to Daddy."

"Put them on." Kane smiled unconsciously. From the day the twins were born, Kane had been absolutely, completely in love with them. They were the most wonderful things that had ever happened to him, and he cherished them as such.

"*Daaadyyy!*" they chimed together on the other end.

"Hey, how are my monkeys?" he said, beaming.

"We wuv you, Daddy," said Rachael.

"I love you both sooo much."

"Mommy is taking us to get ice cweam," Michael said.

"After dinner," he could hear Susan say.

"Aftur dinnur," Michael repeated.

"Yummy! Eat some for me, and be good for Mommy," Kane said.

"Yeth thur," they said.

"Daddy?" Rachael started. "Are you feewing bettur yet?"

Kane felt his eyes tear up and his throat turn to stone. He could read them like open books. Michael had taken it well, knowing that his daddy was strong and would be okay. Rachael, on the other hand, had been wary and, upon seeing him in the hospital bed, had burst into tears. The thought of them having to grow up with him sickly, and eventually not there, was like a cold knife in his heart. He cleared his throat.

"Daddy's feeling better today, sweet pea, don't you worry. I'll see you tomorrow."

Again in chorus, "We wuv you, Daddy!"

"I love you both sooo much!"

"Hey," Susan said taking the phone.

"Hey."

"Are you all set?" she asked. "Don't worry about anything. I'll see you tomorrow."

"Susan I just need to tell you something." He paused "The other day, I...I love you, and I respect your faith, it's just not my faith."

"I know, Kane," she said calmly. "Faith isn't something to fear. When you're ready, I think you will welcome it. I love you." With that, she hung up.

Kane laid his head back and set the phone on the nightstand. This Christianity thing was new with them, and Kane was still unaccustomed to it. Susan had begun going to church after the twins had their second birthday. She had said that God had "opened her eyes to Him" and wanted to talk to him about it. Kane, having turned his back on the Christianity that his mother had smothered him with in his youth, quickly and simply stopped all that nonsense before it got started. Faith and God—and faith in God—did not have any place in his life. He believed in what he could put his hands on; in science, mathematics, and history; in the mental fortitude of a prepared and dedicated individual; and in the power of the human spirit in the face of adversity. He had seen enough pain, death, sorrow, and misery to make him wonder why a good God would do these things to good people. And now this.

He had noticed a change in Susan, though not one that had taken a negative toll on their relationship. If anything, she had been more loving, giving, and content. It was as if the gaggle of problems and cares that the world pitched upon her were not so heavy, because in her heart, the more important issues had already been dealt with.

Kane sighed, shut his eyes, and listened as Charlene lumbered down the hall and knocked on the door.

"Come in."

"Time for your nightly medications!" she said in a singsong fashion that irritated him.

"Thanks," muttered Kane.

He was just so tired, and no matter how much rest he got, he continued to feel the energy flowing from him like blood gushing from an open wound. He was broken inside, and no one—neither man nor God—could save him now.

"Here we go," he said out loud to Charlene as he tossed the pills back and toasted her sarcastically with his water glass. "To the beginning of the end."

APRIL 20TH, 2012.

THE UNIVERSITY OF TENNESSEE
KNOXVILLE, TENNESSEE

Jenny Velasquez walked through the front door of the dormitory with a dramatic womanly swagger, the way only a shapely nineteen-year-old in a dance uniform could. Her raven-black hair swished slightly back and forth with the confident rhythm of her hips. She smiled smugly and checked her fingernails, flicking her hair out of her face as she entered and rode the musky elevator to the fourth floor of Davis Hall, the largest coed freshman dorm on campus. With a "bing," the tarnished elevator doors separated, and Jenny stepped into the fluorescent hall, walking briskly past several guys who made no attempt to conceal that they were studying every inch of her tall, firm frame.

Stopping at room 431, she opened her small handbag and pulled out a bronze key attached to a sorority keychain. Inserting it into the lock with a "snick," she turned the knob and entered her room.

"Oh, hey, Molly. I didn't think you'd be here," she said, tossing her bag onto her twin bed as she began shrugging out of her dance outfit.

"Yeah, just relaxing a little." Molly brushed a small wisp of short blonde hair out of her face and peered over the top of her suspense novel at her roommate.

"Did you get the message from your grandma? The one she left on the machine about sending some money for your school expenses?" Jenny asked as she stepped into a pair of worn jeans.

"Yeah, I talked to her this afternoon, thanks."

"Oh, okay. Hey, you don't have plans with Eric tonight?"

"Nope, he's got a big chemistry test tomorrow bright and early."

"You do too, don't you? Chemistry?"

"No, it's biology. I'm not too good with chemistry."

"You're not going to study?"

"Ugh, no, I've had all the studying I can take."

"I hate science," Jenny said, picking up a lightweight black sweater. "I don't know why you take those classes if you don't have to. You're a religion major, for goodness' sake."

"I think it's fascinating, especially the study of the animal kingdom. Insects and their behavior, for example, are so much more complicated than you might think. It's really amazing to analyze it scientifically, but also know that there was a divine Creator behind the orchestration of it all." Molly leaned back in her chair and kicked her feet up on the desk.

"Yeah, well, whatever." Jenny paused. "Hey, you want to go out with us tonight?"

Molly shrugged. "Who's us?"

"Ben and Allen, a couple of guys I don't know, and some of the girls on the dance team. We're going to RJ Mahoney's to get plowed."

Molly made a somewhat disgusted face.

"If you don't have a fake ID, it's no problem, I mean, we can get you whatever you want."

"Yeah, I know. Thanks for the offer and all, but I'm not really a 'go out and get plowed' kind of gal," Molly said with a smile. "You know."

"Yeah, I know, but I keep asking, thinking that you'll loosen up sooner or later," Jenny said, smiling back.

"It's not about loose. I'm loose," Molly said, reclining. "It's just not my thing, that's all. But if you guys need a ride back later or something, give me a call. I'd rather you wake me than drive when you shouldn't."

"Thanks, Molly," Jenny said, opening the door. "You're very thoughtful, you know that? For two people who don't have a whole lot in common, I think we get along famously."

"Yeah, me too. You guys have fun!"

Jenny gave a wink and a little wave as she allowed the heavy door to latch solidly behind her. Molly took a deep breath and leaned back in her comfy chair, shaking her head. Getting plowed was definitely not her idea of a good time. Besides, she was exhausted, and anyway, she had to finish this novel before it turned to dust. Molly leaned her head back and pulled the open book to her face. With eyes half closed, she breathed deeply the musty scent of the binding. It smelled like quiet libraries and busy bookstores and…Dad. Her daddy had read to her every night as a little girl; even when he had been away on business trips, he would call and read to her over the phone before she went to bed. Molly's eye twitched involuntarily. But that was before. That was before he….

A knock came at the door, and Molly sat up sharply in the chair. Closing the book, she stood and crossed the room and, keeping the security latch in place, cracked the door.

"You and your security latch, you're killing me," came the familiar voice through the crack.

They stared at each other for a moment through the cracked door. "Hey, I just wanted to apologize for being kind of a selfish jerk yesterday," Eric said.

"You know, you *were* kind of acting like a selfish jerk yesterday."

"I know. It wasn't a really good day for me. Coach told me that he's putting me on third string. I took it out on you, so, I'm really sorry," he said humbly.

"Apology accepted." She paused as if deliberating on whether to let him in or not. "Hey! Shouldn't you be studying?" She added with a sly smile.

"Yeah, but I couldn't stop thinking about you." He smiled back as he stuck his arm through the crack and pretended to grab at her.

"Better stop your grabbing; don't think I won't shut your arm in this door. I'm still a little mad at you," Molly said playfully as she unlatched the door. "Besides, *you* could be the campus stalker!"

"You've discovered me! But now you will be my next victim!" he said dramatically as he grabbed her in a bear hug that only a football player could give.

"Okay, you're freaking me out now," she said as she pushed her hand firmly against his chest. "You sure you don't need to study anymore?"

"Nah, I can't take any more, seriously. I'm losing my mind looking at that book. And I wanted to come make up."

"Well, alright, I guess you can stay for a while. But just a while, and then you've got to go," she said as she collapsed into him and laid her head against his chest.

"Go?"

"Oh yeah, you've got to go. Hey, we both have big tests tomorrow, starting early."

"Yeah, I guess so."

"And then..." she mumbled.

Eric looked at her quizzically. "And then what?

"I can't tell you. It's a surprise."

"What? Does it have to do with my birthday? Why can't you tell me?"

"*Be*-cause it's a *surprise*, just like I said. You'll just have to wait and see. It's going to be crazy." She smiled and kissed him.

DAY 1

A flash of light blazed on the horizon, and a deep boom sounded in the distance. The house shuddered. Kane sat up slowly and tried to rub the chemical haze from his eyes. He was having trouble focusing.

What the hell?

He strained his ears, hearing only the night sounds and a strange whining that was growing louder. Kane lay back and shut his eyes once again. He was just so tired, maybe the drugs....

The explosive blast wave struck the house with the force of a category 5 hurricane. The windows disintegrated, sending fragments of glass like tiny daggers in all directions, and there was a terrible splintering sound as the roof peeled away like the lid on a sardine can. Kane was thrown, along with everything else in the room, into the far wall. He was projected violently backward and horizontally into the sheet rock, where he lodged for a moment before slamming to the floor. The early morning darkness around the house had been replaced by a fiery nightmarish thing that bore down upon him and seared itself into his consciousness. He raised his head to get his bearings, gulping lava into his lungs, everything burning. The entire rear side of the house was gone.

Gone.

He dug his fingernails into the carpet and began to crawl toward the door, instinct taking over. Out of the corner of his eye, he saw the truck rolling across the yard as his heart hammered in his ears. Getting out, the only primitive thought in his head, drove him through the door and into the hallway. Kane crawled on his belly, forcing the broken, bloody nails of his fingers into the wooden floor, desperately trying to maintain the only point of stability around him. The wind screamed and his body half floated in the hallway, threatening to blow away at any moment. The structure cracked, lurched, and came apart, tilting and causing him to slide backward into the stairwell and tumble down to the first floor. Kane's body smacked brutally against the marble floor of the kitchen and slid into a pile of mangled furniture. He watched as Charlene's severed upper torso slid past him and into a gaping hole in the floor, the frozen look of shock still on her face. Using the cabinetry, he began climbing up toward the rear of the house. The structure was collapsing. He had to get out. The wind had slacked off enough for him to move, but everything was on fire. Kane winced as hot embers landed on his bare back, and blood poured into his eyes, blurring his vision. He could smell his own skin and hair burning. He climbed with determination and was quickly up at the torn open rear of the structure. As Kane moved to jump free of the house, he heard the sharp cry of an animal in distress. He jerked his head back to the left and saw Barney, the family Jack Russell terrier, trapped in a cubby under a flaming support beam. He was injured but alive. Kane cursed loudly and jumped the four feet down to the opposite side of the split. In a surge of adrenalin, he kicked the flaming beam to the side with his bare foot and scooped up Barney, diving through the open wall as the structure crashed down behind him. Kane fell squarely on the crisp, blackened lawn and rolled to the side to protect Barney as fire fell from the sky like a hellish rain, drowning the landscape in an orange glow.

The storm bunker, surely it's fortified enough to withstand anything.

He broke into a dead run, leaping over the ruined trees and dodging flaming debris in his path. In twenty paces he was at the underground bunker. Placing Barney at his feet, he quickly snatched up the axe at the entrance and swung hard at the heavy padlock, ineffectively spinning it around. The keys had been in the house. Kane glanced up into the dark sky above him and saw, through the smoke, hundreds of long white condensation trails littering the sky with a strange patchwork. Condensation trails like a jet would leave—or a missile.

Missiles.

"Barney, we're being *attacked!*" Kane said, as if this exclamation to the dog would elicit a response. Somewhere in the back of Kane's mind, he thought that if Barney answered him, he could then wake up from the worst nightmare recorded in the history of time. More missiles could mean more blast waves; he had to get into the bunker *now*.

Boom! Boom! Booom! Booooom! More flashes, and the explosions sounded too close. Kane raised the axe again—then dropped to his knees, pressing his palms to his chest as his heart wrenched inside him.

"*Aaagggggh!*" came the guttural sound from his throat.

Boom! Boom! *Boom!*

"*Hooo Ggggod!*" he said gritting his teeth. "*My hearrrt—uggggh!*"

Spitting, drooling, his head spun, stars blinking in the blackness. "*Commeonnngaeeduupp!*"

Kane began to stand, the taloned claws of death digging, tearing into his thundering heart. He stood and grabbed the axe, raised it high, and brought it down, dropping his body weight and severing the lock. The rush of wind grew behind him as Kane pulled the thick metal door open and stumbled into the hatch with Barney. He slammed the door back and barred it as he heard the wind of a new blast wave hammer the door. The door creaked hard but held. Kane leaned against the wall, clutching his chest, his lungs heaving. His mind was racing, and the black hole of pain in his chest only grew bigger as it swallowed more of him. He tried to think logically. Was Susan okay? The kids? His folks? Where had the missiles landed? Who had attacked America, and why? Kane tried to answer these and many other terrible questions that rattled around emptily in his head. But the black mustiness of the bunker was warm and comforting, the drugs were still in his system, and a shot of dizziness coursed through his body. Kane slumped back, half lying against the wall, and closed his eyes to the pain while the black rolled over him in waves, welcoming him down...down...down.

✭ ✭ ✭

"Molly, are you ready for the Great Adventure? Now you must listen, trust, and obey. The time has come."

Molly awoke in a panic, her gargled breaths strangling her in the darkness. She tried to sit up, to move, but a great and unyielding force pinned her across the neck as she lay on her back. In a spasm of terror, she lashed out, thrashing with her arms and legs. Opening her mouth wide, she tried to scream, but the weight upon her throat stifled it before it could leave her mouth.

It was a terrible nightmare, but she knew she was in too much pain to be dreaming.

What happened?

She remembered having to usher Eric out, saying goodnight, and going to bed. That was it. No...wait...that wasn't it. Screams. She remembered the screaming inside her building. And shaking, shaking like an earthquake. Screaming and shaking.

Disoriented in the darkness, Molly tried to slow her breathing. Though it was difficult with the pressure on her throat, she was able to breathe, which meant she could slow down and try to think. Taking a few calming breaths, Molly blinked hard and then opened her eyes wide as she searched trying to yield definition to her surroundings. Nothing, nothing could be heard but the faint sound of water splashing and fire crackling.

It was slowly coming back to her. The dormitory had shaken violently, and she had woken up to all the screaming. The lights flickered, and there was a noise like the sound of a train coming by. Fast and violent it came. The building moved and came apart, cracking under her, breaking. She had screamed and cried out, and then she fell. Fell into the black and the dust and the screams.

As she lay, breathing quietly in the dark, she tried to move the different parts of her body. Moving her right arm slowly, she grimaced as she began to pull it out from under something heavy and rough. With a wince, she pulled her arm free and wiggled her fingers. She then began to bend her knees and wiggle her toes. Everything appeared functional, though her body felt mostly like she had been in a car accident.

Moving her arms slowly, she brought her hands up toward her face to feel the object across her throat. It felt heavy and cylindrical, approximately three inches in diameter. Probing to the left and right, it disappeared into something hard and rough, maybe rock, on her left side. On the right side, she reached down slowly and felt its broken-off end, which seemed to be dribbling something. With her hand, she plugged the end and let it flow again.

A water pipe!

The pipe was not large enough to be overly heavy, though it must have felt that way due to its pinning her from the left side. If the pipe was copper, she might be able to bend it enough to get out from under it.

Molly brought her hands back up to her face and gripped the pipe on either side of her jaw, as if preparing for a bench press. Groaning and straining, she began to push, bending the pipe ever so slowly away from her throat. After raising it a couple of inches, Molly turned her head to the left and scooted down on her back to get free of it.

Breathing a sigh of relief, she thanked God quietly for the small improvement. For a moment she touched her throat, gently probing the soreness. Shuffling to the side, she lifted her head toward the end of the pipe that was dribbling. It could be sewer water, for all she knew. She cupped her hands and cautiously tasted a small handful of water from the pipe. It was cool and bitter and had a soothing effect on her throat that was nothing short of marvelous. Ravenously, Molly began to gulp from her cupped hands, the water running across her face.

If the building collapsed, then maybe there are other survivors. Maybe I can call to them.

Molly opened her mouth to call for help.

"Aaahhhhhoooouuuuuugggggggggg!"

She stopped. Terror crawled steadily across her skin at the sound she had involuntarily made.

What is wrong with my voice?

She tried to call out again, to call for help, to let someone know she was down here, that she was trapped.

"Gggguuuuuuuaaaaaauauuuggggggg!

The horrific sound brought forth a burst of tears that snorted and gurgled through her ruined voice.

"Auguuuuu, aguuuuuuu, aaaaauuuuuuuuggggg!"

The moments of tears and despair grew, forming a tightness in her chest that she could not contain as she continued to rub her throat unconsciously.

She couldn't speak. She couldn't speak at all. How would she call for help or let rescue personnel know where she was?

As she lay quietly, wiping the tears from her face, she shut her eyes and spoke the words of Jeremiah 29:11 within the confines of her mind.

For I know the plans I have for you, declares the LORD, plans to prosper you and not to harm you, plans to give you hope and a future.

As Molly lay silently in the darkness, she began to calm down, the consistent and reassuring words of her Heavenly Father restoring her internally. She allowed herself to relax and breathe until the fatigue and stress of her predicament enveloped her, pushing her into a sleep that crept upon her with an oozing, numbing slowness.

✦ ✦ ✦

Molly's eyes fluttered open, and she immediately knew where she was and that she was still confined. But now a few hours had passed, and the day appeared to have dawned, the dimmest fragments of light piercing through the cracks and giving a small amount of definition to her surroundings.

After taking a few seconds to look around, she could tell that she was lying on a concrete slab, confined in a small enclosure of broken concrete and debris about the size of a coffin. This thought alone was unnerving. It struck her as quite amazing that she had not been completely crushed in the collapse of the dorm.

What could have caused this?

Molly's mind wandered through the possible reasons why a perfectly stable building might collapse. It could be any number of things, ranging from a natural disaster to a terrorist attack; even an accidental fire and explosion within the building itself could do it. Whatever the case, she felt confident that the Lord had spared her for a reason. It wouldn't be long before emergency services would begin sifting through the wreckage to find possible survivors.

So she waited, occasionally drinking small handfuls of water from the water pipe and continuing to mentally recite the soothing words of scripture to herself. But as hour faded into hour, she began to question the active efforts of any rescuers.

Why couldn't she hear anyone talking, shouting, sirens, other people's cries for help? Something. Anything. As she lay there, she was overcome with a dreadful sensation.

What if it's bigger than just my building? What if there's been a major disaster?

Molly mulled it over in her mind and decided that she did not want to believe this was the case yet. Whatever it was, she had to get out.

A strange, resilient strength began to well up in her chest. If the light could get in, then she could get out. She screwed up her face in determination. She was going to get out of her concrete prison, one way or another.

Shifting to the left, she eyed her surroundings closely for any space or rift that she could squeeze through. She found it near her feet—a crack merely two feet wide between two jagged concrete surfaces. Anyone of greater size would not be able to make it, but she would. She had to. Wiggling, squeezing through the gap with silent groans, she moved upward. As she scrambled into each new enclosure, she scanned and reassessed each new space, sometimes having to move laterally before she could continue on her journey upward.

It was severely challenging, and as Molly moved, she prayed for strength and success. She pleaded with the Lord and asked him to be faithful in his promise to deliver her. After countless hours of scrambling, scraping, and shimmying; ten broken fingernails; and more cuts and bruises than she wanted to count, Molly shoved a thin slab out of the way and crawled out of the debris and into the open.

Gasping, lungs heaving, she shut her eyes tightly and praised the name of God for lending her his perseverance during her escape from what would have otherwise been her grave. She crouched there among the rubble, slowing her breathing and listening to the wind blowing across the quietest landscape she had ever heard. After a while, the stillness was so complete that it seemed to scream at her.

Still breathing heavily, wearing only what she had slept in—a t-shirt and shorts—she stood and found that she was unable to shut her mouth as she took in the scene of desolation that assaulted her senses. A single thought echoed across the space of her mind.

Oh, dear God...no....

✶ ✶ ✶

Kane leaned up on his elbow and stared into the dark. Calmly, he righted himself and took a moment to try to get his bearings. His current situation had been caused by some sort of attack. The house was gone; he remembered that. And Charlene was dead, too; he had seen her—or part of her—in the kitchen. He had made it to the storm shelter with Barney, whom he could feel curled up against his left thigh. Okay, at least it was a start. His heart burned and radiated, remembering some terrible past event. He should be dead, according to the doctor. Kane hit the indigo button on his watch and got nothing. He did not know the time of the attack, but if he had to guess, he had not been out more than a few hours. It was a lot quieter now outside, save the occasional unidentifiable "whump" in the distance

Scooping Barney up and cradling him in his left arm like a football, he got to his feet and slowly made his way down the stairs and into the main room of the bunker. Barney whimpered, and Kane was reminded of the animal's injuries. He'd look him over good when he got situated. Navigating was tedious in the dark, and he was only able to move and feel a few feet at a time.

The bunker had been originally constructed many years before as a tornado shelter. It was roughly fifteen feet wide by twenty-five feet long and located six feet underground, which accounted for the set of concrete stairs that led up to the surface. Sometime in the late 1960s, his grandparents had reconstructed it as a blast/fallout shelter, during the fear of the Cold War. In addition to having three feet of concrete on all sides, it was also reinforced with steel beams and blast doors. The owner had gone to great lengths to even tap into an underground well for a fresh source of drinking water. Kane had liked the idea of having it so close to the house and had planned on fully stocking it for emergency events. He had been in the process of putting in the necessities when he became ill.

Kane stepped slowly through the darkness, feeling his way as he went. He tripped over piles of equipment and materials that lay stacked against the walls and on several racks of old plywood shelving. "Thanks, Dad," he mumbled to himself as he moved halfway down the room feeling his way along the shelves. After a few clumsy moments of fumbling in the dark, he pulled out a fistful of glow sticks. Removing two from their packages, he snapped and shook them, immediately filling the space with a blue-white light. Kane tossed a stick on each side of the room, then removed a third to activate for personal use. He'd get eight hours of light out of each of them. Pulling an old military blanket of his dad's from the shelf, he scrunched it up on the floor and placed Barney gently on it, rubbing him and whispering a few words of comfort. Kane stood and moved to another shelf on the opposite wall, picking up a small rechargeable crank AM/FM NOAA radio. The National Oceanic and Atmospheric Administration was always a reliable information source. First, he needed to know what was going on out there before he could know what to do next. He cranked the radio for sixty seconds and snapped it on.

A wash of static flooded the concrete room, followed by a broken and terrified male voice over what sounded like chaos erupting in the background.

"Details are unclear at this time, but first reports are saying...and nuclear...but that's unconfirmed as of yet. The...and damage is wide-spread...are dead and dying. My God, we're just getting reports that New York and DC are completely...."

Kane rotated the knob and found a woman speaking quickly in a squeaky voice, the sound of hurried fear in the background.

"The U.S. government has...and retaliated to the full extent of its arsenal. It's believed...something in the air. Biological and chemical agents…widespread…many major population areas…other areas as well…it's confirmed that Washington DC, Atlanta, New York City, and Miami have all been…EMP…massive damage…The National Guard and FEMA have already begun staging and organizing relief and—."

Kane snapped the radio off, clutching it to his chest.

"*Nnnnnnnhhh*," he groaned. "*Nnnooo*, no, no, no. Please, God, not Miami, please!"

He squeezed his eyes tightly, trying to block the tears. "No, they're alive. They're alive, they're okay. It's okay." He reassured himself, wiping his face with the palms of his hands.

Kane snapped the radio back on. He turned the knob the full spectrum but was unable to get a clear signal on any of the previous channels. After five minutes, he snapped it off in frustration.

He stood in the semidarkness of the bunker, full of pain, confusion, and uncertainty. He needed to stay busy. Keeping focused on the needs at hand would help keep morbid thoughts of his family from creeping into his mind.

Kane's back ached with a superficial rawness, and he reached over his shoulder to probe at the swollen, bulbous areas he knew were burned. He'd take care of them in a minute. He shook his head to clear it. First things first. He had to help himself before he could help Susan, Michael, Rachael, his parents, or anyone else. The broadcast had said that nuclear, chemical, and biological weapons had been used. In the concrete bunker, he was pretty safe from the effects of radiation but still vulnerable to chemical and biological weapons. The first thing he had learned in basic WMD training had been to seal himself off.

Kane turned, holding the light stick in his mouth, and grabbed up the roll of clear sheet plastic and duct tape in the corner of the room. Quickly and efficiently he began rolling out long sheets of the plastic and cutting them with a razor from the shelf. It took about thirty minutes to seal the bunker doors with plastic and hang a second vertical layer of plastic at the bottom of the stairs to create a second line of defense. He also took the time to double seal any crevasses or cracks in the concrete. Not perfect, but serviceable.

Satisfied with the improvised protective barriers, he stood for a moment and did a mental inventory of his situation and what he would need. This whole thing could be over in a few hours or days, or it could drag on and he might have to stay down here for a long time. What were immediate necessities? First was water, then food, first aid and medical considerations, sanitation and sterilization, separation from harmful chemicals and diseases outside, comfort and warmth, and information from the outside.

"Okay, so, water," he said out loud. "This old thing better still work."

Kane moved down the center of the room and into the back left corner, where the old rusty pump was located. There was no drain, so what was pumped had to have a place to go. Kane dragged over the old plastic bucket from the far wall and wiped the cobwebs out of it. He had to pump the old handle fifty times or so before a thick brown liquid began oozing from the pipe.

"Come on."

He continued pumping the handle and filled the bucket half full before the water started clearing. When it had cleared to his satisfaction, he quit pumping, jumped up, and grabbed the new red plastic mop bucket his dad had brought in. Kane brought it back to the pump and filled it up. The well water had rust flakes in it from the pipe, but he was grateful he had such a wonderful resource. Hopefully it would not become contaminated from outside influences. Kane carried the bucket by its handle over to Barney. Using his hands he scooped handful after handful out and let Barney lap it up out of his hands. Kane then drank himself, the cold well water cooling a path down his throat and spreading into his belly. It was bitter and tasted like rust, and he continued to drink until his stomach sloshed with water.

Kane rested a moment as his mind began probe for solutions to his next problem: food. He wasn't hungry right now, but he would be at some point, and he would obviously need food to survive—especially an extended stay in the bunker. The only food he knew he had was a box of emergency energy bars and two fifty-pound bags of dog food.

Well, Barney will be happy, at least.

The ache of his back again reminded him that he would need to tend to his injuries. Kane stood and moved to the new pile of stuff in the entrance area. Waving the light stick over the pile, he took in the new additions. Blankets, a bundle of plastic trash bags, twenty more light sticks, the remaining plastic sheeting, a bundle of old clothing, a six-inch KA-BAR survival knife, a magnesium fire starter, an old military surplus compass, and his dad's military rucksack. Kane looked to his right and noticed a few more items against the wall. First he noticed his grandfather's 30-06 M1 Garand rifle from World War II, which his dad had asked him to safeguard. He also found a stash of various batteries, a compact LED flashlight (which he picked up), and thirty rounds of old Lake City military-issue 30-06 ammunition. Kane grabbed two 3-volt batteries and dropped them into the flashlight, testing the blinding light on the wall to his right. He had to be careful not to waste the battery power.

Where is that brand-new first aid kit? The one I bought over the Internet.

He had put it on the list, and his dad had said that he had put everything on the list in the bunker. Kane moved to the rucksack and opened it. More clothes, including long underwear and a rain jacket. He pushed his hand past them and found the nylon case he had been looking for. Pulling it out, he stuffed the clothing back into the sack and returned to Barney. Having had some basic medical training, he had wanted to buy a deluxe medical kit for a while. Finally, just recently, he had gone ahead and bought it.

Thank God.

He unzipped the nylon pouch and spread the kit open on the floor in front of him. It looked good, and there appeared to be plenty of equipment to work with. Kane clicked the flashlight on. Barney squinted at the light.

"It's okay, Barn. I'm going to take a look at where you're hurt."

Kane shone the flashlight at Barney and was shocked to see how bad the poor animal looked. Covered in blood, with patches of hair completely burned away, he appeared to be in bad shape. Kane shone the light toward Barney's face, finding his right eye to be gone, most likely burned out while he was trapped. Kane reached over and rubbed Barney on his neck.

"Barney, I'm so sorry, buddy."

Barney turned his head and licked the inside of Kane's forearm.

Kane smiled. "Your spirit isn't broken yet, is it? Guess I should take a lesson from you and your good attitude."

He took a second look at it. He wasn't going to mess with the eye socket, as it appeared to be cauterized shut anyway and was, therefore, possibly sterilized. Kane looked closely over the small, furry white body. It appeared that most of the blood had come from the eye. He appeared to be okay, other than favoring his front right foot. Kane tried to touch it, but Barney yelped and pulled it away.

"Okay, okay. I'll get you to sleep before I do anything with that." He stroked Barney's head. "You're a good boy, Barney. Strong in spirit." Kane smiled again.

Barney continued to lie on his side while Kane wiped his bloody fur with a piece of gauze and some hydrogen peroxide to clean him up. That done, Kane removed three 25mg Benadryl caplets from a small bottle and a 200mg ibuprofen tablet from its container, which he broke in half.

"Sorry I don't have any serious drugs, man. These will have to do".

He retrieved a small handful of dog food from the bag and mixed the pills in with it. Barney ate the food mixture gladly.

Kane then removed a small mirror from the kit to aid in looking himself over. He raised it up to his face, and what he saw caught him by surprise. The ghastly, tired, blackened figure in the mirror was not Kane Lorusso but a phantom imposter. Kane stared at himself in the small mirror for what seemed like forever. Most of the hair on his head was burned off, though his eyebrows were mostly intact. Covered in soot, ash, and blood, there was no way for him to tell where he was injured. He'd have to try to clean up a little first. Kane retrieved some small moist towels from the kit and proceeded to wipe himself down. It was a slow process, occasionally making him cuss when he hit a burn or open wound with one of the small towels. After fifteen minutes, he was relatively clean—cleaner at least than he had been. But even after the cleaning, Kane still had difficulty recognizing the figure in the small mirror. The worst of it was all the small burns that covered his upper body, as well as several lacerations, the largest of which was a four-inch-long gash across his ribs on the right side. He also had tiny glass shards embedded everywhere from his forehead to the bottoms of his feet. The large burn on the bottom of his right foot from kicking the flaming beam did not look too good either. He had not felt any of it at all during the craziness of the last few hours.

First, he addressed the glass by quickly pulling the small shards with tweezers he found in the kit, dabbing the sites with hydrogen peroxide and Neosporin. He then addressed the large, weeping gash in his side, which he scrubbed with antibacterial cleanser, cussing and gritting his teeth as he worked. With a hiss he rinsed the wound with a few handfuls of water and let it dry before closing it with butterfly strips.

Picking the mirror up again, Kane reassessed the situation. The burns were the biggest problem, and the fact that they appeared to be partial thickness burns meant there was a high risk of infection. Without antibiotics, infection could easily kill him down in this hole. He closed his eyes and took a slow breath, rinsing the burns with water from the bucket before letting them dry. He took several gauze pads and tore them from their sterile packets. Using medical tape, he attached the dry occlusive dressings to the worst burns across the top of his shoulders and let the others air dry. He did the same with the burn on the bottom of his foot. He then popped four ibuprofen and chased them with a handful of water. He then opened a small bottle labeled *KI Potassium Iodide*. Kane knew that if the blast he had just survived had been radioactive in any way, he would need potassium iodide to keep his thyroid from becoming saturated with radiation. He shook out two small pills and swallowed them as well.

"Nice job, Dr. Lorusso."

Barney was passed out on the blanket, which did not look like a bad idea. First, though, he had to dress the dog's leg. Barney groaned and shifted but did not wake as Kane wrapped the leg tightly with gauze and medical tape, creating a makeshift cast.

Kane took two more blankets from the shelf and spread them on the floor. He went to the rucksack and retrieved some old, worn Carhartt pants. Stepping out of the torn, burned shorts he had fled the house in, he stepped in to the pants and gingerly pulled them up. He decided to go shirtless for a while, for the sake of his burns. Kane lay stomach down on one blanket and draped the other lightly over him. He had never felt so physically and emotionally ruined in his whole life, and he feared it was going to get a lot worse before it got better. He closed his eyes and allowed sleep to overtake him, one searing inch at a time.

DAY 2.

ATLANTA, GEORGIA

Bethany Parsons stopped walking and looked over her left shoulder at her boyfriend Dave, who was shuffling along quietly behind her. She used to think he had good style and was a great dancer. Now, as she looked at him through a lens colored by the dissolution of everything she knew, she realized he just looked ridiculous with all the gold chains and swagger, his hat cocked off to the side and a blue jersey that read "PLAYA" across his chest. Her knees ached, and she was developing a hotspot on her left heel where her shoes rubbed endlessly. She tucked her chin to her chest, stretching her neck, and closed her eyes for a moment.

She was so tired. She had not slept much since all this started. She and Dave had lived together in an apartment in Lawrenceville, Georgia, until the madness had happened. They had been forced to flee their burning apartment, half drunk, only hours after a party had ended. It had been terrible having to watch all their stuff burn, but that quickly dissolved into shock at the realization that everything else was on fire, too. All the trees, the other buildings, cars, everything, everything burned in the semidarkness of the early morning. She had thought at first that it was just a really bad fire, but when the fire department never showed, it began to dawn on her that something much worse was happening. Everyone was trying to flee, packing themselves and what was left of their belongings into their half-burnt cars—but then none of the cars would start. Only the old ones, the ones that didn't rely on computers, and the occasional motorcycle or dirt bike seemed to still function. Planes had fallen out of the sky, cars had driven off the road, and fights had broken out in the dim morning light. There was chaos, screaming, looting, and fire everywhere. It was a nightmare that was all too real, the stink of smoke and fear still heavy in her nostrils. Bethany and Dave had taken off on foot through the woods to avoid the mass exodus of angry, frightened people.

Bethany glanced up, wiping and smudging the stinging ash across her face as it continued to fall in blankets from the dark, ruined sky. She pulled her cracked cell phone from her pocket and turned it on again. It was the only thing she now owned. The cracked LCD screen failed to come to life. She had not been able to reach any family or friends, and she wasn't sure if it was just her phone or if the service was down. She shook the phone with an irritated gesture.

Dave shuffled up next to her. "Chill out, girl, that ain't gonna fix it."

"I know it won't fix it, Dave!" she fumed. "Would you hurry up, anyway? Pull your pants up and quit shuffling. We need to make it downtown before it gets dark."

"Why? This is ridiculous, B. Why are you so bent on going in?"

"Because my family is in Atlanta. Besides…I heard several people say to go into the city because the military was taking in refugees there. What else are we going to do? We don't even know what has happened! Where else are we going to go?"

"Bethany, we've been walking straight since we bailed from the apartment! I mean, have you even seen anything that indicates that there is some kind of relief being organized down here? Seriously! *Everyone is dead!* Look, there are hardly any buildings standing!"

He turned and pointed at a nearby vehicle that was turned on its side. "Do you see what I see? There's a dead person in there! And no one is doing anything. There's no emergency workers. No one! Now, I don't know where the military is, but they *aren't* here."

"Don't lecture me like you're my father, Dave!" she snapped.

"Please, you wouldn't know what that sounded like anyway."

The insult stung, twisting with anger and stress to fuel the boiling rage inside her.

"*Fuck you*, Dave! You're an ignorant jerk. You do know that, don't you? I should have broken up with you a year ago, when I caught you with Tasha."

"Ah, here we go again. World War III has happened and you're bringing this shit up. I bet you're gonna say everything in the apartment is yours too, huh?"

"Who cares about the damn apartment? It burned up along with everything else, and World War III doesn't change the fact that you're a douchebag loser with a moral constitution about as loose as that gaudy chain around your neck."

Dave held his hands up in front of him. "Whoa. Whoa, okay, you know what? Fine. You go do whatever the hell it is that you need to do. I'm getting the *fuck* up out of here," he said, lowering his hands and turning away. "I don't know why I came this far with you in the first place. I never really did like you anyway; you're just good skirt."

"Dave, wait," she said, a slight pang of loneliness flaring inside her chest.

"No, it's too late for that. You're on your own, sweetness."

The loneliness quickly turned to white-hot rage as it flashed across Bethany's face. "Then go, you stupid dick! You're a sorry, wannabe player anyway—and you still think any of that matters? Look around you and think about something other than yourself for once!"

She waved her hands dramatically. "All you ever do is take. Well, now you can take your ass right on back up the street where you came from. And don't *ever* talk to me again!"

Dave must have heard her, because he didn't say a word as he continued walking. Bethany gritted her teeth as she watched him shuffle away through the debris and wreckage of the burning vehicles that littered the interstate.

She was alone now. As the gravity of that thought sank into the pit of her stomach, she fought the urge to call out to Dave again. He was a loser, but he was somebody, and somebody was better than nobody. She glanced around at the complete devastation. The lifeless, smoldering city looked back with cold indifference. The fires, devastation, and half-charred remains of her human brethren stood before her like an otherworldly portal into hell itself.

She wiped at her face again, mixing small tears with the large gray snowflakes as they landed on her face and hair. She looked for Dave one last time and, no longer seeing him, muttered to herself, "Jerk! He'll be sorry when I link up with my family and find all the other survivors downtown."

She believed her own words. Surely it was true. She would find them, and then everything would be alright. The government would be there. Bethany wiped her face one more time and began walking again further into the hateful, ravaged city.

✵ ✵ ✵

In the darkness of the bunker, a repetitive scratching sound slowly began to pull Kane from the tangled clutches of sleep.

"Skritch, skritch," pause, "skritch, skritch, skritch."

Kane opened his eyes, but the dilated lenses of his eyes took in nothing but blackness. The scratching continued.

"Skritch, skritch."

He must have been crashed out for over eight hours. The light sticks were out. Kane felt around in the darkness for his flashlight.

"Skritch, skritch, skritch, skritch, skritch, skritch."

Picking up the flashlight, he shone it in the area of the scratching. "Barney, what are you doing?"

The small animal stared blankly at him from the corner.

Kane began to move slowly. "Ugggggh," he groaned, rubbing at the base of his neck. His back and neck muscles were frozen, and he still felt so utterly tired. Getting to his feet, Kane made his way over to the small dog, who was still scratching at the corner of the dark room. When he got closer, Kane noticed that Barney had been scratching at a loose, cracked area of cement in the corner. What had apparently begun as a small chip was now a sizable depression. Instead of questioning or scolding, Kane watched silently, interested in the distraction. The dog dug for another few minutes at the loose concrete before sitting back to admire his work.

"Just had some nervous energy to get out, huh, Barn?"

Barney stood and turned sideways to the hole, cocked his leg, and began to urinate. The urine trickled through the cracks and disappeared down into the earth. Kane's face slackened into a picture of disbelief.

"Unbelievable," he said out loud. "You were digging us a latrine."

Kane marveled at how smart the dog was. Just like anyone else, he did not want to sleep in his own waste, so he had done something about it.

"Truly amazing, Barney. What would I do without you?"

Barney sat back, licking his lips and yawning as if very pleased with himself. "My turn," Kane said taking his place at the urinal. "We'll have to line this with plastic before making any solid deposits, okay?"

Barney yawned again and gave a leisurely, carefree stretch.

Morning business out of the way, Kane moved slowly toward the front of the bunker. While passing by the unopened light sticks, he grabbed one and tore it from the package. After snapping and shaking it, he tossed it onto the floor to his left. Barney hopped along behind him, carefully keeping his casted foot off the ground. Kane broke the seal and unfolded the top of the dog food. Digging his hand in, he grabbed a handful of the greasy food. He emptied the handful on the concrete, and Barney ate it greedily.

"Breakfast is served," Kane said as he dumped a second handful on the concrete. Kane dug his hand into the food a third time and pulled it out, studying the nuggets in the dim light. The food smelled like nasty old salmon and had a heavy greasy texture as he moved the kibbles between his fingers. Kane squinted and frowned, but his stomach turned and growled, spurring him on. He emptied the handful of salmon kibble into his mouth and began chewing quickly, all the while making a disgusted face. Kane finished the mouthful with a disgusted "ouuugghh." He wiped his mouth.

"Barney, if we get out of here, you're getting better food," Kane said, digging his hand into the bag for round two. Barney had no complaints as he gobbled his food down, making small snorting sounds as he inhaled his breakfast. Kane finished the second handful, and although still not pleased with the flavor, he was happy to have something to put in his empty stomach.

Wiping his palm on the leg of his pants, he stood and stepped back toward the center of the room. Kane had no idea what time it was; in fact, he had already discarded his watch for its uselessness. He sat down and picked up the crank radio, spinning the crank rapidly for sixty seconds. Barney, having finished his food, rejoined Kane and curled up on his blanket.

"Alright, Barney, let's see what's happening outside," Kane said, looking at his companion. He knew that someone looking in on his conversations with Barney would probably think that he had lost it already, but the truth was, dog or not, Barney was his only friend in a situation that had gone bad—and fast. In fact, talking to the animal had been therapeutic for Kane. It helped him to think things through and had helped to ease a significant amount of his loneliness.

He snapped the radio on and was again covered in a wash of static as he adjusted the knob. The NOAA radio had the emergency information channels marked with red triangles. He rolled over the first triangle and heard a frantic, tired young man's voice.

"I can't ex...but it..."

Kane moved the knob with very fine adjustments, trying to find the sweet spot.

"Got it," Kane said as the broadcast came through with unusual clarity.

"There's only a few of us who decided to stay and keep the station up. Everyone else either left or is...well, I did not have anyone, so I felt it best to stay here and continue broadcasting to survivors. Again, my name is Rick Morgan, and I was one of the techs here at the emergency radio substation in Knoxville until yesterday, when everything went wrong. I've found that this station is fortified, and the equipment all still seems to work. I heard that the station had received a grant from the federal government to strengthen it against physical and electromagnetic damage a few years ago. I think that may be why the equipment is working when nothing else is. I think some of the other emergency radio control stations received the same funding, but I haven't been able to raise them.

"It seems," Rick continued, "that the attacks are still coming, but they are much less frequent now. The last reports that came in were over six hours ago and stated that the United States had potentially suffered an estimated 60 percent casualties in the first wave. Many deaths were from nuclear devices detonated over cities to achieve maximum exposure and death. Several cities were vaporized, including New York and Washington DC."

"Miami. What about Miami?" Kane muttered anxiously under his breath. Radio Rick continued his report.

"Those that were missed or not targeted were either crippled, due to the electromagnetic pulse discharge of the nukes, or were hit with other munitions. For example, another weapon that was used in the first wave against us was some type of new prototype weapon called 'The Fire of Allah,' which had been engineered by The Sword. We don't know much about it, but apparently it is a chemical substance similar to napalm—but worse, designed to drown entire cities in liquid fire. This weapon was created to be deliverable via ICBM missiles. The rest of the casualties came from the second wave of attacks, which happened right on the heels of the first. The second wave was comprised of nationwide 'blanket' attacks with various chemical and biological agents, including a supervirus called Chimera. According to this report its a concoction of the smallpox, Marburg, Ebola, VEE, and Machupo viruses. This supervirus was studied at length by the CDC before the attacks and their information shows that its rate of lethality is very high, and that it kills within days. Apparently, it was designed upon detonation disperse into the atmosphere so that it rains or 'snows' down in ash clumps over large areas. This horrible concoction is airborne—and is everywhere. Apart from causing mass casualties, the CDC also reports that the virus had some strange and unexpected effects on certain infected subjects. For example, the information I have here indicates that some of the people infected with the supervirus do not immediately die. Instead, their bodies began to mutate and deform as they slowly devolved into a state of barbaric madness, dementia, and eventually death. At the point of mutation, they became carriers of the disease, but it is unknown how the disease is passed from that point on. Strangely, they also report that a very limited number of individuals exposed to the virus showed no signs of infection. The reasons for this are unknown.

"Last reports were that when the attacks began, many of the world's nations retaliated blindly out of fear and confusion, effectively continuing and expanding the already massive losses of much of the world's population. I...."

The radio hissed static, and Kane hissed back. "Come on you sonofabitch, tell me something more about Miami." He continued to adjust the knob back and forth.

The reception came through again.

"I don't know how long the others and I will make it in here without proper resources, but I'll broadcast as long as I can. Right now I've got to rest for a few and recheck the barricades on the main level; so good luck, everyone, and God bless."

More static. Kane snapped the radio back off as he hung his head in a defeated posture and looked over at Barney, snoozing on the blanket.

"Barney," he breathed in a quiet whisper. "It's worse than I thought."

DAY 5

ASHEVILLE, NORTH CAROLINA

In the dark of the meat freezer, a shadow shifted. A man known only as Malak stood in the cold dark and rubbed his bald head. He'd had enough. His large form moved past and in between the shelves of thawing meat. Though the freezer had been off for days, it had been so well insulated that it had retained its temperature well. Still, it was slowly warming. Malak stepped over several shelves that had toppled over and moved to the heavy door he had barricaded from the inside. This was ridiculous; he had been down in this meat freezer for days. Whatever had happened out there had happened already. Besides, he was tired of eating frozen raw meat. He had stayed as long as he had in the freezer because he knew that if the United States were being attacked, chemicals and diseases would be used. That was the truth of modern warfare without the restrictions humanity imposed upon it: do whatever would kill the most people the fastest, regardless of how inhumane. He began moving the junk that barred the door and pressed his ear to it. Nothing. For all he knew, everyone was dead and everything was gone, which would be fine with him.

Malak had been on his way from Dallas to visit one of his black market arms dealers in Richmond, Virginia. He and his boys had driven all night and had stopped for breakfast in Asheville, North Carolina, when the attacks had started. Without hesitation he ditched his crew and ran across the street. Desperate for cover from the madness, he had kicked in the back door of a meat-packing facility. Three of the plant workers tried to get into the industrial freezer with him. Two he shot to pieces, and the third he beat bloody with a broken mop handle before taking the guy's thick winter jacket. It had been a good choice, the jacket. He would have frozen damn solid without that jacket.

Malak unbolted the door and leaned his weight into it. Even in the dim light of the warehouse, Malak had to squint. The plant was torn open on all sides, and everything was strewn about as if the building had been hit by a tornado. If there was still something in the air, it would probably kill him quickly. He stood just outside the door, breathing deeply and letting his eyes adjust to his surroundings. He was feeling pretty good so far. He took a few more steps and again surveyed his surroundings. Looking to his right, he could see the street outside through a gaping hole in the wall, its jagged edges like the gaping mouth of some beast. Malak took a few steps toward the hole and stopped. At 6'6" and 325 pounds, Malak was a monster of a man, but he was also unarmed.

"Shouldn't have fired all my bullets at the meat packers," he said out loud, laughing to himself at how their title was also an insult. He stooped to grab a piece of rebar with concrete on the end of it.

Better than nothing.

As he stepped through the hole and into the street, the scene before him developed slowly into something not unlike the old Twilight Zone series. The city was a picture of destruction—buildings crumbled, fires raged, cars sat unmanned at dead traffic lights, and nothing lived or moved in the eerie silence. Malak shielded his eyes and looked toward the sky. A thick, churning charcoal sea rolled across the heavens and thundered into the distance.

"Amazing," Malak said in awe as a bitter wind stung his face. He drew the smallish coat around him. He tensed, hearing faltering footsteps approaching from behind him. He turned to see a man in a soiled coat and tie pleading desperately. He appeared to be badly burned.

"Sir, sir, please help me, please! I'm injured!"

Malak spun around, swinging the rebar, and struck the man in the side, knocking him to the ground. The man screamed.

"*Aggh*, no! Please don't!" the man cried out as he slid down the mound of rubble.

Malak pursued him down the slope, a terrible look of satisfaction on his face. The concrete on the end of the rebar had broken loose.

"Wait! Wait! I haven't done anything to you! *Wait! No!*"

Malak stepped up to the man and murderously drove the rebar into his midsection. The air exploded with the man's screams as Malak withdrew the rebar and drove it into him again and again. Blood streamed onto the broken concrete slab as Malak stared with cold intent into the eyes of the dying man.

"Why? Why did you...kill..." The dying man gasped.

"*Because there's no one to stop me!*" Malak snarled.

The man struggled for another moment before succumbing helplessly to the inevitable. Malak looked up and around, anxiously eyeing his surroundings.

"*Hey!*" Malak yelled at the top of his lungs. "*I just killed a fucking guy in the street for no reason!*"

He cocked his head and waited for the screams, sirens, anything. The ashen city failed to move in the following stillness as its fiery master flickered and continued to consume it. Still nothing. Malak took in the devastation of his surroundings and smiled.

More footsteps approached from around the diner in front of him. Two men rounded the corner, one with a semiautomatic handgun.

"Malak! No way, dude, how did you make it?" the stocky Hispanic male asked.

"Good to see you made it, Malak," said the other man, who had dark skin and short dark hair. "Back to your old trade already?" he asked, motioning toward the dead man.

"Sanchez, Dagen. You must have done something right in a previous life," Malak said coldly. "Where'd you get the HI-Point?" Malak motioned for Sanchez to give the weapon to him. The stocky man hesitated but passed the handgun over.

"Out of a car over there, two streets over," Sanchez said, motioning.

"Where's Ashteroth?" Malak asked as he looked the cheap, blocky handgun over.

"Look," Sanchez broke in. "We're through with Ashteroth. Besides, he's probably cooked up like everyone else. It's our time now, boys; this is what we're going to do...."

The group conversation was torn in a fury of sonic rage as the gun recoiled twice in Malak's hand. Dagen looked calmly at Sanchez, who fell to his knees, clawing at the two bloody holes in his chest.

"*Yoooouuuuu!...Fuggguuuugggg...*" Sanchez sputtered and rolled to his side.

Malak swung the gun on Dagen.

"Shoot me." Dagen held Malak's gaze, his face a picture of calm.

Malak continued muzzling Dagen. "Do you hear that?" Malak said in almost a whisper.

Dagen did not reply.

"*Do you hear it?*" Malak snapped.

"I don't hear anything," Dagen said, smiling wildly.

"Exactly! No sirens, no screams. No one cares if you live or die."

"Then shoot me. The world is dead, Malak. Shoot me and be done with it!"

Something dark gleamed in Malak's eyes, like the nothingness behind the eyes of a shark. "Sanchez here was not with me. He was only for himself. Are you with me, Dagen?" Malak pushed the gun barrel closer to Dagen's head.

"I'm with you. I have always been with you. Wherever. So either shoot me, or let's get on with it."

Malak lowered the gun, smiling. "You're almost as crazy as I am."

"That's not news...so what do we do now, boss?"

"Find Ashteroth," Malak said. "And when you've found him, we'll begin."

"And if he's..." Dagen started.

"He's alive, just like the rest of the cockroaches. Just find him."

"Specifics on recruits?" Dagen asked.

"See if we can find some working vehicles. Food. Water. When you find them, gather a few women and children as slaves and hostages, just in case there is some sort of police or military presence that we need to overcome. Recruit murderers, rapists, sickos, psychos, and anyone willing to do what I command without question." A look of grim pleasure crossed Malak's face. "I need soldiers."

✧ ✧ ✧

Bethany Parsons had never felt so ill in her entire life. She stopped in the street and closed her eyes as each beat of her hammering heart caused her head to throb painfully. Her stomach turned, and a feeling of nausea overcame her. The rancid, uncooked meat she had found and consumed in the ruined food market had not agreed with her, but she had craved it, she had *needed* it. Her vision blurred with the pain, and she was overcome with a terrible weakness that threatened to steal her balance. She wiped more tears from her face and began to cry bitterly.

How is this happening? Where is the National Guard?

Her family was gone. The modest apartment downtown where her mother and younger brother had lived was now nothing more than a pile of smoldering rubble. The building was gone, and her family was nowhere to be found. Bethany wiped a few tears from her eyes as she tried to get a grip on the terror and loneliness that surrounded her.

She had been in Atlanta for three days and had yet to find any organized assistance like she had hoped she would. What she had found were people—others who were stranded or had come into the city to find help. Hundreds, giant masses of them were strewn across the city. But they weren't okay. Everyone appeared to be sick. Many refused to talk to her, and the ones that would spoke incoherently. Some lay lifelessly on the sidewalk and in the street, while others wandered aimlessly through the wreckage as though they were sleepwalking. It was a terrible dream that she couldn't wake from. She stumbled around a corner and onto Peachtree Street, where she saw a man dressed in the army combat uniform digital fatigues just ahead of her.

"Wait! Sir, please!" Bethany called out with a croak to the silhouette that began shuffling away from her and into the smoke and debris.

"Sir, please, are you with the army? Where do I need to go? To get help?" she said, half pleading as the man stopped and began to vomit into the street.

Bethany began to lower her outstretched hand and winced as the man continued to wretch, expelling a greenish-yellow substance from his mouth. She picked nervously at one of the many giant pus-filled boils that had risen up on her arms, face, and body—everywhere the poisonous ash had touched her.

"Hey, are you okay?" she asked as she slowly approached and reached out her hand again. "Are you sick too? We should find some help. You're with the Guard...."

"*No!*" came the ragged reply. "No one left. They're all gone. Gone. Gone away." The man crouched, hiding his face and rocking slightly as he wiped away the greenish slime that hung from the corner of his mouth.

"But...the other people..." she began, her tongue stroking across blistered lips. "They said to come here. Where's the rest of..." she mumbled as the man turned his back to her.

"Sick. Sick. Everyone sick. Dead already. Sick and dead. Sick and dead." He vomited again with a terrible groan, his body shaking violently as the bloody slime mixture splashed onto the concrete.

Bethany gasped and stepped back as he retched again and again. The man scrambled across the ground on all fours and wiped the sleeve of his uniform across his mouth. He continued to hide his face.

"Leave alone. Sick," he muttered roughly.

Bethany took two steps and came within an arm's length of the crouching man. "Please...."

The speed at which the man rose, swiping broken fingernails across the flesh of her face, utterly startled her. Bethany screamed and fell backward into the debris-filled street, clutching her face.

"*Leave alone!*" he screamed in gravelly tones. He raised his emaciated head and stared her in the face, the hollowed, bleeding sockets of his eyes emanating a ghoulish appearance. "*You leave alone!*"

"Okay!" Bethany cried out as she slowly stumbled backward, holding a hand to her bloodied face.

"Sick. Everyone. Sick and dead. You too," he said as he turned and moaned, shuffling away into the smoke.

Bethany began to weep as the blood dribbled down her face and dripped onto her shirt. She looked around as she cried and tried to process what was happening. It was all too much. The vicious desolation of the dead city closed in, smothering her with the smell of decay. She struggled to her knees and used her shirt to dab at her face, noticing the diamond tennis bracelet that her mother had given her. It was still so beautiful and seemed like such a foreign object in her current state of desperation. The diamonds and gold sparkled slightly as her tears mixed with blood and splashed across them.

Bethany coughed, gagging as her insides twisted. Rolling with mad contortions like a wounded serpent, her stomach writhed, and she dropped to all fours as she began to vomit.

DAY 13

Kane slowly lowered himself down to rest on his stomach on the cool concrete floor. He had just finished his second set of 150 pushups. He would do a third set before he went to bed later. He had been in this bunker for what seemed like forever. In reality, it had been more like twelve days—but that was just an estimate, as he really had no way of keeping time and no daylight to go by. He guessed that it was most likely late April or even May by now, but beyond that he could not be sure. Time was slipping away from him; and as the days passed, the human concept of exact time began to diminish as its importance faded.

He had started doing the pushups, sit-ups, and squats to keep from going crazy. That and the practice of karate forms and technique had been a good way to expend restless energy. Kane rolled over and sat up, looking around. He was down to about half of the glow sticks and a third of the way into the dog food, even though he had tried to go sparingly. The radio still worked, but there was no longer any radio traffic. That guy, Rick Morgan, at the emergency radio substation in Knoxville, had been the most reliable, but something had happened to him. The station had gone dark. During his last transmission, Rick had said something about not going out or they would get you. This final transmission had really disturbed Kane. That had been three days ago.

Kane looked over at Barney, asleep on his blanket. The dog had been whining a lot lately. Kane was beginning to think the animal's wounded eye might have become infected. It now had an oozing yellow film that covered it. He reached over and began to rub him along his back. Barney stirred and whimpered.

"Hey, buddy, we doing alright?"

Kane exhaled and stood, closed his eyes, and took in the silence. Nothing moved in the musty darkness of the bunker, nothing but the smallest drip-drop of water into the bucket. He could not believe this was happening. Every day he went through his routine—eat, medicate, redress his wounds, work out, check and rub Barney, meditate, work out, check the radio, meditate, work out, organize and prepare the items in the shelter, and so on.

For what?

His wounds were healing well, but his days were numbered anyway with a terminal heart condition, which he was sure had worsened since the attack. He unconsciously rubbed his chest. It endlessly ached day and night. What was he going to do if he was able to leave? Where would he go? His mind swam with the dire hopelessness of the situation. He shook his head. He needed to be here and now. The two most important things right now we're taking care of his only friend and checking the radio for the possibility of news or information. Hopefully, it wasn't really that bad out there. The government would adjust, reorganize, and assume control again. Kane knew that the government planned and prepared for things like this. Surely they had all the major officials underground somewhere. When it was all clear, they would emerge and reestablish a governmental structure, at which time they would begin broadcasting on the state of the nation and the government's well-being. Citizens would then be clear to begin rebuilding their broken lives. There was no way to know how long that would be, but hopefully soon he would be able to get out of the bunker and begin trying to fix the things that were no longer right in his life.

Kane stood in the semidarkness, thinking about his family and what had become of them. If the devastation was as great and wide spread as Radio Rick had portrayed, there was little possibility that they could have survived. How could he possibly go on with his life without them? That was a problem that had no solution, a problem that loomed endlessly, until Kane felt utterly hopeless in its shadow.

How can I deal with this? Where do I start?

Whatever the case, he needed some resolution to his current situation. This unending state of isolation and distress was desperately driving him toward madness.

DAY 17

ASHEVILLE, NORTH CAROLINA

Malak sat in a plastic chair at a metal desk on the top floor of an abandoned, burned-out concrete structure, drumming his fingers restlessly. The structure, which was now referred to as "The Compound," was surrounded by a wall of stacked concrete chunks, which were reinforced with steel rebar. Two roaming squads of perimeter patrols checked and rechecked the wall as they made their rounds. So far he had been successful at recruiting almost fifty men. This did not include the women who were rounded up and forced to serve and service the men. Any children found would be killed, because they only consumed resources and could provide no service. The order had been simple enough for men and women alike: join and serve—or die. Men who were recruited were required to fight Malak himself in unarmed combat. Malak had never lost a fight, so the men who fought him were either slaughtered or saluted by him for their savagery and recklessness in battle. This ensured no weak links in his crew. Each of the forty-six men he commanded were crazed, vicious, psychotic men, men who were hell bent on the destruction of others.

It amused him that the likelihood of these men having been this way before the end began was very low. Sure, a few of them had been twisted from the start, like his lieutenant, Ashteroth. But many of the men who now served him had most likely been regular, everyday people. They had been people with families and jobs and structure to their silly routines. Maybe the worst they ever did was to take something that was not theirs, or hit their wife, or drive while intoxicated.

Malak smiled. How fast they resort to violence, murder, and force when "the man" isn't standing over them. They had not followed the law and acted with restraint in their previous lives because they had liked it that way. They had done it because society had told them that if they did not, they would be punished. Malak smiled again. He had saved them. He had set them free from their fragile moral compasses, and they worshiped him for it.

"Malak," came a voice from behind him.

Malak blinked as he was pulled from his thoughts.

"You wanted to be notified of any contact with Lurchers."

Malak turned and glanced at the painted man behind him. "What about it?"

"Third patrol made contact with a sizable group, 'bout thirty of 'em on the east side of the compound. Creatures tried to breach the wall."

"And third patrol put the disgusting filth to rest?"

"They did."

"You're dismissed." Malak waved his hand, and the man disappeared back the way he had come. They were coming in higher numbers now. He knew them to be nothing more than cannibalistic animals, but there was an unnerving, calculating intelligence there, some remnant of the mind that had existed before. They were more organized than he had first thought. It was no matter. His structure was fortified, his men were prepared, and the monsters would be put down like the dogs they were.

✡ ✡ ✡

When the voice finished speaking, Malak stood and moved to one of the holes in the wall of the structure. He gazed out upon the ruins of the city and breathed in deeply through his nose the burned smell of a dead civilization heavy in the air. It was his time now; that's what the voice had told him. He had heard the voice for years now, but he had always dismissed it as a hallucination brought on by the usage of "Z," a new and powerful narcotic. Now it was different. He was not under the influence of outside substances. Even though the withdrawals he was going through raged in his body and tortured his mind, the voice still whispered to him.

It's your time now, Malak. Build your kingdom as you wish.

It spoke to him as clearly as any human being could, and he trusted it more than the desperate humanity that surrounded him. It spoke truth without the life-draining poison of the human tongue. It was pure and strong, and it promised him breathtaking power, asking only for him to do what was right in his heart.

It had been just over two weeks since the end had begun; everyone had even called it the "end war" because of the complete destruction that had followed. He had heard that the government had not survived in the least as one might assume it would, down in a bunker somewhere. In fact, he'd heard that nothing had made it—no president, no governmental branches, no societal system, and no military. No one was left except the lone and powerless few and the disgustingly rabid monsters that tried to breach his compound by wave after wave. They were no obstacle, though. The true power now was held in the hands of the fearless and the violent. Malak's hands.

Modern humanity had all but been destroyed. Most of the politicians, doctors, teachers, artists, philosophers, lawyers, and other civilized people were gone. They had not survived the first few weeks without running water, power, food from the store, and medical attention. They had simply lost the will to live. Possessing no valuable survival skills, those once deemed society's most important had become the most unnecessary. Everything they had known and every modern convenience that they had ever relied upon was stripped from them in one terrible instant. Life as humanity had known it had been violently torn from its place in history and thrown back into the dark ages. The world now was one of savagery, death, greed, and basic survival.

Survival of the fittest.

A smile crept across Malak's face as he thought of things to come. The voice had been right all along. It *was* his time now. Using the power of the darkness that flowed within him, he would build a new world. It would be a world that thrived upon the death of the weak, the indulgence of lust, and the strength of those who served the darkness. It was his world now. His world.

DAY 24

GREEN COUNTY, TENNESSEE

Kane took his shirt off and sat back, wincing slightly as the uncomfortably cool concrete block wall touched his bare skin. He placed the M1 Garand rifle butt down between his knees and glanced at Barney, lying quietly on his blanket across the room. The little sentinel watched his movements silently with a single inquisitive brown eye. Facing the bolt toward himself, Kane pulled back slightly on the charging handle to reveal the chambered 30-06 round inside the weapon. He released the charging handle and let the bolt seat back into place before closing his eyes and leaning his head back against the wall.

Why am I still here? Why am I trying so hard to survive?

There was nothing for him to return to if he lived. No family, no familiar way of life, no friends, no purpose. There would be nothing left of the Kane Lorusso who had gone into the bunker those many days before. God had stolen almost everything from him—everything but his life and the life of his furry friend. Kane racked his mind in the black silence of the claustrophobic bunker. He pinched his eyes shut and wiped tears from his face as he moved the barrel of the rifle under his chin.

He would do it. He would end this miserable existence now.

Breathing in deeply the dank, musty air of the bunker for the last time, Kane slipped his right toe through the trigger guard and began to straighten his leg. Slowly, ever so slowly, he pushed as his muscles quivered in anticipation of the report.

He thought of his childhood, fishing with his dad on Lake Cleary in the dead of summer. The crickets chirped as he and his dad threaded bloodworms on their hooks. That had been their time together. He loved those days. They laughed and talked about girls and sports and "man things," as his dad had called it. His dad rested a heavy hand on his shoulder, and Kane caught a whiff of his father's scent. It smelled of Speed Stick deodorant, sweat, and a hint of beer. It was as familiar as anything he knew.

"You're growing into a fine young man," his father had said. "But always remember, it's the choices you make that will determine who you will be as a man."

It was the mid-1990s, and he was graduating from police academy. His parents and his sister crowded closely as his uncle took their photograph. He had been so relieved to be done with it after all the weeks of rigorous training. He looked off to the side and became irritated at how slinky his sister had dressed and that his classmates were eyeballing her.

His mother whispered over his shoulder. "We're so proud of you, Kane. We love you so much."

It was early December, seven years ago, when he had gone on his first date with Susan. She was so beautiful and full of life. He had been irresistibly drawn to her. They were smiling and flirting together in the corner of a quiet coffee house. A fire crackled nearby, and the air smelled of good coffee and spice.

She reached forward and lightly touched the top of his hand, smiling slyly and winking as she spoke. "I think you're the most mysterious man I have ever met."

It was February sixteenth, three years ago, as he paced at the head of the hospital bed as his wife was in labor with their first two children. They had decided to wait, to not know anything about the twins until they were born. It would be the greatest surprise, and Kane had endured about all the waiting he could stand.

"One more push!" the doctor was saying. His wife was screaming. "And here's number two!"

"So, Doc? Boys or girls?"

"You've got one of each!"

"Really? Fantastic!"

"Congratulations, Mr. Lorusso! You are the proud father of fraternal twins. Do you have your camera ready?"

He froze. In the darkness of the bunker, Kane froze completely, refusing to stiffen his leg another fraction of a millimeter. After a moment, he slowly pulled his toe from the trigger guard and released the trigger. Kane opened his eyes and slowly looked down to see a familiar warm, furry little body that shifted again and shuffled even closer to his leg. Barney whined, a low, sad sound as he adjusted his head to rest it on Kane's thigh. Kane wiped his arm across his cold, sweaty brow as the puppy slowly rolled his head to the side until his good eye angled up to look Kane in the face.

"Barney? I'm so sorry, buddy. I'm so selfish for trying to leave you alone in here." He quietly choked on the words as he set the rifle to the side and scooped up the small furry creature and hugged him under his chin.

"I won't leave you, Barney. That's a promise."

In the dim artificial light of the bunker, Barney, revealing some slightly salmon-tinged puppy breath, began to deliver a host of wet kisses to Kane's lower jaw. Kane pulled the small dog close.

"I love you too, Barney. More than you can know."

DAY 26

ATLANTA, GEORGIA

On the ground floor of a wrecked, rubble-filled Jackson's department store, a lonely wisp of a female figure crouched close against the interior wall. Though still a fairly young woman in years, the scarred, drooping, grey flesh of her face indicated she was an elderly woman on the brink of death.

Silently she rocked from toes to heels, moaning ever so slightly, as she pulled fistful after fistful of hair from her balding head. The injuries she had sustained and the wasting appearance of her fragile frame offered up an absolutely wretched appearance.

A raspy, guttural hiss scraped past her vocal chords as she shuffled and scooped up a shard of glass with a skeletal hand. Squeezing the shard tightly, she began to moan again as she began gouging something into the partially burned plaster of the wall with rapid movements. As she dug through the burnt surface with the giant translucent claw, the inner plaster began to reveal itself, stark white against the blackened surface. Blood trickled down what was left of her arm and dripped from her elbow onto the trash beneath her feet.

With frenzied motions she worked, moaning softly as she moved and scratched deeper into the white undersurface of the wall. The blood continued to run from the palm of her hand, slipping across and under the diamond and gold tennis bracelet that hung so beautifully from the bloody arm.

After a few moments, she gave a low growl, peeling shredded lips over broken teeth, and stood to stare at the wall that was now covered in a mad, almost illegible script. "SickAndDead.ItchySkin.ItchyHotNever-Sleeps.FleshyPersonTastyMeats.NeedsFleshy-GoodTasties."

Giving another hiss of satisfaction, the ragged figure shambled from the burned-out storefront and into the street, mixing and mingling with so many others as they sauntered aimlessly through the despoiled wreckage of the city.

DAY 30

ASHEVILLE, NORTH CAROLINA

Dagen moved to the compound wall and looked out upon the desolate wreckage of downtown Asheville as evening began to set in. Fishing out a cigarette and placing it between his lips, he fumbled with a nearly ruined book of matches. He flicked half a dozen sodden stems against the striking pad before one caught in a flash of flame. Mumbling his discontent at using up so many, he quickly lit the cigarette and shook the match out inhaling deeply the fragrant tobacco smoke.

Small tendrils of smoke drifted about his face as he stared aimlessly into the encroaching darkness. It had all gone down so fast; entire societal collapse, chaos and madness followed. It was perfect. Gone were the days of rules and militaristic order and... The Jay Lee Sloot School for orphaned children in Hagerstown, Maryland.

Dagen grimaced and rubbed his face, the rotten memories of his previous life bobbing to the surface like so much trash.

Sons of bitches, he thought as he took another long drag on the smoke.

He had never known his father, an ignorant teenage crack head who had knocked up his mother then disappeared without a trace. His mother, not believing she could handle a child on her own, had abandoned him at a nearby fire station. Fitting that he should start his life with nothing.

A small fight broke out in the courtyard behind him. Two men were struggling over a worn survival flashlight.

"Enough, you disgusting trash! I swear, if you don't stop, I'll tear both of your throats out and keep the trinket for myself!"

The men abruptly stopped and dispersed whispering curses at each other. They knew better than to invoke the anger of Malak's second in command. He turned back to his cigarette and his thoughts.

Jay Lee Sloot had seemed an honest man, a Christian man, a man devoted to helping and restoring the lost children of society – at least that's what he wanted the world to believe. The truth was much uglier. The School had been a hell hole filled with violence and oppression where children were badly beaten or had their daily rations taken for the smallest infraction. Jay Lee Sloot seemed to be a bright spot in an otherwise miserable existence for Dagen.

Dagen had been six years old when Sloot had first befriended him at the boarding school. He had a charming way about him, something fatherly and warm, and Dagen had been ravenous for the man's attention. Sloot was attentive to many of the boys at the school, but he was especially fond of Dagen. He spoke of how great the Lord God was and that Jesus had overcome the grave for the sake of mankind. He said that God's truth would set him free and that God had orchestrated their special friendship. The man had an easy, disarming personality and with a wink here and a treat there, he won the boy's unbridled affection.

"Praise God for you, Dagen. You are such a blessing to me," he had crooned as he lovingly stroked the boy's thigh.

DAY 33

The dog food was gone. Kane had tried to make it last, but there wasn't any more now. There had not been any for the last three days, and a terrible boiling hunger rolled through Kane's stomach. The man who had entered the bunker those many days ago was a different creature now. Physically, any extra fat or heavy muscle had been used by his system for fuel long ago. Mentally and emotionally he was standing at a giant precipice, just inches, moments from toppling into the depths of insanity. As much of a mentally fortified individual as Kane Lorusso was, he was at the breaking point on every level. He sat in the darkness and sipped handfuls of water from the bucket, the only temporary reprieve from the aching in his stomach. The light sticks had run out, as had most of his other necessary supplies. Kane had decided to only use the flashlight for emergencies, which relegated him to scrambling around in the dark for most of his waking hours. The darkness of the bunker was overwhelming; it felt murky and eternal. It slowly sucked away at his soul and threatened to change him into something monstrous.

Kane paced in the confined space, grabbing handfuls of his hair and talking to himself, the pungent odor of bagged feces stinging his eyes and nose.

"It's fine, it's fine, everything is fine. I'm going to make it out of here, and I'm going to find my family." He continued pacing. "Isn't that right, Barney? You and I are going to make it out of here. We're going to be just fine."

Barney wheezed and chuffed as he shuffled and changed his position on the blanket. He was not doing well, and for the last week he had not gotten up off the blanket. Kane now spent most of his waking hours sitting and talking with Barney, who seemed to appreciate Kane's words and soft rubbings under his chin. All they had was each other in the thick blackness of the bunker. Kane sat next to the animal again and scooped him up off of the blanket. Barney made a long, sad whining sound as Kane tucked him close in to his chest. He could feel the small animal's heart racing inside his narrow chest.

"I know you feel terrible, Barney, but you're going to be okay. You're going to beat this infection, because you're a fighter. Remember when we first took shelter in here? I was so bent out of shape, and you with your bad eye had the best attitude. I appreciated you for that."

The animal shook violently and wheezed deeply, his lungs laboring.

"And when I was going to kill myself, you didn't give up on me then either. You've been my very best friend, Barn, and I need you to keep going a little while longer. I need you here with me."

The small dog raised his head, and in the darkness Kane felt the small pink tongue licking the side of his neck.

"I love you too, Barney. I love you, too."

The puppy gave a series of small whimpers and grew still. Kane drew Barney close, trying to feel the animal's heartbeat, and whispered, panicking, in the dark, "Barney? Wake up. You can't go yet. Come on, Barney, come on, buddy. I *need* you to stay with me." He paused, listening for any noise from the small dog.

Kane burst into a wail.

"Barney? Don't go! You're all I've got! You're the only family I have. *Pleeease!*" Hot tears of grief ran down Kane's face as he continued to clutch the lifeless animal. *"Baaarneeey!"* His sobbing cries echoed and disappeared into the dark. He doubled over and continued crying bitterly, gasping for air, grieving for his only friend.

After a few minutes, Kane laid Barney back on his blanket and wiped his face with his sleeve, his pain morphing into a violent rage. He stood, raising his arms in the air, and screamed at the top of his lungs.

"You hateful bastard! This what you want? To take everything from me? Well, God, *you win!* You've broken me, and I hate you for it! Why don't you just kill me?" he yelled with blind fury. *"Kill me,* damn you! If you hate me so much that you would do this, then just kill me now and send me to hell, because I will *never* devote myself to a sadist! Do something real for once, and kill me like you killed everyone I ever loved!" Kane screamed. "Look, I'll even help you do it!" he yelled as he began stomping wildly toward the front of the bunker, his chest throbbing.

Kane reached the first wall of plastic and tore it down, flinging it angrily to the side. He stepped quickly up the stairs, his heart gaining momentum in his chest. He clawed at the second barrier and stripped it from the door, tears streaming from his eyes. Unbarring the heavy door, he pushed his way through and out into the open, squinting his eyes shut against the light as he screamed.

"Do it! *Do it!*" Kane gulped the poisoned air into his lungs and slapped at his chest. "Show yourself to be the all-powerful God everyone thinks you are and *do something*! Answer me, you fraud!"

Suddenly, something moved inside Kane's chest. It crinkled and then moved from left to right with an audible popping sound. He grunted as the air in his lungs was physically knocked out of him. Kane clawed madly at the air, his legs pinwheeling as he elevated slightly from the earth and hung suspended for what seemed like an eternity before being forced down onto his knees on the hard, blackened ground. Any fight left within him immediately surrendered, evaporating like the morning mist under the gaze of a heavy sun.

In the stillness that followed, a stiff breeze blew up and ruffled Kane's shirt and hair as he gasped to refill his lungs. The pain in his chest was gone, completely gone. With his hand pressed tightly to his chest, he rocked back onto the turf outside the bunker and sat for what seemed like forever as tears formed streams down his grizzled face. He began rubbing his palm in a circular motion over his heart, trying to analyze what had just happened. He had been manipulated by some invisible force. His heart had moved, quite physically, as though some internal malfunction had been restored. He tried to choke back the sheer brokenness of the moment, to master himself, but his own burden crushed him even as he felt it lifted away. Minute flowed into minute as the tears poured from his eyes until at long last his system refused to continue their production.

Something had changed inside him.

For the first time he opened his eyes, squinting in the dim light, feeling as though he had never used them before. The scene that greeted him was one of desolation. Not one single aspect of the landscape seemed familiar to him. Mouth agape, he stared at where his home had been, the trees in the yard now burnt, barren stalks, the dark gray sky churning above him. He breathed deeply, and the air continued to sustain him. It smelled of smoke, destruction, and second chances and was the purest scent he had ever breathed. He closed his eyes again and took the sweet new life into his lungs. He slowly made it to his feet, wiped his face, and ran his hands through his hair, exhaling.

"Okay, God," he said quietly. "I'm listening."

✫ ✫ ✫

The wind had kicked up and was biting through his clothes. It was cool, very cool for early summer. Kane guessed it was about fifty-five degrees, roughly thirty degrees colder than it should be at this time of year. He squinted at the rolling black cloud cover that turned the day into a perpetual twilight. It was hard to tell what time of day it was, but he was unwilling to stay in the bunker another night. Now that he had emerged, he had no desire to return to its musty depths.

Resolving to go back in only to get Barney and any gear he would need for his journey, Kane stepped back into the bunker. He quickly gathered the army duffel and began stuffing a few items into it: his and Barney's blankets, some extra clothing, the six-inch fixed-blade knife, magnesium fire starter, compass, crank radio, leftover batteries, an old water skin, and the remains of the first aid kit. He then shrugged into a fleece jacket. Exhaling a loaded sigh, he began making his way out, stopping at the bottom of the stairs. He looked over his right shoulder at his grandfather's M1 Garand. The world he knew was gone. He would need some protection and a tool to hunt with, if he could find game. Kane went to the rifle and picked it up, working the action a few times. It looked functional, but he could not be sure. The rifle needed to be cleaned and lubricated, but he did not exactly have the resources for the job.

He'd have to test it first. He grabbed up the thirty rounds of old military ammo in their old paper boxes and carried it all to the surface. Setting the pack and rifle down at the entrance to the bunker, he stopped and sighed again. He hated that bunker. Every time he reentered, he had the distinct feeling that the doors would slam behind him and he would once again be trapped—this time, forever. He took a deep breath, let it out, and entered for the last time. Moving quickly to the rear of the bunker, he emptied the water bucket onto the floor, refilling it with rapid pumps of the handle. He picked up the bucket and, taking two steps, bent and scooped up Barney, the furry body limp in the crook of his arm. Kane quickly stepped back up the stairs to the surface, setting first the bucket and then Barney gently on the ground. He stood and surveyed the wreckage where his house used to be. Starting toward it, he began scanning the debris for something he could use to dig with. After a few minutes of searching, Kane retrieved a broken, jagged half of a ceramic kitchen bowl. Satisfied, he returned to an area near the bunker, where he dropped to his knees and began digging through the scorched grass to the soil below. Ten minutes of hard work rendered a depression in the clay approximately two feet deep. Kane reached over, picked up his friend, and lowered him gently into the hole. Using the broken bowl, he scraped the excavated dirt onto Barney until he was completely covered. Using the flat underside of the bowl, he smacked the dirt down into place and shifted back on his heels to sit for a quiet moment.

"Thanks for lending me Barney. He was a really smart, good-natured little guy. He was my last true friend. I'm grateful for the time we had together. I guess you have your reasons for taking him from me." Kane paused and wiped his face, smiling sadly. "He loves bacon...and...and when you rub his belly, but you'll never get rid of him if you do that."

Kane smiled again weakly and sat for a while longer in silence in front of the small grave.

"So....Amen, I guess."

After gathering his equipment together and filling the water skin, he shut the blast doors to the bunker. He threaded the sheathed knife onto his belt and slung the pack over his shoulder with a grunt. The full water skin added a good bit of weight. Kane picked up the rifle and dropped eight rounds into it, loading it to full capacity. He shouldered it and aimed at the splintered trunk of a fallen tree about thirty yards away. The rifle felt solid and had a good weight to it. The nature of the thing spoke to him; the familiarity of shooting was like breathing as he slowly squeezed the trigger. The rifle cracked, echoing across the barren valley, and a chunk of burnt bark exploded from the base of the tree. It was right on target.

"They sure don't make them like they used to," he said to himself.

Kane slung the old rifle over his shoulder and set off in the dim light, down in the direction where he knew the main road should be. He had to find survivors.

✲ ✲ ✲

The hollowed-out general store would have to do for the night. Even with the dimness of the day, Kane could tell it was getting darker, and the temperature was dropping fast. He stepped into the burned-out Western Auto store, which only had three walls and no roof, and glanced around. It would at least provide some protection from the wind. Kane loosened the rifle and leaned it against the wall, followed by his pack, which went next to it. He stepped back outside to rummage around the immediate area for stuff to burn and returned with an armload of chunks of charred wood and bits of paper and cardboard. Making a small pile with the scraps of paper, piece by piece he made a teepee with the wood slivers over it. After completing a decent little structure, Kane retrieved the magnesium fire starter and, with the knife, shaved a small pile of the silver flakes right next to the paper. A few flicks of the blade against the striker lit the magnesium with a white flash, and the paper soon followed. In a matter of minutes, Kane had a more than adequate fire going. He let the blaze settle a little before setting a hubcap he had found on top of the fire. With a small smile of satisfaction, he reached his left hand into his jacket pocket and pulled out a slightly burned can of chicken noodle soup he had scavenged during his walk. He cut the top of the can open and poured its contents into the hubcap. Leaning back against the pack, Kane rubbed slowly at his face and allowed the warmth of the fire to spread over his body.

He had walked nine or ten miles along the broken, burned highway toward Knoxville. Now he was just on the outskirts of the city. It had alarmed him how much destruction there had been, and he feared that if the whole nation had suffered as badly as the Knoxville area, it might never recover. The lush, rolling green hills were now hollow, barren, and black. Cars sat as if frozen in time, their blackened skeletal drivers' hands still clutching desperately at the wheel. Everything had happened so fast, no one could react. He had seen no people, few animals, and no living vegetation since leaving the bunker. He had been very fortunate to find the canned soup intact during his journey. He furrowed his brow as he contemplated the fact that he had not seen another single living person all day long. He began to wonder if he was all that was left of a ruined world.

A cold wind blew across the room, and Kane pulled his blanket up and drew it close around him. He removed a small bottle from the pack and shook out a potassium iodide tablet. There was just no way of knowing how irradiated the environment was. He popped the pill in his mouth and swallowed. Bending forward, he removed the boiling hubcap from the fire, using a strip of torn cloth, and set it next to him. He was just so tired. He had already been through so much, and each new step seemed to draw him closer to some unforeseen destiny. How he had even survived the initial attack had been a miracle, but the true miracle had occurred when he emerged from the bunker. Something supernatural had happened, something ridiculous that completely defied all logic. His heart felt great, which was impossible. He had felt it physically move as if someone had reached into his chest and grabbed it. In his terrible moment of personal desperation, he had reached out, and someone had reached back. God had reached back. Was he losing his mind?

He could swear he had heard a whisper on the wind that had spoken to him. Listen, trust, and obey, it said. The words seemed to permeate his very being.

He had thought about those words all day long, and there was no other explanation for it. The God that he had rebelled against for so long wanted him to listen, trust, and obey—but to what end? Kane reached down with the cloth strip and checked the soup to find that it had sufficiently cooled.

"Thank you, Campbell's," he said as he tipped the hubcap of steaming soup into his mouth. The broth was hot, and Kane closed his eyes as he savored each noodle and fragment of processed chicken that touched his lips. It went down easy and had a rejuvenating aroma; it reminded him of his childhood and how a dose of chicken soup had the power to cure all.

Whatever was in store for him, he could not imagine, but he was confident of one thing: the God who had saved him from himself was far from being finished with him. He tipped the hubcap again, and the wet noodles tickled his whiskers.

DAY 34

KNOXVILLE, TENNESSEE

Among the rubble and ruins of the Southern town, a slight figure glided easily in between the fires and through the smoke. Slowly and carefully it moved, each step calculated, each movement planned, stopping occasionally to listen. The young woman continued to slide through the wreckage, looking like a spirit trapped in the mortal world.

She took two striding steps and arrived at a cement wall, leaning her body against it and cocking her head to listen again. She nervously tugged the stocking cap on her head down around the back of her neck and pushed several renegade strands of blonde hair back up under the dirty cap. Her eyes darted left and right, searching. She was sure she had lost them. She was faster and smarter, and her brain wasn't scrambled like theirs. She did not think it correct to even call them people. People were what they *had* been. Not any more, not now. She strained her ears over the crackle of a nearby Volkswagen beetle that was burning. Craning her neck slowly around the edge of the building, she tried to get a look down the next street. It appeared clear. She moved quietly, walking on her toes to avoid excess noise, and entered a ruined consignment clothing store with an illegible name scrawled in broken letters across the entrance. Moving as fast as possible, she crossed to the stairs and went up to the small room that had most likely been a studio apartment above the desecrated establishment. She moved to the corner and sat down, drawing her knees up to her chest.

She had nothing anymore, nothing but the clothes she had found and a constant string of prayer running through her head. That was the only part of her old life that had not been taken from her. Nothing could take that from her. Even though she could not speak the words, she prayed them anyway in her mind. It gave her comfort to know God had not forgotten her.

Molly shifted and leaned her head back against the wall, shutting her eyes and exhaling slowly. She had not seen another healthy, living human being since she had dragged herself from the wreckage of her dorm room several weeks ago. Everyone she had come across was dead, dying, or had mutated into one of *them*. She had been so confused at first why these other survivors had tried to kill her. They had first appeared to just be sick people, but after a group of them had tried to eat her, she had changed her mind. Something had altered them. Something chemical had fried their rational brains and had turned them into rabid, cannibalistic creatures. It was disgusting how their skin seemed not to fit anymore, sagging off their starved frames, and how they were always scratching and coughing. Most of them seemed completely oblivious to major injuries, burns, and trauma that would have a normal person concerned. She called them "Sicks," because the name was fitting.

She put her hands over her face and rubbed her eyes. She had slept very little and eaten even less in the weeks since she was tossed into the nightmare. Something about the constant fear of being found by one of them had her terrified of spending too much time in the open or accidentally falling asleep in an unsafe place. She knew she needed to get out of the city, but she was also terrified of what she might find outside of it.

A muffled coughing on the street below caused Molly to freeze and cover her mouth with her hands. She had heard what sounded like only one of them, but they never traveled alone, never. Molly sat as still as she could, hardly breathing, waiting. There it was again, more coughing, coughing and moaning out in front of the building and in the alley behind her.

The coughing was everywhere, and one of them was in the building below her now, shuffling and moaning. How did they always find her? It was like they could smell her out. Molly pinched her eyes shut and began praying in her mind. *Heavenly Father God, hear me please! I'm so tired, I can't...I just don't know where to go...there is nowhere that's safe.*

One of them was moving up the stairs, coughing.

Father, send your angels. Send your angels, Father! If it is your will that I live, send your angels to protect me, because I can't do it. I can't do it anymore.

The Sick was nearing the top of the stairs, scratching and coughing.

She opened her eyes but continued praying. *Jesus, Lord God, Your will be done. Your will be done.*

The thing shambled through the door, bloody, burned, and half naked, and for one terrible instant they locked eyes. The creature emitted a blood-curdling shriek and began pointing at her. They were running. She could hear them in the street and below her in the building, running, coming up. Coming for her.

Move!

Her brain screamed as the figure with the bloody, sagging skin lurched at her. She was up and moving, dodging under the grasping arms, and in three steps she vaulted through the busted-out window to her right, spinning and grabbing the windowsill. It was a fifteen-foot drop to the street, and she dropped as the creature came through the window after her. Falling, she hit the stone alley and pitched forward onto the ground, knocking the wind out of herself with a grunt. She rolled to the side, seeing stars, the shrieks growing louder in her ears. Hoisting herself to her feet, she began running, blindly running away. She knew if they trapped her in the alley, it was over. She burst out of the alley in a dead sprint and saw the lot of them streaming out of the building to her left. There had to be twenty of them, maybe more. She groaned in terror as the muscles of her legs began to cramp and she struggled to catch her breath.

Lord Jesus, save me!

Molly was slowing considerably as the rabid, nightmarish gang descended upon her. She dashed into another building, hoping to find something she could use to barricade herself in, but as soon as she cleared the opening she knew she was in trouble. The building had an upper floor that had mostly collapsed onto the first with multiple holes in the walls and no ceiling. It wasn't going to work. She bolted for a gaping hole in the far wall. Taking a few running steps, she leaped over a pile of junk in the floor and landed on the uneven concrete surface, her right ankle twisting violently under her weight. Molly gasped and took two more steps, her leg buckling under the stabbing pain. She stumbled and went to all fours, scrambling into the corner and collapsing to face her pursuers. Tears cut fresh paths down her dirty cheeks as she balled her fists and cried a desperate sound. The awful burnt, bloody monsters poured through the wall and did not slow as they came at her, mouths wide in horrible screams.

Jesus SAVE!

Something flashed from the hole in the wall to her left, as the butt of a rifle struck with a gooey smack against the side of the closest Sick's head. A man. He was swinging the rifle and kicking wildly at the freaks. Three, four, five of them were down. The man continued fighting them off with devastating blows, standing between her and the madness. He brought the rifle up, and she watched in a strange slowness as the rifle glowed and cracked over and over, the Sicks falling in a gory display. Molly was frozen, her limbs anchored in stone. The stranger continued fighting, ducking and dodging, shooting and smashing with the butt of the rifle. He fought with a savageness that shocked her as he moved, shooting and striking the vile creatures to the ground. After what seemed like an eternal instant, it was over.

He continued to stand with his back to her, breathing heavily and watching for movement. He squeezed off a few more rounds until the few who were still thrashing became still. Slowly he scanned the immediate area, watching, waiting. Nothing moved in the urban twilight. After a time, the man slowly turned to face Molly, and she was able to see him well for the first time. He looked solid and capable, a man in his early thirties with a motley head of dark brown hair, grey-blue eyes, broad shoulders, and a bearded face stern with the stress of battle. As the barrel of the M1 smoked, he set it against the wall and extended his hand to her, the stern look melting into something softer.

"Are you okay? What...what the...what is going on here?" he said, still out of breath. "Why...why were they attacking you?"

Molly continued to stare, uttering not a sound. God had not forgotten her. He had sent her an angel.

The man smiled slightly and continued to hold out his hand, his face a reflection of a strangely ancient, fearless character.

"Okay, let's backtrack," he said. "My name is Kane, and I'd like to be your friend."

Molly erupted in a choked, wheezing gurgle of tears that sounded like a toad being squished as she reached for the offered hand.

✲ ✲ ✲

The dim streets of what was formerly Knoxville, Tennessee, had an eerie appearance in the fading dimness of the day. Nothing stirred in the rubble-filled streets save a lonely bit of paper floating on the wind and the constant flicker of a burning city. The acrid smoke of many fires rose up ever higher to mingle and disappear into the collective blackness that was now the ceiling of the world.

Kane moved cautiously, picking his way through the marred streets with his rifle held low, at the ready. The girl followed close behind him, mimicking his every move with a slight limp. She had not yet told him her name—or anything, for that matter. He had decided that it was most likely because of shock and that she would speak when she was ready. As he moved, he scanned left to right and continually glanced behind him and the girl for possible threats. As he glanced, he noticed her watching the ground and stepping carefully, her mouth forming silent words as she walked. Under the ash and filthy clothes, she appeared to be a naturally pretty girl with blonde hair, not older than nineteen or twenty, and with a hard, natural athleticism that showed in her slim figure.

He stepped to the corner of a broken Central Commerce Bank and quickly peeked around the corner. The street was clear. He motioned for the girl to follow and moved with purpose, deliberately trying not to focus on the occasional arm or leg or child's shoe that protruded from a collapsed building or overturned vehicle.

Initially, his thought had been to go into the city and attempt to find survivors or means of communication, but he had quickly decided that neither might ever be found. He had resolved to backtrack and leave the city when he heard the girl's cries a few blocks away. The madness he had seen in those creatures' faces had been something far from human. The sunken eyes, sagging skin, and burnt bloodiness had shocked him. Seeing them converge on the girl had left him no choice. No choice at all.

Kane had been steadily trying to make it back to a multistory investment firm building that he had passed on his way into the city. Being in the shadow of a great hill, it had seemed to weather the violence fairly well, and he had marked it in his memory as a good spot for taking refuge if things went bad. As they moved, the structure came into view around the corner with a partially destroyed sign that read, "Singular Investments: We take pride in every single one." The building was about five stories tall, and although the brick façade had mostly come off, it still appeared to hold its structural integrity. Kane surmised it had survived because of the large hillside just beside it that had blocked a large portion of the initial blast wave. He motioned toward the building.

"We'll move to that building and stay in there for the night."

The girl nodded in agreement, and the two of them moved without a sound across the street and into the darkened structure.

Just inside, Kane motioned for her to stop and wait at the entrance as he removed the flashlight from his pocket. She watched as he moved with a measured fluidity down the small corridor, snapping the rifle left and right and using the flashlight to flood the rooms with white light. She waited in silence as he disappeared down the hall of the abandoned office building. Moments later he emerged from the shadows at the end of the hall.

"All clear; come on."

They moved slowly to a set of stairs and began climbing. At every turn Kane made a slight pause at the corner and quickly snapped his upper torso around the corner, rifle and light pointed upward.

Kane moved methodically with Molly in tow, having her remain behind while he cleared, then calling her forward as they progressed. After what felt like a long time, they arrived on the top floor and moved to a large conference room that looked to be in complete disarray, with a big wooden table and wooden chairs strewn everywhere with all the windows blown out. Molly entered the room and stood, rolling her hands over one another and looking about.

"It's alright," Kane said, seeing her uncertainty. "The light and smoke from a fire will be visible, but I'll barricade the door well first. We should be safe in here."

Molly moved to a wall and sat, drawing her knees to her chest as Kane shut the heavy oak door and turned the deadbolt. He then grabbed one of the chairs and shoved it up under the handle. Propping up a second chair, he stood on it to reach up into a hole in the wall and grasped a protruding 2x4. With easy back-and-forth motions, he worked the board free without bending the nails too badly. Kane surveyed the room. He needed something hard, and preferably metal. After a moment of rummaging around in the debris, he came up with a length of one-inch diameter lead pipe.

"Not ideal," he stated, "but it will work." Kane went to work, removing the chair from the door and replacing it with the 2x4.

Molly remained still, an unmoving shadow in the darkness. Kane, flashlight in mouth, went to tapping and then banging the nails through the plank into the wooden floor. After procuring a few more nails from various locations around the room, Kane returned to nail the top part of the board down through the door itself, just under the knob. He grabbed the 2x4 and tugged vigorously a few times. Satisfied, he began to build a fire out of available debris, and after a few short minutes, the room was ablaze with the warm light of burning chair legs, the smoke wafting up through jagged gaps in the roof.

Kane sat back to another wall and began pulling necessary items out of the pack, aware of the girl's penetrating gaze. He stopped while pulling a blanket from the rucksack and met Molly's stare.

"Okay, look," he said, looking down with a sigh. "Let's just get something out of the way." He set the pack down and looked her in the eyes once again. "You don't have to worry about me. I'm not going to hurt you or...or try to...you know, take advantage of you or something. That's not who I am. I'm just a guy. And I'm as scared and lost as you are, so maybe we can keep each other company for a while."

Kane watched as the vigilance in her face drained and her shoulders visibly slumped.

"Here," he said. "You're welcome to share anything that I have." He extended the blanket to her. "If it smells like a puppy, it's because that's who it belonged to last."

He dug into the pack and, to his surprise, found one last energy bar. He halved it and gave half to her. Through the dirt, ash, and grime shone the most genuine smile Kane had ever seen. It was a smile that radiated with the thankfulness of being safe for once, for simply having someone who was willing to share a fire, a blanket, and a meager meal. Kane couldn't help but smile back, a big smile—the first time he had really smiled in a very, very long time.

✵ ✵ ✵

Molly made a chopping motion with her hand toward her throat. She did it again, wincing as she brought her hand to her throat as though playing a game of Pictionary.

"I don't….What are you trying to…?" Kane said as he watched.

She brought her palms in and down, making a rumbling sound with her throat as though something was collapsing. The she suddenly raised her hands up, as if trying to protect her head.

"Alright," he said. "So you were in a building that…what? Fell down on you?"

She nodded her head rapidly.

"Okay."

She raised her hands again and made the chopping motion to her throat again. This was followed by her opening her mouth and moving her lips without sound and making a forward motion with her hands. She shook her head and touched her throat again.

"Something fell on you and hurt your throat?"

She nodded.

"And you can't speak now?"

She nodded vigorously and dropped her hands to her thighs, as if all done.

"Oh. I thought you were in shock or something." He paused, thinking. "Can you write?"

She nodded again, and Kane began digging into the pack until he found the first aid kit. Pushing through to the back of the kit, Kane removed a small notebook and pen, which he handed over to her. She immediately began writing at a frenzied pace, and after a minute she handed him back two small sheets of paper with the following message:

THE BASICS

My name is Molly Stevens, and I am/was a 19-year-old freshman at UT.

When the attack happened, I was trapped in/under my dorm.

That's how my voice was injured.

For the last few weeks I haven't eaten or slept much.

I've just barely survived, hiding from those monsters.

I did not have much living family before the attack, so now I have no one, really.

I'm not sure what to do now, where to find food/water or where to go.

If you see me moving my lips, I'm praying.

I love Jesus.

God sent you to help me, and I'm thankful for you.

Thanks for sharing what you have with me.

Kane smiled and looked up.

"Nice to meet you, Molly. You went to UT? Are you familiar with the downtown area?"

Molly nodded.

"You don't know where an emergency radio broadcast station is down there, do you?"

Molly nodded and scribbled on her pad. "Third and Finley I think. The building with the huge antenna."

"Excellent! We'll check that out tomorrow." Kane rubbed his chin. "Well, guess it's my turn now. My name is Kane Lorusso, and I lived with my family in Green County, just outside of town. I was a police officer, a father, and a husband." He paused for a long silence. "I was a lot of things that I'm not anymore, I guess." Another long pause while Kane rubbed his face. "When the attacks happened I took refuge in a fallout bunker on my property, and I stayed in there until two days ago. My puppy, Barney, survived the attack too, but he didn't make it out of the bunker. He was my friend. I was told a few days before the attack that I have a fatal heart condition, so, I'm not sure what's going on there."

Kane paused and tapped at the paper. "I see that you wrote that you love Jesus, and you like to pray. I think those are good things. I think that God has given me another chance at life so I can use it to do something for him, but I don't really know what that means or what exactly I am supposed to do. So…I'm trying to figure it out as I go, day by day."

Kane decided to omit the part about God talking to him and what happened to him outside the bunker.

Molly smiled at him again, that brilliant smile. She then looked down and scribbled something out quickly. She handed it over to Kane.

"Is this damage just local or what?" it read.

Kane shook his head with a grimace. "No, Molly, I'm afraid that the entire country, maybe even the whole world may be like this. In the last few months, before the attacks, did you hear about the Sword of Destiny?"

Molly nodded.

"Well, it seems they were the ones who started it all. When they unleashed what they had, most every other country in the world did the same. They used nuclear, biological, and chemical weapons all together, the combined effects of which might help explain your friends that tried to kill you in the city."

Molly scratched against the paper with the pen and revealed her work again. "Your heart, how bad is it?"

"Well, I'm not really sure. The doctor seemed to indicate that it was most certainly fatal and that I would need a transplant. How much time I have is really unknown; I mean, it could just give out at any time, I guess."

He meant the last statement as a sort of lighthearted attempt at humor, but as he watched her reaction, he saw a mask of fear and abandonment flash across the young woman's face and realized something for the first time.

She needs me.

He continued quickly, "But you know, since I came out of that bunker I've been feeling a lot better."

Molly nodded, acting unconcerned, and started scribbling again. She showed it to Kane. "Where's your family?"

Kane swallowed hard and gritted his teeth. "I don't know. They went to Miami just before the attacks, to get things ready for my initial heart surgery, but I don't know what happened to them. I do know Miami was hit...."

He stopped and leaned back, taking in a deep breath. "I'm a realist, Molly, so I'm not going to lie to myself or you. They are all probably dead."

Molly hung her head, and the room was quiet except for the light popping of the fire and the brisk wind pushing through the hollow windows.

After a moment, Kane said, "It's hard to think about, but I have to believe that everything happens for a reason."

Molly nodded again, looking down to write once again, "God has saved us for his purpose. He will tell us what he wants us to do."

"I think he will, Molly," Kane said. "I'm sure that he will." With a quick smile, he added, "We should get some rest." He shook his blanket and pulled it up tight around him. "Rest well. In the morning we'll head over to that emergency radio substation on Third and Finley. See if we can find anybody else. If you need something, just reach over and shake me."

Molly nodded and laid down, curling up with her blanket. Kane sat with his eyes half closed, looking into the fire. He watched the flames jump and dance as they swirled and spun with each other. Swirling and dancing like the memories of his family. Memories of his children giggling and squealing as they ran, the security of his wife's embrace, and the warmth of her kiss. It all seemed so far away and dreamlike, and he just wanted to hold them in his arms again. The fire glowed and fizzled, and Kane began to drift and float away into a different time. A time awash with golden light and the love of his family, a family that could not be further from him now as he sat huddled in the barren wastelands of civilization.

DAY 35

NEAR COLUMBIA, SOUTH CAROLINA

Courtland Thompson walked through the endless field of tall golden wheat at a leisurely pace. The blue sky radiated with crystal clarity, and the wind rustled the stalks of wheat like golden waves on an open sea. He closed his eyes as he walked, breathing deep the cool breeze and enjoying the sun on his face. He belonged here; he had always known it deep in his soul.

"Courtland."

The gigantic black man stopped, opening his eyes and looking to the left where he had heard the voice. He stared at the endless wheat stretching into the horizon. He looked to the right and then turned to look behind him. That was strange. He could have sworn someone had called his...

"Courtland."

Courtland spun back to the front and found nothing that had not been there before. The wheat continued to gently bow as the wind cascaded over it. He squinted his eyes, trying to see.

"Courtland, are you listening with your eyes or your ears?"

"But I can't...see."

"Then *listen*."

The giant black man became still. "I am listening."

"Who do you say that I am?"

Courtland stammered, his knees shaking, "I...I...who *are* you?"

"Who do *you* say that I am?"

Courtland's knees buckled, and he dropped down onto them among the tall wheat. A brilliant bright light burst forth and surrounded him, causing him to gasp and tears to flow down his face. *"My Lord Jesus!"* he exclaimed, squinting into the light.

"The one you've had visions of is coming. He will be a fugitive and an outcast, but you must help him to understand his purpose. He will come in my name, bearing the sword of justice. It is at his side that you must combat the darkness in my name and for my sake."

"Yes, my Lord," said Courtland, forcing the words from his throat.

"Be vigilant, for the time is at hand," the voice whispered.

Courtland sat straight up in the darkness of his small room. The padded wooden table he used for a bed creaked under his weight. He exhaled and rubbed his hands over his head, trying to slow his breathing and the hammering of his heart. Had it been real? It sure had felt real; the memory of the vision still burned in his mind.

His knees crinkled and popped, and Courtland winced as he swung his feet over the edge of the table. He rested them on the cold floor and turned his head to look out the window. The ranch was completely quiet except for the occasional walking of a sentry along the fence.

"Combat the darkness?" he whispered to himself.

Courtland could feel the fear and doubt creeping up in his chest. Even though he was immense in size, a true modern-day giant at eight and a half feet tall and over five hundred pounds, he was no longer a young man. After his sports career, he had successfully retained a good bit of his athletic prowess but had been unable to keep from aging. Now he began to digest the words that had just been planted in his mind. He was to become some sort of warrior at fifty-three years old? He knew that his doubt was a result of his sinfulness as a fallen man, but even now he was unable to make it leave him.

He wondered if his mind was going bad on him, or if the short-term memory loss he had suffered after the attacks had something to do with the visions. They were becoming more and more frequent to the point where they seemed more real than his own memories. He felt as though he was going crazy. He remembered the week before the attacks; and then the next thing he knew, he had woken up here at this ranch outside of Columbia, South Carolina, as a part of "the Family," as they called themselves. He couldn't though for the life of him recall what had happened in between. When they had found him, he had been in the middle of the burnt, blackened woods, lying on a ten-foot square patch of pristine green grass. He had been neatly dressed and unharmed during the attacks. They had said it had been the strangest thing any of them had ever seen, but Courtland knew stranger things were coming. Great and terrible changes were on the horizon. The United States was in shambles, and the wicked would rise to power without the constraints of the law to bind them.

"Combat the darkness," he said again to himself, as he lay back down on the table. "To God be the glory, forever and ever." He closed his eyes and lay still as the strength of righteousness began to fill his heart once again.

"I will combat the darkness."

✡ ✡ ✡

Molly pointed toward the large blackened building with a half-toppled radio antenna pointing up from the roof and motioned for Kane to follow her. After checking the street, they stayed together, moving and scanning, vigilant in their security measures. Stepping into the doorway, Kane checked the handle on the door and found it to be locked. He jiggled the knob a few times to get Molly's attention. She nodded her understanding. They had agreed to limit any talk or verbal noise as much as possible to lower their chances of being noticed by Sicks. Kane pointed to his eyes and then up to indicate for her to look for a way to climb up. After spending a few moments looking, they found a bolted drainpipe that showed possible access to several windows. Molly went first, easily scaling the pipe, grabbing and stepping with grace. Upon reaching the height of the second-floor window, she leaned to the right, away from the pipe, to test it. She was going to have to jump for it.

"Be careful," Kane whispered, stating the obvious.

Molly leapt from the pipe with a cat-like smoothness that took her straight to the window ledge. She snagged it, pulling herself up and into the opening without using her bad ankle. The girl was strong and able.

No wonder she's survived as long as she has.

Kane ascended the pipe slowly and with careful movements. It creaked loudly under his weight and the added weight of the pack made his movements significantly clumsier. Molly reached out the window and caught the pack as Kane swung it over to her. He jumped and grabbed the ledge and, after a bit of scrambling, was up and through the window. In the twilight, the building was dark, and it stank with the smell of rotten death. Kane looked at Molly, who had her hand over her nose and mouth.

"Stay here while I check it out," he said.

Molly nodded. Kane stood, rifle raised, listening for any sounds of danger. He walked slowly, checking his corners, sweeping from left to right and snapping the flashlight on when needed. He stepped through the doorway to a larger room and stopped still, the smell of death over-whelming. On the floor in front of him was a pile of six bodies, lying all haphazardly on top of one another, with one body lying out to the side. It looked like one of those strange suicide cults where everyone died all at once. Upon closer inspection, each person had a carefully placed gunshot wound to the back of the head, execution style—all but the one off to the side, who had been shot in the chest. The weapon lay a few inches from the lone man's hand, a 9mm compact Glock. A dirty ID tag on the man's shirt read "Rick Morgan."

"Radio Rick," Kane muttered under his breath. "Did it really come to this?"

Kane picked up the weapon and checked it, only to find it completely empty. Rick had killed everyone, at their request, while they had knelt in a circle and had then shot himself. The death of civilization was not an easy thing to handle. Some people didn't even want to try.

"Rest easy, bro," Kane said quietly and stuffed the Glock into his pack.

He called to Molly, and she hesitantly appeared around the corner, still covering her nose and mouth.

"It's alright; you don't have to look. Come on past," he said.

She slid past and moved to the stairs.

"Think it's up there?" Kane asked.

Molly shrugged.

"Okay."

They moved up the stairwell and onto another floor, which consisted of a large control room that looked to control the broadcast system. Kane let out a small sigh and shook his head. A fire axe protruded from the center of the main console, its handle angling up at a perfect forty-five degree angle. All the control panels had been destroyed, and their internal wiring and circuits gushed forth from them like the guts of a great robotic beast.

"Jeez, Rick, was this necessary?" Kane paused as he looked around. "Well, I guess coming here was a good idea, but none of this equipment looks functional."

Molly shrugged again, a slight look of disappointment on her face. She turned and, quickly scanning the room, stepped to the far wall and pulled down a map. Kane watched with interest as she stepped back over to him. He looked over her shoulder as she held forward a map of the Southeastern United States. Molly started tapping rapidly with her finger at the map.

"What?" Kane said looking closely. The map appeared to be geographically detailed and had certain points located with stars. "Look at the legend; what do the stars represent?"

She flipped the map over and brushed her finger over the different stars on the legend.

"Okay, I see it. The small stars are labeled EMRSS, or emergency radio substations, and this big star is labeled EMRCS—emergency radio control station." He looked at Molly and then back at the map. "The sub stations are all inside cities, but this control station is on the coast between Savannah and Charleston. I even read in the news a while back that some emergency radio stations were being fortified to protect them in case of some sort of event. It's possible that this station could be intact and functional."

Molly looked at Kane with questions in her eyes.

"Okay, it's like this: the United States has been torn to pieces, but there still have to be pockets of survivors out there," he explained. "These people need to know that there are others out here too, others who are trying to survive in the wasteland. If we can make it to that radio control station, we might be able to broadcast messages to survivors over the emergency channels, or make contact with someone."

Kane looked at the map and thought for a moment, sighing. "I don't know what to do. What I want to do is go to Miami and look for my family. But how would I get there? How could I cross that distance on foot? What about the danger? Even if I had a working vehicle, many of the roads and highways are going to be in ruins, and fuel would be limited. It's not logical. It might not even be possible.

"Check this out," he said suddenly, pointing at the EMRCS on the map. "This is something I can do. There is something happening here that's bigger than you or me. I have to accomplish some purpose before I can move on. I know that sounds crazy."

Molly nodded.

Kane hurried to add, "Don't get me wrong, I haven't forgotten my family. If they're out there, maybe they'll hear the signal that we broadcast. Right now, though, I know God has awakened my heart for some purpose." Kane pointed to the EMRCS on the map. "And I think...I think this is where I have to go."

Kane rubbed at his chest unconsciously and then gestured with his hand.

"We both know what complete isolation can do to a person. It's the lack of hope and fear of that continued isolation that kills a lot of the ones who survive a catastrophe. We have the opportunity to spread some hope and reach out to others out there, if we make it there and the equipment still works."

Molly nodded and smiled.

"That is," Kane added, "if you're still in?"

Molly smiled but shook her head no.

Kane smiled too. "No? Alright, I see how it is."

Molly suddenly put her hand over Kane's mouth and grabbed him hard on the bicep with her other hand. Kane became quiet, and as they listened, a muffled coughing was just audible above the thump, thump, thadum-thump of many savage fists banging on the door to the outside.

☆ ☆ ☆

Suddenly the stern look returned to Kane's face as he looked directly at Molly. "How weak is your ankle?"

She shrugged.

"Write," he said. "Can you run on it?"

Molly pulled out her pad and scribbled, "It hurts, but I think I can run."

"Okay," he said.

Kane looked down and checked the rifle. There were six rounds in the Garand, and he had another reload of eight ready to go, but that was all the ammo he had left. The encounter when he had first met Molly had expended over half of his ammo supply. Unlike modern AR-15 style rifles, this rifle's design made it impossible to reload midstream without unloading the rifle altogether. Instead, all of the loaded rounds had to be fired before the weapon could be reloaded. That was valuable time wasted—time in which the fight could be lost.

Kane looked at Molly again, saying nothing, and saw the fear beginning to creep up into her face.

"It's alright. We'll make it. We'll figure something out," he said. "Let's go. Stay close to me."

They moved down the stairs and through the room with all the bodies on their way back to the window. Kane gestured for Molly to stop. He stepped to the window and cautiously peered out and down the side of the building to the door. He stood staring for a moment, then whispered to Molly, "There's got to be at least forty or fifty of them down there."

Molly put her hands over her mouth and shrank back against the wall.

"We won't have a chance if we take them head on, so we'll have to outsmart and outmaneuver them," he went on.

Molly had seemed to freeze. Kane continued to peer out the window and then at the surrounding area. "I'll be right back," he said, stepping away from the window. Molly grabbed his arm, the fear vivid in her face.

"I'm coming right back. I'm not going to leave you, I promise."

With those words he stepped away and passed through a few rooms to the opposite side of the building. Molly watched as he looked out the window on the opposite side for a few moments and then returned. The banging was growing louder as fetid bodies slammed against the door, which creaked under the blows.

"Molly, I know you are scared of them, and I understand it's because of what you've been through. But now you are going to have to use your fear to motivate you, not slow you down." He looked her in the eyes. "Are you going to be able to kill one if you have to?"

Molly nodded unflinchingly.

"Good. Remember they're monsters. They're not people anymore."

She nodded again.

"Here's what we have to do. Listen closely, because we don't have much time before they get in here." He pointed across the hall. "You're going to go across the hall and climb out that window. There's a large pile of junk below it, so you're only going to have to drop about ten feet. When you hit, run to the body shop that you can see from the window. It's built into the hillside and should provide you with a good hiding place. Do not stop running. You hear? Your ankle is going to hurt, but you are just going to have to leave that behind and push through it."

Molly nodded silently.

"The garage looks pretty solid, so get in there and close yourself in. Stay there, and I will come to get you later. Oh, and you're going to take the pack with you, in case...well, you might need it if I don't..."

Molly began shaking her head rapidly.

A splintering sound made its way to their ears, and the two could hear a rustling sound below them. They were in the building.

"Look, I've got to distract them from you, because you're not very agile right now. I'll meet up with you later when we lose them, okay? Now, take the pack and go!"

Molly grabbed the pack from Kane and moved quickly across the hall to the window. She popped her head out and glanced left and right. It was clear. Dropping the pack out the window onto the junk, she slipped out and dropped the ten feet and half stumbled, half rolled down the slope, coming to rest on top of a baseball bat, crusted black with carbon. She groaned slightly as a swell of pain rushed through her ankle. She knew the bat would probably only be good for a few licks, but it was better than nothing. She snatched it and the pack up and began moving.

On the other side of the building, Kane could hear them moving through the building, searching. Some were even coming up the stairs, and he could hear their deep, ragged breaths as they labored to find their prey. Kane slung the rifle over his shoulder and ducked out of the window, stepping onto the ledge. Now he had to jump back to the gutter pipe, which did not look so easy from this direction. He heard the scrambling in the hallway behind him and leaped from the window, snagging the gutter in the process and tearing it from the structure. It splintered away with a sharp metallic sound as the pipe folded in half. Kane rode it halfway down and released it, tucking into a forward roll as he landed. The Garand smacked the ground, and Kane thumped hard on his back and slid a few feet. He began to raise himself as he heard the creatures' shrill, moan-like screams from around the building. They had seen Molly.

Flames of pain streaked up Molly's calf and into her thigh as she ran. *Don't look back. You're almost there.*

She ran as fast as she could manage, with each step bringing on a rollercoaster of pain that screamed up her calf, twisted around the back of her thigh, and drove up into her spine.

Don't look back.

She was now within a block of the body shop, but the screams behind her were growing, ever growing. She could no longer stifle the urge to look back. As they closed in on her, she was able to see the hollow eyes and the bloody, blackened sagging of their grayish skin. Their lips peeled back over jagged teeth in a terrible wailing moan like the sound of a wounded soul damaged beyond repair. Molly let fly a wail of her own and pushed for the final stretch.

Kane pulled himself to his feet and grabbed the rifle, its stock falling away from the broken frame.

"Damn!" he yelled. Tossing the stock aside, he began running around the side of the building. The rifle still appeared functional. He rounded the corner and saw the mass of disgusting creatures converging on Molly as she reached the door. Only two of them had toppled out of his window and were now righting themselves in the street.

"No way! *Come on*, Molly, get in there!" The two Sicks that fell from the window behind him were now scrambling toward him quickly, mouths wide. Kane raised the broken rifle and supported it as best he could. a jarring crack, the first shot veered left, but the subsequent rounds hit the first Sick in the chest, and it moaned as it toppled over. Quickly acquiring the second target, he fired. The shot opened the creature's head like a ripened melon, spilling its contents in the street as the ghoul fell.

"Molly!" he gasped as he dashed around the corner.

She slammed her shoulder hard against the garage door and turned the knob, but it did not budge. They were inside fifty yards now, closing fast, their screams heavy in her ears. *Gunfire. Kane, please be okay.*

She rammed against the door again, still finding nothing but resistance. She turned and fled up the small embankment behind the shop. There a small two-foot-by-two-foot window was just visible right at ground level, but she could not see through it. There was no telling what was on the other side of that window. Maybe she could...but there was no time. The monsters flooded through the gate and crossed the yard at a rapid pace. Molly ran to the window and kicked it out with her good foot, shoving the pack through the small opening. She then stepped back as the monsters approached, cocked the bat over her shoulder, and bared her teeth. The first one came in, and Molly swung with everything she had, snapping the creature's head back so hard she thought it might come off. It dropped to the dirt, squirming. She cleared the second and third out with hard licks to the head, but on the fourth creature the head of the bat broke away with a snap. Holding the jagged handle like a wooden stake, she ducked the grasp of another and rose, jamming the spike up and into its chest. The dreadful moaning of the ghouls drowned her very thoughts as she turned and ducked, diving headfirst through the low window. Clearing the window, she fell across the top of a cluttered table before going to the floor. She was immediately up on her feet, grabbing and shoving a tall cabinet in front of the window, cutting off hosts of groping shadows from entry.

Two rounds were left in the Garand, and the reload of eight jiggled in Kane's pocket as he ran. Molly had to have made it inside for the creatures to be swarming around the garage like they were. They screamed and banged and climbed all over it, and suddenly the structure did not look as robust as it once had. He had to get them away from her.

"Hey!" he yelled as he ran. *"Over here! Look! I'm over here!"* He continued running toward the mob, the creatures oblivious to his presence. Weaving through the junk and lifeless cars in the street, he continued forward.

The garage was coming apart, crumbling under the force of the masses outside. Molly scrambled around in the semidarkness, trying to find something she could use to protect herself. She stepped forward, bumping into something hard and metallic. Squinting her eyes in the dimness, she tried to get a better look at the large shape in front of her. She grabbed hold of the cloth covering; pulling the cover to the side, she dropped it on the floor and reached down to feel padded leather, metal, and...handlebars. She had found a motorcycle. Molly groped downward and felt the keys in the ignition, but there was no way to know if it would start.

Kane stopped short and raised the broken rifle, firing twice into the crowd, the steel clip ejecting with a singing sound. He jammed his hand into his pocket, grabbing the other steel clip and shoving it into the top of the rifle. He raised the weapon again. Some of the mob had separated and turned toward him, but the others were remaining. They seemed to be congregating in front of the shop's rollback door, banging and howling. Kane began firing again into the approaching fiends.

More gunshots. Kane is still out there.

She had to do something to help him. The dusty, aged cruiser rumbled steadily next to her. It was holding up for now. She made a quick pass around the room and grabbed a large cylinder of compressed gas, pulling it by the top and dragging it to the rollback door. She paused; the banging was stopping, and she could hear them moving away. More gunshots sounded from the outside. Molly unlocked the rollback door and slid it open slightly. She groaned with the effort, pushing the cylinder out as it fell with a clang and listened as it rolled toward the street.

Kane had three rounds left. As the creatures began to move toward him, he stood his ground, holding the rifle ready. As he stood, he watched as the sliding door on the garage rose slightly and a red cylinder rolled from under the door and into the street. It rolled down the slight incline right into the thick of the creatures. Kane's mind snapped into focus. This needed no explanation. He took a few running steps to the bumper of a burned-out minivan and supported the shattered rifle against it. Aiming at the cylinder, he fired a shot, just as a Sick stepped into the line of fire and had its leg blown off at the knee.

"Come on!"

He took aim again and fired the last two rounds quickly in succession. The scene was suddenly bathed with a blinding flash, followed by a deafening concussion. The Sicks, now just shadows, disappeared against the backdrop of a fireball. Kane dropped behind the bumper of the van for cover.

Molly flung the door up and ran back to the bike, grabbing the pack and slinging it over her shoulder. She straddled the bike and revved the engine. It had been a long time since her grandpa had taught her how to ease the clutch on a motorcycle. She stalled it out. Nerves racking in the silence of the blast, she cranked the motorcycle again. This time she took a deep breath and secured her grip on the throttle. Cranking it heavily to the rear, she popped the clutch, squealing the back tire as she shot from the garage like a missile.

Kane stood and saw Molly coming at him on an older model Honda Shadow 1100.

As she pulled up with a wild look of satisfaction across her face, he dropped the rifle, took the pack from her, and slung it on his back as he climbed onto the bike. Kane glanced over his shoulder to see the Sicks beginning to stand on their feet again. Some of them were fully engulfed in flames.

"*Go!*" he yelled. "Get us out of here!"

The bike growled, and the rear tire barked again as they took off down the ruined street, weaving through the burning wreckage as they went. It was time to get out of the city.

DAY 35

SOMEWHERE IN NORTHWEST SOUTH CAROLINA

Wellsey Littleton sat with his back pressed against the hard, cool rock. Other than a dead wind blowing through a barren landscape, nothing moved and nothing lived in the darkness that engulfed him. The short, fat man spat into the fire without regard to the string of tobacco juice hanging from his chin. The juice dripped off his chin and left small dark stains on the tattered mechanic's uniform that read in cursive "Lucky's Auto."

He didn't care anymore. Had it been weeks or months? It felt like an eternity had passed since the world had gone straight down the tubes. Wellsey folded his arms across his chest and listened to the nothingness. No crickets, owls, or small animals scurrying about, no sounds one got used to in the darkness. Not anymore—just a hollow wind blowing endlessly, a product of man's ultimate violation of the earth. He had known it would happen. Eventually it would have to. All that business of global warming, the depletion of the ozone, and man's destruction of the environment had some folks all worked up. But Wellsey Littleton had known for a long time that before the world died due to those things, the human race would destroy itself, and the planet along with it with a plague of war. Mankind was just too rotten at the core to continue coexisting in this world peaceably—especially once they developed the ability to cause mass destruction with modern weapons.

He sat quietly, contemplating his circumstances by the fire. In his forty-two years of life, he had not found many people he had even cared to even speak with. Most people thought he was an antisocial hermit, but he had always just enjoyed his own company better. Funny. Now that he was truly alone, he kind of wished he had somebody to share his black, smoky tire fire with.

Wellsey looked up and tried to scan the sky for some trace of the moon in the boiling blackness. The landscape was dark except for the flickering of his fire on the nearby tree-stalks. The leafless, branchless poles dug angrily at the sky, blaming it for their fate like bony skeletal fingers. He had not met many survivors of the disaster, and the ones he had found were disinterested in him—or the other way around. He could probably find more people if he tried, but he was out in the country and had no desire to venture toward the cities. He wasn't sure he'd find anything anyway after hearing that most of the urban areas had been wiped away with a wave of God's hand. But they were just stories, and he wasn't sure he believed any of them anyway, especially the stories of folks disappearing up here in the mountains. One woman he met had wailed and said that the evil had come up from the ground and took her son. Crazy old hag. He *would* rather be alone. He spat into the fire again and watched the black juice sizzle and harden in the coals.

Wellsey suddenly looked sharply to the left. Had he seen something in the blackness beyond the fire? He lay still, straining his eyes at the dark world beyond his small bright bubble. The rubber on the fire fizzed and buzzed as it burned.

"Jiminy Christmas," Wellsey said out loud, turning back to the fire and crossing his arms again. The shadows were playing tricks on him. It was all those lame stories that gave him the creeps and put him on edge.

It moved again with a shuffling sound in the dark. Wellsey was on his feet in a surge of adrenalin, tightly gripping the tire iron that had lain beside him.

"Who the hell is it? Who's there?" he yelled into the night. As he stood there, trying to focus his eyes and ears, he had the strangest feeling that as he looked into the nothingness, it looked back into him.

"What do you want? I don't have anything!" he yelled. It moved again, and Wellsey bent down, quickly grabbing a half-burned tire off the edge of the fire. He spun, throwing it like a discus toward the movement. The tire slapped and smacked the ground with a wet sound and slid a few feet, dragging the flames with it. Wellsey's jaw dropped open and the hair on his body stood on end as the thing retreated from the flames.

"*Skreeeeek-k-k-k-k-k-k-k.*"

"*No! Get back!*" He screamed, his own voice sounding girlish and high-pitched. The silent night air now filled with a chorus of sound.

"*Skreeeeeeeeeeek-k-k-k-k-k-k. Skreeeeeee…Skreeeeeeeeee…Skreeeeeeeeeeee-k-k-k-k-k-k-k.*"

They were all around him…those…*monsters.* He spun, turning wildly as the screeching continued to envelop his every sense. Dropping the tire iron, he grabbed a flaming log from the fire as a rapid skittering sound approached. He swung the log back and forth in a shower of sparks as the beast came around the rock toward him.

"*Nooooo! Get back! You're not real! Not real!*" He screamed wildly as it dodged and moved from the flame. "You can't be…you're a…"

The one he never saw came in so fast from the left that he did not have time to adjust his footing. It rammed him hard, and the sheer impact caused him to slam down in the dirt. Wellsey tried to raise himself, choking on the swirling dust that flew up his nose and into his eyes. Something suddenly clamped down on his bicep so forcefully he heard the bone snap, and from his throat came a sharp cry of pain. He was dragged forcefully away from the fire, and then the pressure was gone as quickly as it had come, dropping him fiercely to the ground.

"*Skreeeeeeek-k-k-k-k-k-k-k...Skreeeeee...Skreeeeeeeeee-k-k-k-k-k-k-k.*"

The shrieks were all around him, moving in the darkness. Wellsey reached with his right hand over to his left bicep to check it as he tried to move the fingers of that hand. His right hand moved slowly, shaking as he touched his arm at the shoulder and slid it down. In the darkness his fingers dropped away from contact. He felt the torn shirt, wet, wet with....

Why is it wet?

The warm liquid flowed into his hand. He continued to grope at the ragged stump and choked out a gasp at the realization that his arm was gone.

"Oh, shit...*shit!*"

"*Skreeeek-k-k-k-k-k-k-k.*" They were close now.

"Please," he gasped. "Please, I'm not ready to go yet," he pleaded, cradling what was left of his arm. "I'm not ready."

Something struck him from behind and knocked him flat, facedown in the dirt. The vice closed over the back of his neck and pinned him against the scorched earth. Wellsey cried out as the thing made a whirring sound that burned the back of his neck. Light exploded across his vision with a popping sound, and beams of light burned through his mind. The warm spray of his blood poured into the dirt, and he realized he had stopped breathing. In a detached sort of way, he knew he was dying, but he felt weightless, dropping away from the world, flying. He had always wanted to fly, ever since he was a child. Just like Peter Pan, he was flying away into the night, into the dark, to Never Never Land.

DAY 36

OUTSIDE ASHEVILLE, NORTH CAROLINA

A thumping sound broke the silence of the dim day as the motorcycle crested the top of the hill and began to wind down into the barren valley. Molly and Kane had done their best to avoid Asheville, but they had encountered so many blocked roads that they were going to be forced to cross under I-26 just south of the city. Molly stared straight ahead, focused, leaning slightly here or there to avoid the debris in the road. It had turned out to be a very good idea to stick to state and county roads, as they had seen very few Sicks. They had been driving almost straight since they left Knoxville the day before. Even after alternating drivers the going had been slow and it was starting to take its toll. They needed water, food, and fuel—in that order. The wind blasting they had received during their ride had not helped their dehydration. In the mountains of North Carolina, they had found many streams and rivers, but not a single one appeared safe to drink. The water rolled and tumbled downstream with an orange tint and an unnatural thickness. Something had gotten into the natural water sources and ruined them. As they crept into the valley, Kane watched the black and twisted metal road signs as they approached. The first indicated State Highway 64. Directly behind it was another sign that read Hendersonville/I-26, six miles. Kane pointed to the sign, and Molly nodded as they passed it. They were going to have to pass through a small town outside of Asheville called Hendersonville. Kane hoped that there would not be any nasties to encounter there, and for the first time he wondered why he and Molly had not become sick or mutated into one of them, as they had most likely been exposed to whatever had changed those poor people.

The road wound and twisted through the dead mountains with only the occasional abandoned vehicle or body to avoid. They hadn't seen anyone, not a single living person on their journey. Kane liked it better that way. The people you might run into in these circumstances would most likely be untrustworthy, smiling to your face and then stabbing you in the back to take what you had.

"You okay?" he yelled over the wind to Molly, who nodded her head in answer.

"Alright, keep your eyes out for a good place to rest for the night."

Molly nodded again.

As they rounded the corner, coming into Hendersonville, a convenience store stood out on the right side of the road, battered, burned, and in bad shape. The damaged sign above the parking area hung down to the left and read, "Bart and Debbie's One Stop Shop—The best hot dawgs and boiled peanuts on earth!"

Kane pointed to the store, and Molly nodded, turning smoothly into the parking area and hitting the kill switch. Kane stepped off and dropped the backpack, bowing his back, stretching.

"Where'd you learn?" Kane indicated the motorcycle.

Molly dismounted and gave a little stretch herself and mouthed "My grandpa," patting her chest.

"Who?"

"Grandpa," Molly mouthed again more dramatically.

"Ah. Right on, grandpa," he said.

Kane did a slow 360, checking out the area and noticing that the interstate was about two hundred yards away. Satisfied, he picked the pack up and said, "Shall we see if Bart and Debbie are home?"

Molly stepped in behind him as he walked to the front door and noted that broken glass littered the interior and exterior of the store.

Kane peered through the shattered out glass door and yelled, "Hello? Hey, is anyone there? Bart? Debbie? Are you back there with the famous peanuts?"

Molly nudged him hard, a look of impatience on her face.

"I couldn't resist," he said with a delirious smile. "Come on, let's check it out."

The two stepped into the darkened building, Kane playing his flashlight over the store. The sharp smell of human decomposition hit them, and Molly gasped and pinched her nose. Kane became serious again, looking at Molly.

"Stay on me," he said and turned, moving silently through the store. Molly looked back and forth, noticing that the shelves were mostly bare except for a few lone items.

"The place has been looted pretty badly," Kane began but stopped short, seeing the boots protruding from the door that read OFFICE at the rear of the building. Stepping around cautiously, Kane looked at the heavyset older man in coveralls and a NASCAR t-shirt, holding a double-barrel, side-by-side coach model shotgun across his lap. By the looks of him, he had been dead for a long time and was the cause of the stench. Molly peered over Kane's shoulder with a grimace as he bent down to try to retrieve the corpse's wallet. Pushing the body to the right, Kane pulled the wallet from the dead man's pocket, opened it, and peered at it for a moment.

"We found Bart," he said, looking over his shoulder at Molly. As he went to fold the wallet back up, a key slipped from an inner pocket of the wallet and fell to the floor with a jingling sound. Kane looked down and picked up the key, examining it slowly in his hand.

"Huh? What do you think it goes to?" Kane wondered aloud.

Without hesitation Molly pointed directly at a large, heavy-looking door in the back wall of the office.

"Well, that would seem to be the obvious choice, wouldn't it?" he said, stepping over the body and taking the shotgun, which he opened to find two full chambers of 00 buckshot. Snapping the shotgun closed, Kane inserted the key in the door and turned it. The deadbolt slid free with a clink, and the door moved, exposing a narrow opening. Kane slipped his fingers into the gap and pulled the door open toward him. It opened with a light creaking sound, and Kane snapped the flashlight on, disturbing the darkness. He stood a moment in silence before moving forward and whispering, "Jackpot."

Molly struggled to look around Kane, but he stepped to the side and waved his hand like Vanna White revealing the requested vowel. What greeted Molly's eyes may as well have been an oasis in the middle of the Sahara. Large quantities of canned and dry goods and tanks of stored water sat neatly on shelves, along with some survival items and firearms. Bart had been well prepared. He had been well prepared indeed.

DAY 36

OUTSIDE OF COLUMBIA, SOUTH CAROLINA

The rolling landscape was smothered in a blanket of smoke, the haze so thick in some places that it had become hard to breathe. The forest fires had burned out of control with no measures to protect against them. It had been two days of nonstop work for those at the ranch, digging trenches, cutting trees, and scraping back the ground cover to keep the fires from overtaking it. Courtland continued to labor, but as hard as he worked, he thought it strange that he never broke a sweat. Because of the fires, he had also not slept in over two days, but he felt strangely unaffected by the deprivation. The truth of it was that he felt rather well physically.

A thin man with gray hair stood up a few yards down the line and propped a hoe over his shoulder, breathing heavily.

"Courtland, why don't you take a break with me away from the rest of the family for a minute," the man said.

"Sure, Vincent," replied Courtland, setting his rake down.

Vincent had been elected the leader of this family.

Family. It was more like a militia.

Whether that had been a group election or a self-appointment, Courtland could not be sure, but the people here seemed to go along with it okay. Vincent seemed to be a decent guy, if not a little arrogant and pushy. Usually, his reasoning for doing something seemed mostly rational.

"Listen up, everyone," Vincent said to the line. "The fires seem to be past us now. Let's finish up what we've started, and we'll call it quits on the fire line."

Everyone nodded and murmured in approval.

Vincent motioned for Courtland to follow him, which he did. They walked across the farm through a ruined orchard and into the main building, where Vincent stopped at a door and motioned for Courtland to enter first. The giant man stooped and turned sideways to squeeze through the standard doorway. Vincent followed him in and shut the door.

"Courtland, I am not a theatrical man, so I'll just get to the point," Vincent began. "In the few weeks you've been here, you've worked hard, given freely of yourself to others, and been just an all-around positive influence on our family," he said. "All that said, you still don't appear to be at home here."

"That's because I'm not home, Vincent...not yet," Courtland stated.

"Well, I know I can be overbearing sometimes, but I have to make tough decisions for the good of the whole. This may irritate some under my care, but several hundred men, women, and children are depending on me to keep them alive. That's quite a responsibility. I'm sure you understand."

Courtland was silent, his wheels turning.

"We need you *here*, Courtland, and not just physically. Have you spoken with the new woman, Christine, who arrived here two days ago? Not only do we battle the elements, food shortages, and rampant forest fires, but this woman tells stories of how there are beasts that come up from the ground and prey on survivors. She says they are creatures born of darkness that seek out human victims. She has seen them with her own eyes. She also had a run-in with the Coyotes, you know, that gang we've had to bribe several times. The only reason they haven't attacked us yet is that for the time being we have superior numbers. I fear, though, that if they did, they would still overcome us. Psychopaths—all of them. They captured Christine up near Asheville. This was before she was able to escape and find her way here. The things she has seen and been subjected to at their hands would put a chill to your bones. She says their leader—"

"Is a cutthroat demon of a man named Malak," Courtland interrupted. "I have already been spoken to about him...but not by Christine."

"Courtland, listen," Vincent said. "We are in desperate times, and we will not be able to survive here on this farm forever. In the coming days, we...I am going to need your counsel on difficult matters, matters that will affect all of us."

"Vincent, you know that I will help you in any way I can, but something is happening out there that is bigger than you or me or this family. When it calls me to take up my place in the cycle, I will be obligated to answer and leave this place. There is still much about myself and God's purpose that needs to be revealed."

Vincent stood with a questioning look of confusion on his face that slowly ebbed into something indiscernible.

"I am concerned with the here and now, not all this business of God and prophesy," he said with irritation.

"And this is what separates us," Courtland stated, a look of weariness on his broad face as he looked down at Vincent.

The two men stood quietly, staring at each other for a moment in a silent showdown of wills.

"You do as you must, but do not forget us," Vincent said briskly and opened the door. "The world you knew is gone, Courtland; there is nothing left for you out there among the ashes."

"God is there. He has gone before me."

Courtland squeezed through the door again and moved slowly toward his quarters without a sound.

The Family existed because that's what these people desired—a return of community, friendship, and family in the days after these things were taken from them. Courtland, though, try as he might, had never been at home here. With the exception of two individuals with whom he had felt a strange and distinct connection, he was an outsider, and the people here treated him differently. The reason for this was crystal clear—the things they longed for were not the things he longed for. Courtland felt a deep nagging and the unanswered call of purpose within him. The recurring visions had only served to enforce these desires. Things that bent the mind—visits of angels with instructions from God, visits from the Lord himself, or the one where the moon turned to blood and the stars fell from the sky and the earth dissolved into the belly of the fire worm. But the vision that frequented him the most was the one about the serpent-man who commanded an evil army. He was the one who would wield the dark power and bring death and suffering before him. He would call himself the "Champion of the Darkness," and his name would be Malak. And in his vision, Courtland and the nameless warrior were commanded to stand against him in the name of the King of Heaven. The message was the same every time, as loud as the tolling of Heaven's bells. Listen, trust, and obey. It was what he had to do when the time came. And he would do it.

DAY 36

BART AND DEBBIE'S
HENDERSONVILLE, NORTH CAROLINA

Molly sat and smacked her lips in the light of the fire. She never in her wildest dreams would have thought that SPAM in the little metal container could taste so unbelievably good. Kane had cooked it on the small propane stove that he found in the storage. The potted meat was the appetizer, and now canned beanie-weenies were cooking in a small pot on the burner. The aroma wafted up into her nostrils and activated her salivary glands. She felt as though she had not eaten in a month—actually, it had been about that long since she had really eaten something worth eating. Kane looked at Molly over by the fire as she watched him cooking a few feet away on the stove. He had never seen someone so interested in food.

"Can I help you with something?" Kane asked

Molly gave an annoyed look and motioned for him to hurry it up.

"Okay, okay," Kane said. "Soup's on."

He picked up the pot with the clamps and poured the beanie-weenie mixture into Molly's outstretched cup, which she quickly drew back and sat in front of her on the ground. She retrieved a small piece of paper with writing on it from her pocket, and handed it to Kane.

Kane filled his own cup and then read the note out loud. "Thank you, God, for this meal you have given to us, for the company you have blessed us with, and for your grace that saves us daily. Amen."

Kane smiled as he finished Molly's prayer.

Molly looked up and smiled as she began her meal. The two sat for a few moments, quietly gulping down hungry mouthfuls until they had eaten their fill. Kane packed up the stove and cleaned out the pot as well as he could with just a little water. He poured some more water into the pot and set about boiling it. Reaching into the new stash, he withdrew a .45 caliber Springfield Operator 1911 pistol. Kane looked the weapon over and worked the slide a few times to be sure it functioned, then disassembled the weapon and wiped the parts down with rag he had found. Dabbing his finger in a small bottle of motor oil, Kane methodically lubricated the friction areas of the handgun and reassembled it, wiping it down again with the cloth. He cycled the slide and checked the trigger pull, causing the hammer to snap forward. He then picked up a seven-round magazine and began loading the 230-grain jacketed hollowpoints into it and the two extra magazines he had. Molly watched silently from the other side of the fire.

"It helps me relax," Kane said. "I used to be anal about my guns being clean, back when I was a cop."

He dropped the magazines in his pocket and tucked the Springfield into his waistband. He also took the time to saw the barrel of the shotgun off to twelve inches and the stock down to a pistol grip, which he wrapped in duct tape. Satisfied with his craftsmanship, he set the converted shotgun down beside him.

"If you want," he began, "you can come sit over here and help me decide what we want to pack to take with us to eat."

Molly got to her feet and stepped around the fire with her blanket. After sitting next to Kane, she began picking out the canned goods she liked, stuffing them into the satchel.

Kane watched as she picked and chose the cans she wanted, scrunching her nose in disgust from time to time at a can of mystery meat or other unknown substance. She had such a girlish look, and yet she was very much a pretty young woman. He liked her, but not in a romantic sense. He felt responsible for her. The warrior in him, the protector, felt responsible. Just like a big brother charged with the care of his little sister, Kane took his charge seriously.

The pot was at full boil, and Kane turned the stove off and withdrew his prize from the stash: a safety razor and shaving cream.

"Okay, Molly, you're about to find out what I look like without this beard. Are you ready?"

Molly nodded slowly, smiling.

"Here it goes, but you're going to have to be my mirror, and tell me if I missed any spots."

Kane worked slowly and with short strokes, the razor tugging, pulling, and yanking at the coarse beard. It hurt, but the process of shaving felt wonderful, almost as if he could close his eyes and be in his bathroom at home. The careful work of a few minutes, with the corrections of his assistant on the missed spots, produced a clean-shaven and significantly less barbaric-looking man.

Molly gave him the thumbs up and mouthed, "Looks good."

Kane set the razor aside, dumped the water, and then set some more water to heat for personal cleanup.

After taking turns cleaning up with the warm water, they found themselves sitting bundled up around the fire once again. Molly sat enjoying the warmth of the fire as Kane quietly sketched something on a blank piece of paper. Kane tried to not think about the things from normal life that he selfishly missed. Good coffee, a hot shower, the way a beam of sunlight felt when it soaked into him, his family all snuggled together on a sleepy Saturday morning. But they were great things, things worth thinking about. So Kane took a few minutes, closed his eyes, and pretended he still had them, and then he thanked God for allowing him to have had them at all.

After a few silent minutes, Molly drew out her pad and wrote a note, which she passed over to Kane. "Do you think that God is leading us to the radio control station for some reason?"

Kane read the note and thought for a minute, then said with a sigh, "I don't know, other than that I feel led to this place. I can't say exactly what it is that God wants me to do other than what he told me. He said listen, trust, and obey."

Molly stared with a strange expression at Kane, then looked down and began writing furiously. She handed him the pad, which read, "Why did you use those words exactly?"

Kane did not blink. "Because that's exactly what I heard when he spoke to me."

Molly wrote again and handed the notebook to Kane. "Those words, exactly, are the last thing my father said to me before he passed."

Kane paused staring at the fire. "No way we would have survived this long if God didn't have a purpose for us. I think he will tell us what he wants us to do as soon as he knows we are ready to follow those three commands."

The distant sound of a vehicle's exhaust backfiring brought Kane to his feet with a sense of purpose. He motioned for Molly to remain seated as he moved out toward the trash-filled street, where he stopped and focused on the small pinpoints of light positioned on the I-26 overpass. He strained to make out the dark outline of a figure standing outside the vehicle, looking back at him from the top of the bridge. They both stood rooted in place for what seemed like minutes before the stranger quickly turned and jumped back in the vehicle with a whoop as it peeled out down the broken highway. The vehicle faded from view as it turned and started down the on ramp. Kane turned and jogged back to the fire as the motor grew louder.

"Molly, there is some sort of vehicle coming down here from the high-way. For now, we have to assume we can't trust whoever this is until they show us otherwise, okay?"

Molly nodded.

"Grab that shotgun and set it beside your leg, and pull the blanket up over you, but keep your hand on the gun."

Molly nodded again and did as Kane had said. Kane stepped back and allowed the fire to be between him and the street. He tucked his shirt up in the back over the Springfield and clicked the safety off. Kane had been a police officer for eleven years at the time of the attacks; and in that line of work, eleven years was more than enough time to ruin anyone's noble ideas that human beings were naturally good. Kane knew, especially in a desperate situation such as theirs, the chances of meeting up with some-one who had not devolved to some form of barbarism were scarce. He stood in a natural stance, knees slightly bent, with his weight just for-ward on his toes, and waited.

A dune buggy, rusted and beaten with a ram grate welded to the front, sped up into the parking lot and screeched to a stop with its brakes locked. Human skulls with little bits of flesh still attached hung on the steel bars of the grate. Quickly jumping from the vehicle, four men fanned out and into the light of the fire. Kane's sixth sense was blaring and waving every red flag that he owned. These men had come to take something, maybe everything. Kane adjusted quickly and began the diversion.

"Heeeeeyyyyyy! What's up, guys? I can't believe it! We haven't seen anyone in days. Where'd you guys come from? Are there other survivors there? Can you give us a ride?"

Kane continued to rant in the softest tone he could muster.

The front man shuffled up and into the firelight but said nothing as the others began boxing them in. Kane continued to blabber ridiculously as he analyzed the four men. All four of them were dressed in a strange mix of clothing, except for the front man, who was in all black with a black leather jacket and a black ski mask over his head. The two on the left and closest to Molly had the look of wild uneasiness in their paint-covered faces. They were the new guys. The one on the far right, closest to Kane, had a purple mohawk and a lot of chains and spikes, and was covered in war paint. Kane watched as the front man's lips peeled back, revealing white teeth in a wicked smile that gleamed in sharp contrast with the black. These two were more seasoned. There was also a driver still in the buggy, but he was covered in shadow. This was definitely some sort of gang, and they were not here to sing Kum-ba-yah. Kane stopped babbling.

"Well," he said as he lifted his hands up in a helpless gesture. "You're, ah...welcome to share our fire with us if you want. We don't have much food or—"

"Shut the *fuck* up!" spat the front man, the spittle clinging to the mask in a long string. "You squawk like a bitch," he snarled as he drew out a black handgun. The other thugs brandished crude, barbaric-looking weapons.

Kane shifted uneasily and allowed a look of fear to visibly cross his face.

"Okay, um, I'm...I don't know, can we help you with something?" his voice intentionally weak with the sound of frail emotion.

Kane watched the two on the left eyeing Molly with lust in their eyes. He clenched his hands, the sinewy muscles of his forearms binding against each other like steel cables.

Not yet.

"We're here to take from you what you value most," the front man said just above a whisper.

Kane let his voice crack when he spoke. "But...we...we don't have anything."

"Oh, you have something. Everyone has something to lose," he whispered and looked at Molly.

Molly remained motionless, a faint look of terror behind her steely eyes.

"Please, please, you...you don't have to hurt us. We just...we're...we just..." Kane continued to babble.

The front man pointed sharply at Kane. "If I have to tell you to shut up one more time, I'm gonna spill your fucking guts in that fire while we take your girlfriend here for a little test drive."

He paused, seesawing the gun back and forth as if thinking. "Actually, we're just gonna do that anyway," he stated with a sinister smile, perfect white teeth behind the fire.

The deception had worked and had made the thugs feel in a position of power. In the middle of a pleading, babbling sentence, Kane dropped to his right knee behind the fire and drew the Springfield. He fired three rounds at the front man. The air shattered with human screams. Kane adjusted and drew down on the one with the mohawk as the crazed man came through the flames at him. With a crack, the .45-caliber round slammed into the goon's upper right chest before the wild man sacked Kane and sent the gun sliding into the dark. Molly was groaning and thrashing on the other side of the fire, but he was unable to see her as he struggled madly with the vicious man who was now upon him.

Molly kicked hard at the skinny one's groin but struck his thigh instead, pushing him back with both legs as she scrambled for the shotgun. The skinny thug lunged forward and smacked her in the side of the head hard with his forearm. Molly's world reeled as the thug pinned her neck to the ground with his forearm. The other thug was on her now, tearing at her pants. Molly struggled and thrashed, but felt as though her head was going to pop from the pressure on her neck. The skinny one was suddenly up in her face as he shifted more weight onto her. His warm breath washed over her face and smelled like spoiled milk and old hate.

"You're not going to enjoy this," he whispered in her ear. "But we will."

Molly could feel the other one tugging at her, trying to loosen her pants. Her vision grew red and hazy as she bucked and gasped for air.

"Just cut her damn pants off already," the skinny one was yelling.

Molly gave a final desperate, shuddering surge against her attackers as she flailed her limbs wildly, gagging. The skinny thug leaned back and drove down, hitting her hard in the face with his free hand, bouncing her head against the pavement. Light blazed in her mind from the impact, and she whimpered and became still as the energy continued to flow from her. With a far-off tearing sound, her pants came free and floated lazily in hazy slow motion across her field of vision to land clumsily in a pile in front of the fire. The jingling of a belt buckle and the sound of canvas pants sliding down became drowned in the thundering of her own heart. A single, lonely tear streamed out of her right eye as she slowly lowered her hand beside her body in defeat—and felt her fingers touch the shotgun.

Kane and the thug rolled and rocked across the concrete as the mohawked man yelped and fought like a cornered, rabid dog. Kane braced the man's right hand, which held a crude spiked mace that continually pressed down toward him.

"Tricky, tricky, getting Fagen like that! But a bullet won't stop me!" Mohawk said in a crazy, high-pitched tone.

Mohawk broke free and came down with the medieval weapon, screaming wildly. Kane rolled to the side as the spikes dashed off the concrete. Mohawk swung again, but Kane blocked the blow with his left arm. He grabbed the wild man's arm and struck it with the bony part of his forearm, knocking the club free. A shotgun blast tore from the other side of the fire, followed by more wild screaming. Mohawk grabbed Kane's shirt with both hands and dropped his forehead fast against the bridge of Kane's nose with a crack. Kane's eyes involuntarily clouded and he could feel the blood run across his chin. Molly was groaning and crying.

"You diseased pigs better leave some for me," Mohawk yelled across the fire.

Kane's right hand clamped down behind the thug's neck and pulled him in.

"You're not going to make it to the party!" Kane hissed through bloody, clenched teeth.

Lashing out, Kane punched the gunshot wound and kicked the screaming man off of him. In a flash, he was on his feet, stepping in front of the man and grabbing a handful of his mohawk. Sweeping the man's legs back, Kane drove the man off balance and headfirst into the coals of the fire. The wild man gave a girlish shriek and thrashed his hands deep into the burning coals as his head cooked. He pushed and writhed as Kane bared his teeth and shoved the man's face further into the fiery embers until the man gurgled and relaxed. Releasing him, Kane was up and moving around the fire, drawing the Ka-Bar knife from his waist. To his right, the front man lay dead on the ground, a trio of holes in his chest. The dune buggy was unmanned. There was also another groaning, dying thug, naked from the waist down, with a bloody shotgun pattern across his abdomen and genitalia.

A half-clothed Molly was scrambling and kicking at the skinny, painted thug who was raging and choking her.

"You think you're a fighter, you little whore? You're gonna die!"

The thug picked up the shotgun and moved to point it at her. In two steps, Kane was there, stomping the thug's gun hand against the brick wall next to him and twisting his boot to the sound of popping fingers. A frenzied scream shot from the man's throat as he launched himself at Kane, his mangled hand clutched to his chest in the flickering light of the fire. Body slamming against body, they hit the ground hard and rolled across the concrete, struggling with each other. Kane snatched the man hard against his own body, yanking his head to the side. Letting loose a fearsome cry, Kane drove the knife down behind the thug's collar bone and worked it right to left, severing the carotid artery. Terror and blood mixed in the air as Kane bore down and held on with desperate, primal groans. The man shook and gasped violently, his eyes widening and then rolling back in his head as his frenzied movements slowed to a stop. For an eternity, nothing moved in the flickering light of the scattered fire. After a tense moment of silence, Kane withdrew the knife with a spray of gore and rolled the body to the side. The dune buggy cranked up and squealed out in reverse with Kane's duffel in the passenger seat. Kane jumped to his feet and ran blindly out after the buggy, but it was gone, taillights disappearing into the night.

Balling his fists in the flickering light of the dying fire, Kane threw his head back and screamed. He screamed a terrifying and ferocious sound, threatening the darkness that surrounded them as the blood of another man dripped from his chin. Chest heaving with uneven breaths, he stood in the dark alone. Motionless, his weary eyes searched the darkness for unseen monsters as he and the knife dripped red splashes of color steadily onto the ground.

It had been a long time since he had been forced into killing men like this. The gravity of what he had done began to soak into him, the weight of death and old feelings heavy on his shoulders. He felt weak, light-headed. It was one thing to kill at a distance, pulling the trigger on your target and watching him fall. It was something else entirely to kill a man in hand-to-hand combat. Up close, you could smell your enemy's sweat, see the fear in his eyes, and feel him struggle as his life flowed from him. Those things never left a man, not for the rest of his days. Kane wrestled with his conscience as he tried to figure out if this level of violence, even if for noble reasons, was what God had wanted from him. In the darkness he whispered a quiet prayer.

After a moment, he straightened and listened as the dead wind continued to blow restlessly. He exhaled forcefully and turned, still trying to get his breath as he walked back toward Molly.

Kane stepped back into the firelight, covered in blood and looking like he just stepped out of the slaughterhouse. He turned his attention to Molly. She was sitting with her back against the wall and her knees drawn up to her chest. Tears poured out of her eyes as she cradled her legs with her arms.

"You okay?" he asked quietly, as he wiped the blood from his face.

Molly sniffled.

"You're not hurt? I mean, they didn't..."

Molly shook her head.

Kane knelt and handed her the blanket to cover up with.

Molly choked and coughed, and the tears poured out as she sobbed.

Kane slowly sat next to her, wiping his hands on his pants.

"You did the right thing," he said and paused, looking at his hands, hands that just took three lives. "You did what you had to do," he said quietly, almost as if to himself.

Molly did not respond, and they sat for a while, embracing the cold, silent dark.

After a few moments, a slight wheeze came from the other side of the fire. Kane rose and reassured Molly. He then cautiously stepped around the fire to find the terribly burned mohawked man wheezing. His eyes were burned out, and his face and head were burned all the way through to the bone, giving him a disgusting skeletal look. Kane stooped over the man and looked at him.

The man rocked back and forth slowly, whispering in raspy undertones through charred teeth. "You don't know what you done. What you done. What you done. You don't even *know*."

Kane remained silent.

The man continued. "Malaksssss gonna burn your world for zhis. Everyshang you know, anyones you ever love. Everyshang gonna burn in the darknessssss. No one can shtand in the darknessssss witshout bein' swallowed by it."

"We'll see about that."

The man chuffed and gave a dry, painful laugh. "You shhink yer a tough guy? You don't shtand a chancessss. You don't evensss know what you done. You don't eeeevvveeennnngoooogggghttt...."

The man stopped rocking and became still, his skeletal jaw hinging open. Kane turned back to Molly and spoke with urgent concern in his voice.

"Get your stuff together, Molly. We're leaving."

DAY 36

DOWNTOWN—ASHEVILLE, NORTH CAROLINA

Malak rolled the Z-laced tobacco cigarette between his fingers slowly and deliberately. He leaned against the wall as he moved his fingers, his eyes scanning the large concrete area around him that had come to be known as "The Arena." It was an immense pit within the compound, carved out of what had been part of an underground parking deck. It was here that all the initiations for the gang took place as well as the matched fights for entertainment and other killings that were necessary. Even though it was physically made of concrete, the blood and brain and bone that had soaked into it over the weeks was as much a part of it as the concrete. Malak looked down at the dark pink hue in the concrete, smiled, and licked the paper, rolling the crude joint up tightly.

Retrieving the Zippo, which never left his pocket, he lightly burned the end of the cigarette and inhaled deeply. He still could not believe how lucky he had been in finding the stash of Z in the storage vault in the basement of the compound. Malak had ordered his soldiers to dig through the pile of rotting police corpses to get to the door. The security indicated that whatever was behind the doors would be something valuable in the context of the world, but he had no idea it would be an item whose value would transcend the death of civilization. The building had been so disfigured that he had not recognized it as the state headquarters for the DEA, which currently housed the proceeds of some of the state's largest narcotics busts. He had unearthed large amounts of drugs, evidence in cases waiting for a court appearance that would never happen. It was his good fortune. People would always need drugs. He took another drag on the drug-laced cigarette.

Z had been created in the early years of the twenty-first century. It was an extremely powerful, hyperaddictive drug—a mix of PCP, methamphetamine, ecstasy, steroids, and several other choice drugs. It had been created by accident but was found to have several desirable effects for criminals, such as numbness to pain, prolonged adrenaline surges, heightened awareness, and rapid muscle growth. Z was such an intensely powerful concoction that it was known for killing nearly two-thirds of its users during their first trip. The DEA had cracked down, calling it "poison" and starting a nationwide campaign to stamp it out. They were never completely successful, however, which was good, because Malak liked to use it as a proving ground, a place to test a person's constitution.

Malak required his soldiers to use it. This worked in his favor for three reasons: first, their surviving the first trip meant they lacked any shred of weakness; second, his soldiers gained the power of the drug and had to be killed outright to be stopped; and third, it maintained their allegiance to him because they needed it. He knew that sooner or later it, or something like it, would become available by other means, but until then they needed him to provide it.

A gentle yellow haze began to penetrate the corners of his vision, and small beads of sweat sprung up on his large, bald head. He shuddered once and took the final hit on the joint, allowing the smoke to penetrate deeply into his lungs. His muscles began to contract rapidly, and he braced against the wall as he and the walls and the floor and everything else began to slowly melt together in a yellow fog. The initial ten minutes and the final ten minutes of the high were the hardest part, but the ride was in the middle—and it could last for days. A series of hard tremors shook Malak, causing him to gasp and claw at the wall. His vulnerability during this time was why he demanded solitude while entering and exiting. After a few minutes, he slowly straightened himself and breathed deeply, allowing the yellow thickness to fade and his mind to clear.

He looked around the room. Everything had a slight golden sheen around it that sparkled and winked at him. He called it the glow, and when he saw the glow, he knew he could hear the voice when it spoke to him. After the attacks, he had found that he could hear the voice without the aid of the drug. But under its influence, it spoke to him clearer, deeper, and his consciousness was void of other distractions like hunger, sleep, anger, and sex. He felt almost as though he could see the future.

A sharp pang racked through his mind, and Malak shook his head as it swam with an unusual sensation. He supported his head and tried to focus and get hold of himself.

It was then that the voice spoke to him.

"He is coming," it said.

"Who?" Malak asked, holding his head.

"A man whose only purpose is to mock you, to destroy what you've built, and to steal what you've earned,"

"What? What man?"

"He will ride a steel horse and keep company with a silent witness."

Malak listened and continued holding his head.

"You must not underestimate this man, for he comes to take the power from us, that he may enjoy it for himself."

"How will I know him?" Malak asked.

"You will know. He is the one who soils your throne room at this very moment. Seek him and the girl out, and destroy them before you are destroyed yourself," the voice said, fading away.

Malak relaxed and breathed deeply a few times, allowing the glow to return. "I will find them, and they will fear the darkness," he said.

✿ ✿ ✿

"Daddy," the young woman called. "Daddy, are you there?"

Courtland strained his eyes through the dense fog. "Marissa?" he said.

"Daddy, I can hear you. Come this way," the young woman said. "I need to show you."

"Show me what?" Courtland said.

"Come," she said.

"I still can't see you."

Courtland stepped slowly through the dense fog. It wrapped and swirled and clung to him as he waded through it, unable to see even inches ahead.

"I'm here. Watch your step now," she said.

Courtland took a series of small steps and stopped short of a giant precipice. He stood staring out into the thickness and then down at the ledge. He felt a smaller hand grab hold of his own, and he looked over to see the smiling face of his daughter Marissa. At sixteen years old, she was the best of his wife Teshauna, who passed away while giving birth to her, their only child. The loss of his wife had nearly destroyed him, but he had gained a wonderful, smiling, intelligent, beautiful gem of a girl. And she loved the Lord. Because of his faith, Courtland knew everything happened for a reason. He had been determined to make the best of it.

"Daddy, can you see?"

"No, dear, I can't," he replied.

"Look again."

Courtland turned his head and peered over the chasm again. As he looked, the fog began to clear and he was able to see deeply into the chasm.

"What am I supposed to see?"

"Look closer," she said.

Courtland squinted, and as he looked, a scene began to develop in front of him. He saw a large red SUV traveling down a dark road at night. It was his custom Cadillac Escalade, tailored to fit his enormous size. He and his daughter were driving home from a dinner date. Courtland watched and knew that even though he was experiencing a vision, he was also uncovering some of what he had forgotten.

They were laughing and talking as they drove.

"No way, Dad, I don't believe you," she said.

"It's true, I promise. I couldn't make that up," he protested.

"Why did I never know that about how you and mom met?"

"I don't know. I was sure you knew that."

"And this was during your Crushball career?"

"Yeah."

"And mom didn't have a problem with you playing a violent sport like that?"

"No, your mother was very supportive of me and my many injuries. She knew I loved it and was good at it. Actually, it was the only thing I was ever really good at."

"That's because you were 'The Sledge,' right?"

Courtland smiled. "That was just a nickname."

"There's something you're better at, though," she said.

"Really? Enlighten me."

"Being my dad," she said, smiling.

Courtland smiled, and his heart melted as he looked over at his daughter. "That's because you're so precious to me, Mar..."

"*Dad!*" she yelled

Courtland's focus snapped forward, and he instinctively jerked the wheel to the left to avoid the large buck standing in the middle of the bridge. The guardrail provided no resistance as the large Escalade crashed through the rail and over the bridge, tumbling with screams of terror as it plummeted toward the water.

DAY 37

DOWNTOWN—ASHEVILLE, NORTH CAROLINA

In the center of the Arena, the chained man sat quietly, drooling blood and staring without focus at the ground. Malak and his two elite officers, Dagen and Ashteroth, stood in front of the man as the tightened chains held him to the concrete column. Malak stood shirtless behind the other two with his arms crossed, his giant bulging arms only slightly covering the large tattoo of a coiled viper in the center of his chest.

"Well, what's your answer?" Dagen asked.

The chained man refused to respond.

"What was that?" Dagen said.

Ashteroth lunged in, snapping a left punch across the man's pulpy face with a crack. The man drooped his head and drooled more blood and teeth.

"Friend, you can't have many teeth left in your head. When they are all out, we'll have to find something else to remove from you," Dagen said. "So, be a good boy and tell us where the fuel reserve is, because we know that's where you were coming from."

The man did not respond. Malak shook his head.

"He must be sleeping," Dagen said.

"Ashteroth, give him something to wake him up," Malak said.

Malak knew that Dagen and Ashteroth would do a good job with the interrogation. They were the two most cruel and ruthless men he had ever known. Though he knew they could never hold a candle to himself, he also knew they would do their jobs well as his lieutenants.

Ashteroth, whom the men called "Tattoo" for his full-body decorations, was a true psychopath whose only medication was his dosing of Z. The wild interlocking bands, sleeves, flaming heads, and tattooed designs covered his whole body, even his face, giving him a wild, tribal appearance. This man was known for his psychotic outbursts, which everyone feared. Even Malak never knew what to expect from him and almost had to kill him once when, in a fit of rage, he overstepped his position.

Dagen, on the other hand, was as cool and collected as any human man could possibly be. Dishonorably discharged from the Marines, he had done time in the USDB at Leavenworth for cutting the guts out of a superior officer after the man called him a faggot. An unusually sharp reaction for a single insult – especially for Dagen, but Malak felt sure that the roots of the situation ran much deeper and Malak didn't care to question the man about his past. As it turned out, the officer lived, and Dagen was released on parole after spending a number of years in the box with good behavior. He was Malak's planner; battle commander; and even-headed, wise counsel. As serene and smooth as he appeared to be, Malak had run with him for a long time and was aware of the depths of evil the man was capable of. He had once watched Dagen, during a simple home invasion, personally torture a whole family to death, all the while explaining to them that if God loved them, he would not allow them to endure such pain and terror. A man after Malak's own heart.

Ashteroth finished giving the man an injection of adrenaline from a dirty syringe and pulled the chained man's shoe off as he brandished a small scalpel-like knife. As he went to work, the air filled with the screams of the tortured man.

"See," Malak said, smiling wickedly. "He's not asleep."

"Where is the fuel reserve?" Dagen asked again, but the chained man whined and murmured quietly without answering.

Malak nodded at Ashteroth, who went to work on the man's other foot.

The man continued to thrash and scream.

"You stupid fuck! Why not tell us where it is and let us have it? It's not worth all this," Dagen said.

The man moaned and hung his head, determined to keep the secret to himself in his final hour.

Dagen shook his head and looked at Malak.

"Bring out his family," Malak said.

Ashteroth motioned to a goon at the doorway.

"Noooooooooo. Not them!" the man moaned sadly.

Ashteroth spat in the man's face as he hissed, "Whatever happens to them is your fucking fault! You did this to them," he added, an evil smile on his lips.

A woman was walked out to the Arena, bound together with a young girl. The thug walked them out in front of the chained man and forced them to sit. The little girl cried quietly.

"I'm getting tired of hearing myself say this," Dagen said. "Where is the fuel reserve?"

The thug was now dumping gasoline over the woman and child as they wailed.

"Wait, wait, don't do this! They have nothing to do with this," the man said with sudden vigor.

"Then answer the question, or they'll burn!" Ashteroth yelled as he struck a match.

"I can't. Lives are at stake," the man moaned.

"You got that right," Ashteroth said as he flicked the lit match at the gas-covered woman and child. The match went out before bouncing off the woman's shirt and falling to the ground. Ashteroth, annoyed by the new chorus of wailing, was cursing and striking another match.

"Wait! Wait! I'll tell you. I'll tell you, just don't hurt them anymore."

Ashteroth was preparing to flick another lit match when Malak stayed him with a motion of his hand.

"Then speak, you worthless piece of trash."

"South, south of Atlanta, uh, I mean where Atlanta was. The reserve is south on I-75 about twenty miles. Look for the high-reinforced walls that protect the compound. It's visible from the interstate. The reserve was a government facility constructed for emergencies, but...families have taken refuge there. Don't hurt them," the man said and hung his head.

"Are there ways to transport the fuel out?" Dagen asked.

"Yeah, they have operational tanker trucks there," the man whispered.

"They weren't disabled in the attacks?"

"No. They were housed in an underground storage along with the fuel. It was hardened."

"Excellent," Malak murmured. "But you should have told us all of this the first time we asked."

"Malak!" a voice came from the doorway.

"What?"

A disheveled man came forward. "I need to speak to you, boss...about scouting party three."

"Fagen should be giving this report, and you should know how this works by now, Nelson. It can wait," Malak said, turning back to the sniffling family.

"It's about Fagen and the others..." Nelson said.

Something in the man's tone turned Malak back around. He looked at Dagen. "Handle this for a moment," he said, walking over to Nelson. "This better be good."

"We found some people south of town."

"So what?"

"We..."

"Where is Fagen?"

Nelson was silent.

"Where are Fagen and the rest of them? I swear I'll pull your fucking lungs out!" Malak spat the words with a growl in his throat.

"They were killed," the man babbled.

"How many were there for them to overtake you?"

"It was a man and a woman."

Malak seized forward, grabbing and lifting Nelson and slamming him to the wall. "You're not making sense. Come clean with it, or you're a dead man."

"The...the man, he and the girl killed them all." The man was shaking.

"You're supposed to be crazy, bloodthirsty killers, and you can't handle one civilian man and woman?"

"He wasn't just a civilian. He fought like a cornered Comanche Indian. He had training. But it's okay, boss, it's okay. I've got his bag."

"And tell me why I give a *shit* about his bag!" Malak snarled, squeezing Nelson's throat.

"Guhhh," Nelson gasped. "Because there's a map that shows where he's headed," the man said, holding up the radio station map in his left hand.

Malak released the man and snatched the map from him, suddenly regaining his calm.

"Tell me everything. Spare no detail," Malak said.

While Nelson recounted the story, Malak looked over the map, noticing black arrows along certain routes and that the control station had been circled.

"The one who soils my throne room," Malak recited under his breath. "Was there a motorcycle?"

"Yes."

"And the woman, his company, did she speak?"

"No."

An involuntary tremor of excitement shuddered through Malak. They were the ones he was looking for.

"Nelson, your intel has been worthwhile, but…" Malak paused.

Turning quickly, he grabbed him again by the throat and slammed him forcefully against the wall. Nelson gagged as he was pushed upward, his feet kicking tiny circles in the air below him as Malak began to slowly crush his trachea.

"Fear is weakness, and neither will be tolerated. When you run from a fight, you drag the name of the Coyotes, *my name*, on the ground behind you. Think about that as you steal that last bit of oxygen," he whispered as he slowly pushed Nelson to the ground. The man struggled fruitlessly as Malak drew himself up and began driving Nelson's head into the concrete with violent repetition.

"You disgust me!" Malak said in a whispered growl as he continued to reshape his victim's skull against the concrete.

He slowed and released Nelson's lifeless body. In the quietness that followed, Malak half closed his eyes and breathed in deeply the rusty scent of fresh blood.

Leaving Nelson's body on the floor, Malak stood and turned, motioning for Dagen and Ashteroth to join him as he wiped his bloody hands on his pant leg.

"Dagen," Malak said as he wiped his hands, "gather three squads and assault the fuel reserve. Follow the directions given by our prisoner. We need that fuel. Meet up with us at this radio control station." He pointed to the map. "I'll have a copy of the map drawn up for you."

Dagen nodded.

Malak turned to Ashteroth. "Ash, someone believes they can spit in our faces and walk away. A man in the wasteland near Hendersonville managed to murder one of our scouting parties. I need you to take another two squads and find this man. He will be riding a motorcycle and traveling with a young woman."

Malak held up the map again.

"This route is where he should be traveling. When you find them, remind them why they should fear the Coyotes. Do as you wish with the girl, but keep the man alive for me to deal with."

"Yes, Boss," Ashteroth said, with a joyful gleam of insanity in his eyes.

"And them?" Dagen asked, motioning to the sobbing family behind them.

Malak glanced over his shoulder, irritated.

"Force him to watch his family burn, then cut out his eyes and leave him there. I want their death to be the last thing he ever sees and their screams to haunt him into eternity."

✵ ✵ ✵

Courtland breathed in sharply and stepped back from the precipice. "I remember," he said.

Marissa continued to hold his hand.

"It's okay, Daddy."

"But we crashed. I mean, how did we make it?" he asked.

"We didn't, Dad. We died that night, three days before the attacks."

Courtland was silent, scrunching his brow as he tried to process this news.

"But I don't understand. How did I...?"

"It is you that the Lord has chosen for his work on Earth. You were returned from the in-between just after the attacks," she said.

"How...?" he started.

"The answer to that question you will not be able to grasp," Marissa said.

"What about you?

"I reside in the house of the Lord, where I belong."

"Marissa, I want to be with you again," Courtland said, his throat tightening.

"The time is not right for that, Daddy," Marissa said. "Now it is time for war."

"And this old man is supposed to be a warrior?" Courtland said, pressing his hands to his chest.

"Yes, Daddy. You are faithful, wise, strong, and courageous. It is the Lord who commands you to use these gifts for his glory. During your absence from Earth, your human form was altered. You passed through heaven when you returned to Earth, and though you retained your mortal shell and the pain that accompanies it, you were imbued with something else."

"What exactly?" Courtland asked.

"The strength of heaven. Your physical strength has been enhanced far beyond that found in earthly men. But to maintain it, you must keep your strong faith in God and in his plan, or it will fade."

"It's all so much to try to understand," Courtland said.

"Be strong, Daddy, for the nameless warrior you seek is fast approaching. He will need your strengths and you will need his, for only together and united in the light will you be able to hold back the darkness."

"How will I know him?"

She smiled. "You won't be able to miss him."

"And the serpent man, Malak? What of him?"

"Don't focus on him, for he is empowered by the darkness but does not control it. You will have to confront him, but it will not end with him."

Marissa let go of Courtland's hand and began to fade.

"Thank you, Marissa. I will serve the Lord on this earth until I see you and your mother again. Then we will sing his praises together," Courtland said.

The girl smiled as she faded into the fog.

"I love you, baby girl," Courtland said into the thickness.

"I love you too, Daddy."

In the darkness of his room, Courtland opened his eyes and sighed deeply.

DAY 27

SOUTHEAST OF SPARTANBURG, SOUTH CAROLINA

Kane steered the bike under the overpass and brought it to a halt. It was only the second time it had rained since he had emerged from the bunker, and it was not wasting time becoming a downpour. The black rain fell like a curtain of tar drippings from the foul sky. Kane made a disgusted face as he dismounted and shook his arms to free them of the oily substance. He stopped and watched as it oozed and slid in globs off his sleeve, creating small black pools on the ground.

Molly was stepping off the bike, setting her things on the ground, looking like she'd just been dunked in a tank of diesel fuel. Her left eye was black, and she had red marks around her throat from their encounter with the bandits. Kane gingerly touched his broken nose and glanced around. There were a few charred vehicle remains and some skeletal human fragments under the overpass, but not much else. He shrugged off his jacket and wiped his palm across his face a few times, trying to remove the goo.

"This stuff is disgusting," he said, glancing at Molly. "It can't be good to have it on us."

Molly nodded as she slid out of her top layer, tossing the soiled shirt in a heap on the ground.

"You know, I used to dislike getting caught in the rain, but this…this is not right," Kane said, shaking his head.

They quickly removed some of their ruined clothing and tried to get as much of the black substance off of them as possible.

Kane moved back to the bike and unloaded the rest of the meager supplies out of the bike's saddlebags along with the five-gallon container of unleaded fuel he had siphoned from the pump at Bart and Debbie's. It was only half full. He went ahead and filled the bike up, mentally inventorying what they had left. That thug had taken almost everything they had when he drove off with that duffel. Kane still had the Ka-Bar and had taken the Springfield .45, the shotgun, and a few other items from good ol' Bart's stash of equipment. He had not been able to load up on food and other items, because they had no way to carry them and were under the considerable time constraint of needing to leave before the dead thugs' buddies came looking for them—as they most certainly would. It had turned out to be pure genius, making a copy of the map of the radio station, as it too was gone.

He unloaded a smaller jug filled with water and took a long drink from the nozzle. He passed the water to Molly. No matches or lighter meant no fire tonight. Kane stepped over and inspected the remains of one of the vehicles, a van. It was not cozy or comfortable, but it would provide shelter from the elements. He opened the door and began cleaning some of the junk and burnt debris out of it. Molly stood close behind him, shivering slightly. The rain continued to pour down, dripping off the overpass around them, creating a thin black sludge across the ground.

"We won't have a fire, so we'll have to sleep in here to keep warm tonight. If you're okay with that," Kane said as he looked at Molly.

Molly nodded in affirmation. Kane reached in and began tugging and pulling the busted front seats out and tossing them onto the ground. He then allowed Molly to climb in and secure a spot first. He then climbed in and sat next to her, leaning against the frame and draping the last remaining blanket over them. Kane produced a small can of tuna and showed it to Molly.

"You hungry?"

She nodded.

Kane cut the top open with the knife, and they shared a quiet meal together, picking the tuna chunks out of the can with their dirty fingers.

Kane surveyed the look on Molly's face. "You alright?

Molly looked back at him.

"We've had some pretty bad stuff happen recently. I just want to make sure you're okay."

Molly made a sorrowful face and shrugged her shoulders as she chewed.

"Well, I want you to know that I'm committed to you as your friend, and you can trust me. I couldn't victimize us both by doing nothing; that's not my nature."

Molly's eyes looked teary in the fading light.

"That's not the first time I've had to kill men like that," Kane sighed. "Before I worked for the county, I started with the city of Knoxville and worked just over three years with them. My beat was an area of the city called East Riverton. You know it?"

Molly nodded slowly.

"Then you know it's a rotten ghetto full of druggies, crazies, and gangbangers. One November night, around two o'clock, I was dispatched to a call at an abandoned hotel in East Riverton called Hotel Florentine. Florentine had been a real nice fancy hotel back in the 1930s, before they closed it up. In more recent years it had become home to the scum of society. This was the reason the city planned to tear it down, but they never did after the state declared it a historical landmark. By then it was just a shadow of its former self. When we took a call at Florentine, we never went by ourselves. We went three or four deep at minimum, and ideally, we took five or more. The reason was, every time we went, we were guaranteed to run into a lot of really bad people who really hated our presence as a symbol of the law. So, around two in the morning, a streetwalker had heard screaming coming from the place. My partner and I were not really concerned, because weird stuff happened there all the time. Really weird stuff." Kane shifted in the less-than-comfortable rusty vehicle and wrung his hands.

"Well, my partner Max and I had been out of academy about a year and a half, and we were young and full of it. Anytime anything went down, we were in on it. Fights, chases, dopers and crazies, we'd been up to our eyeballs in it and had come out clean. We were invincible. On our way to the call, Max went to call for another unit to go with us, but I stopped him. I told him it was no big deal and that it was just a noise complaint. We'd be back in service for calls in ten minutes."

Kane swabbed the bottom of the tuna can with his finger and transferred the remaining morsels to his mouth. He set the can aside and pulled the blanket up around him.

Molly continued to listen closely.

"We arrived, got out of the car, and crossed the trash-filled gutter and sidewalk to get to the front of the hotel where we could enter. Funny the details you remember from a critical incident – like how the city was humming faintly, singing its usual song, and how the cold, humid night soaked through our jackets and into our bones. I remember nodding to each other, our flashlights at the ready, as we announced our presence and made entry through the front door. We weren't halfway into the main lobby when we saw her. It was the thirteen-year-old girl from the nice part of town that had gone missing from The Village, the downtown shopping district two days earlier. It had been all over the news. I remember her name - Rebekah Sims. She had been raped and beaten to death only moments earlier. Her body was... It was... Terrible. I'll never forget it, how it played out in slow motion like I might be able to stop what was about to happen. Max was trying to call out on his radio when he took an old fire ax in the chest as we were ambushed by a bunch of half-naked junkies. I was first struck in the side with a baseball bat and then the head. The first blow shattered my walkie-talkie. My gun belt was yanked so hard that it hit my boots. It took me only a second to realize how screwed I was and that help wasn't coming. In the next two-and-a-half minutes of terror that followed, I fought for my weapon and shot two of them before a major malfunction occurred and the gun became a hammer. It worked pretty well in that capacity for a minute, until it was knocked from my hands into some dark corner of Florentine's trashed lobby. They came for me, and I fought them with everything I had. I had to put my thumbs through one guy's eye sockets, and then beat the last two into submission with the broken leg of a small coffee table." Kane paused.

Molly sat unmoving, eyes wide with anticipation.

"Well, then I got to helplessly hold my partner's hand as he slowly bled out and cried his young wife's name. I wouldn't ever be the same after that. Not after all the lawsuits, attorneys, and the use of force hearing where they claimed that I had been negligent and used excessive force. But worst of all was Max's loved ones accusing me of getting him killed. His wife, Amy, slapped my face and told me that she had trusted me to look after him. She said I was a good-for-nothing cop if I couldn't protect the people who depended on me."

Kane stared deeply into the growing wet darkness around him, clinching his jaw and pausing.

"That poor little girl had no chance, and those junkies, they had it coming, but Max...Max was my fault. I never forgave myself for that," Kane said as he wiped a runaway tear from his face. "I turned everything off and got hard real quick. I knew the hardness would help me to do the job better after that. Not caring. That I could kill, if the bad guys needed killing. The job had a way of putting calluses over your emotions so you didn't have to care about the terrible things and people you dealt with. But the one thing I could never turn off was the desire to be there, to protect and defend those people who needed me, the ones who would otherwise be victims. It wasn't until Susan and the kids that I began to feel again, only for them to be...well..."

He cleared his throat.

"I guess....I couldn't protect them either."

Molly and Kane sat quietly together in the enveloping darkness.

Molly took his small flashlight and scrawled a few words in the notebook before showed it to Kane. It read:

The fate of others is God's responsibility, Kane. What you are able to accomplish is by his admission only. All you can do is your best and trust that the rest is up to him.

"But I'm a black sheep, Molly," Kane said as he looked up from the note. "Like God picked the wrong guy for whatever this is." Kane motioned with his hands. "Why me? I'm cynical and rough around the edges, and I rebelled against God for so long. I feel like I want to do the right thing, to live a life of peace and compassion. You know, leave that junk behind. Yet, on every side I'm pressed with violence and injustice and evil. And I am driven to stand against it."

He shook his head, questioning his own words.

Molly wrote on the damp notebook page for a long moment. She handed it over to Kane, who took the flashlight from her to read it:

The right thing is doing what God calls you to do. You have the heart of a hero, and God has called you to be his, to fight for him. History has shown that God uses imperfect, ordinary men like you. These are men of faith, men who are willing to trust, who are willing to sacrifice everything for him. These are the men he uses for his purposes, whatever they may be.

Kane was slightly taken back by what he read. He smiled slightly. "You know what, Molly? I think I really needed to hear that."

Instead of responding, Molly leaned slowly to her right and shifted her body up against his, leaning her head over onto his shoulder. Kane breathed deeply and once again thought about what his purpose could possibly be, and why God had saved him and this young woman from certain death. As much as he tried, he was having trouble seeing the big picture. His faith felt so small and fragile. He had struggled with himself over releasing control of it. If only there was someone who knew the answers that could clarify it for him. If only God would openly speak to him again.

Molly was breathing heavily, and Kane knew she was asleep already.

"Well, Suz," he said quietly to himself. "My faith found me, just like you said…and I'm desperately trying to cling to it," his words disappearing into the cool wet night. "I just hope. I hope that I have the willingness to do whatever it is that God wants me to do."

He almost choked on the final words as he looked upward. The black rain continued to slurp down onto dark landscape, and the pitch black night was held at bay by two friends, huddled together in the smallest light of hope.

✡ ✡ ✡

The golden summer sun drifted low on the horizon and filtered nimbly across the tops of the evergreens and hardwoods as the day came to a close. Molly Stevens was a tomboy. She had always been a tomboy. The only child of her hardworking father, when she was not in school or otherwise engaged, she was outside. The other girls in her neighborhood teased her and called her names like Joe and Bobby to allude to her lack of girliness, but she didn't care. She had always loved it outside. The trees, the animals, and the soft breeze were her closest friends. As a young girl, she spent countless hours running, dancing, climbing trees, and playing make-believe. In her imagination, she conjured up the most wonderful and magical tales. They were tales of princes, castles, terrible monsters—and, of course, beautiful maidens. The maidens were always saved by the prince, who always slew the monster. All was as it should be in the mythical lands of her mind.

On this particular evening, Molly had climbed high into the arms of an old oak tree in the front of her yard and had sat for a while to converse with the tree and the squirrels and watch the neighborhood, as was her custom this time of day. Lazily, the sun drooped further behind the trees as the evening creatures began to trill and call and make all other manner of night sounds.

She was waiting for her father to arrive home from his weeklong business trip. He was the love of her life, her hero, and her bastion of strength. She had never known her mother, who had died during her birth. On these special days, she would sit and watch for his faux wood–paneled station wagon to round the corner and begin its journey down the long straightaway to the end of the cul-de-sac. When her father pulled in, she would quickly climb down, dropping to the ground and running to him as he caught her, wrapping her in his great big arms.

"My darling girl," he would always say as he hugged her tight.

Her grandmother opened the front door and stepped onto the front porch.

Molly continued to wait, swinging her legs back and forth under the large tree branch on which she sat.

"Molly, dinner's ready," her grandmother called.

"I'm waiting for Daddy," Molly said.

"Well, bring him in with you when you find him, and be careful up in that tree like that. You could hurt yourself."

"Yes, ma'am."

As if on cue, the station wagon appeared around the corner and eased into sight, its headlights gleaming pin pricks against the dark vehicle. Molly swung her legs more rapidly now, the anticipation growing with her excitement. A slight screeching and wailing sound reached the edge of Molly's ears in the fading light as her grandmother went back inside and shut the door. As the station wagon idled slowly down the street toward her, the strange wailing grew louder as well. It was a siren of some kind, like she had heard in the old black-and-white movies her daddy liked to watch.

From her height in the tree, she could just see the red and blue lights flashing and coming down a side street to her right. There the screeching sound was again, rubber tires sliding on asphalt. Molly winced as the sirens and lights came closer and the screeching continued.

The police were chasing someone. Molly squinted her eyes to see her father, who was still steadily approaching. She waved at him to get his attention, and he gingerly returned a wave out the window. The car that was being chased ran the stop sign at a very high speed and slammed into the station wagon, flipping it over and grinding it across the neighbor's yard.

Molly couldn't breathe. "Da...da...*Daaadd*," she slurred as she scrambled down out of the great tree.

She hit the ground and was running. Running as fast as her little legs would take her to her daddy. As she ran, the man in the other car got out and began running. Then the police were running and shouting as they chased him down the street. Molly was only slightly aware of this as her focus continued to center on the upside-down station wagon that her father was now crawling from.

"*Daaaadyyy!*" she cried in desperation, falling to her knees next to him.

"My darling girl," he whispered.

Her father had a faraway look in his eyes as the blood poured in buckets through Molly's hands and across her flower-print shirt. The neighbors were coming from their houses, her grandmother screaming hysterically behind her.

"Just....Just...I," her father stammered as he clenched his bloody hands.

"Daddy, you're bleeding," Molly sobbed as she watched her father squirm in pain.

With a sudden clarity that made her gasp, her father lunged upward, grasping her arm with his hand, his eyes wide.

"Molly! Are you ready for your great adventure? Just like the ones you dream about?"

Molly continued to cry, her shuddering breaths sucking the tears from her face as her father spoke.

"Love your grandmother, but obey the Father. Listen, trust, and obey. When he calls to you, you must answer him and fulfill your purpose."

Molly's father released her and gave a final shuddering sigh as the paramedics descended upon the dying man. Her grandmother scooped her up and clutched her closely to her chest, her breasts heaving against the child with each sob. Time slowed as the frenzy of people and emergency workers swarmed and moved around her father, trying to sustain his waning life. But sustain him they could not, and the blood continued to flow, seeping into the sidewalk cracks and spilling into the street.

The great adventure had begun.

DAY 38

SOUTHEAST OF SPARTANBURG, SOUTH CAROLINA

Molly awoke with a start, sitting up sharply. The dream had been the same. It always was. It was a cold reminder that she was still alone in this world and that even now, some unknown purpose still awaited her. Her white-knuckled grip held the blanket around her with a strong remembrance of unpleasant fading memories.

The dimness of the morning poured through the cracked windows of the van in shades of dark blue and gray. Kane was gone. For a moment she panicked, believing that she had once again been abandoned. Throwing the blanket back, she clamored out of the rusted van. In a quiet frenzy, she scanned back and forth and quickly located Kane crouched at the edge of the overpass. She closed her eyes and pulled her hands to her chest, taking deep breaths as she tried to slow the pounding of her heart. He had not left her.

Picking up her damp jacket, she shrugged easily into it, making an uncomfortable face as the cold and slightly wet material touched her skin. She looked toward Kane again. In the gloominess of the grey morning, she could see him tilting his head and listening to something. Molly approached, and Kane motioned her in with an open palm pumping downward—a gesture for her to be quiet.

Molly quietly approached as Kane cupped his ear and then pointed up. Voices. Molly heard them now, multiple voices talking angrily just above them on the overpass.

"This is where the track stops, and by questioning me you're calling me incompetent," a male voice was saying.

"You *are* incompetent," another male voice said.

"I'm telling you, they are around here somewhere, I've been tracking for longer than you've been alive, you sonofabitch!"

"You're a..."

"Shut your mouth, Leach, and do something productive for once in your miserable life," a commanding voice broke in. "If you weren't such a valuable fighter, I'd have killed you a long time ago. But that doesn't mean I won't cut out your tongue from your throat if I hear so much as one more word spill from your filthy sewer."

"Yes, Ashteroth."

"Now, tell me what you've found, Drake," Ashteroth said.

"See," Drake was saying, "when I kick up this black crusty stuff you can see the motorcycle track right there as it veers toward the exit ramp."

"And?"

"Well, I'd just bet," Drake scraped with his boot again at some of the dried black, crusty ground cover left by the rain, "if this stuff was falling from the sky, they took shelter somewhere close."

"Fan out in groups of three and search the area. If they're close, we'll find them," Ashteroth said. "If you find anything, leave it for me."

Kane grabbed Molly's arm and physically stood her up.

"Get on the bike!" he said in a forced whisper, pulling her away from the edge of the overpass. Molly made a move for their things, but Kane pulled her back.

"*No time!*" he hissed. "Leave them and get on the back of that bike, now!" Kane grabbed the sawed off shotgun and the box of shells, sticking the gun in his waistband and dumping the shells in the left cargo pocket of his pants. He stepped back over to the bike and handed the Springfield .45 handgun to Molly.

"You know how to use this gun?" he asked.

Molly shook her head, her face a portrait of sheer anxiety.

"Okay, I'm driving, and you're keeping them off of us, understand?" He cocked the hammer back and clicked the safety on. "This is the safety. Click it down like this and point and shoot," Kane demonstrated, then brought out two magazines filled to capacity with seven rounds each. "Fresh magazines with seven bullets each, okay? Eject the magazine with this button here and slap a new one in, facing this direction, and hit this slide catch. Understand?"

Engines roared to life above them, the sound of angry tires squealing against the pavement.

Molly shook her head rapidly, showing her uncertainty.

"You can do it," Kane said straddling the bike and pulling the choke all the way out. "Action is faster than reaction. We are going to get the jump on them, but they will be right on top of us. Wait to shoot until they are within close range, and hold on tight."

Kane started the bike and dropped it into first gear, goosing the throttle as he popped the clutch. The motorcycle jolted so hard that for a second, Kane thought they would both be thrown off. The hardened black substance crinkled and shattered like brittle plastic in the wake of the bike as it shot from under the bridge.

From the top of the overpass, Ashteroth was screaming, "Over there! That's them! Get 'em! *Go! Go!*"

Vaulting onto the back of the rusted dune buggy, the tattooed man grabbed hold of the roll bar as the dune buggy began squealing away down the off ramp.

Kane maintained a death grip on the handlebars as the bike half slid across the crunchy black film at just under fifty miles per hour. He teased the throttle but was afraid of losing stability on a surface that felt like ice as the bike continued to slip and catch. Clinching his jaw, he looked in the left side mirror, only to see that the motley entourage was definitely pursuing them. He guessed them to be about twenty to twenty-five men strong with about eight vehicles—a few bikes, some beat-up cars and trucks, an ambulance with its rotators flashing, and a rusted dune buggy. *The* rusted dune buggy.

Kane focused back on the road. He should have known it was the same gang, and like any organized gang, they wanted revenge for what had happened to their boys earlier.. He could have kicked himself for not thinking to take a different path to the radio control station. He had even known that they had the map that had been in his bag.

The back tire slipped again, and the bike wobbled unsteadily as Kane and Molly shifted their weight together through the slight turns. Another glance in the mirror showed the vehicles behind them fishtailing. That was good; at least they weren't gaining on them. The barren hills rose up around them as they began their descent into a small canyon. Suddenly, the black film ended, and the motorcycle fully grabbed the road with a bark. Kane exhaled with relief and torqued the throttle back, sending the 1100cc Honda screaming down the winding county road. Kane could feel Molly's fingernails digging into the flesh of his ribs through his jacket as she clung to him.

"Hang on, Molly!" he yelled over the wind and the thump of the motorcycle.

The vehicles behind them hit the paved road with a multitude of barking tires burning against the pavement. Ashteroth jumped quickly into the main cab of the dune buggy and pulled his upper body up through the roof.

"Get up there!" He swung his arm at the two motorcycles in front of him. *"Get up there and take them down!"*

The charred, dirty motorcycles chugged ahead, leaving trails of black smoke, their cloaked riders' dark garments flapping behind them. The brown El Camino and the old rusted GMC truck, loaded with painted, tattooed freaks, followed.

The curvy nature of the road and the breakneck pace was keeping the majority of the group off of Kane and Molly, but the two black motorcycles were gaining on them, their dark riders appearing like angels of death. Molly slapped Kane on the shoulder three times in rapid succession.

"I see them. Get ready!" Kane yelled.

The thumping of the Honda was joined by a cacophony of growling exhaust pipes approaching from the rear. Molly squirmed on the seat behind him. They were getting close. Kane swerved to the left and shot down the centerline between two rusted, disabled vehicles. The black riders followed suit, merging single file to thread the needle. The two bikes then separated again and began to flank Kane and Molly.

Out of the corner of his eye, Kane could see the rider creeping up on his left, aiming some sort of revolver across his chest at them. A bullet zinged past his head. Kane instinctively ducked, steadied the throttle with his right hand, and drew the sawed off shotgun with his left as he looked over his shoulder at the man.

"Now, Molly! Now!"

The rider's wild masked grin of satisfaction faded to a look of shock just an instant before Kane fired both barrels of the weapon simultaneously at the rider's front wheel. The tire disintegrated with the sound of metal distorting, the front forks folding under the bike as it began to tumble. The rider's head struck the asphalt and exploded like a water balloon dropped from the hand of a child, the red mist lingering in the air behind them. The .45 was bucking wildly in Molly's right hand as Kane hit the shotgun's breach break with his left thumb and ejected the spent shells over his shoulder. Weaving left and right, the second rider began backing off to avoid Molly's fire. Kane pinned the open shotgun under his leg and brought his left hand back to the handle bar as he accelerated again. Molly was waving the Springfield over his shoulder, its slide locked back to the rear.

"Good! Now reload like I showed you!" Kane yelled.

The truck plowed through the partial barricade and sent the disabled vehicles spinning off the road. The engine groaned as the old truck made gains on the bikes ahead.

Kane slowed and decelerated into a sharp turn, noticing the ravine that dropped away sharply on the right side of the road. Accelerating again, something cracked against the rear of the cruiser, the sound like the snap of a bullwhip. He shot a glance in the side mirror only to see the black rider and a full-size truck gaining on them. Flashes of light burst from the over the cab of the truck. Muzzle flashes. Molly was going to get shot in the back. Kane cranked the throttle back, and the bike's speed increased to eighty miles per hour on the curvy road. Dodging quickly left and right, Kane zoomed around and in between the dead cars and scattered junk in the road. Leaning quickly to the right and hard back to the left around a long gradual turn, Kane avoided a burned out sedan in the left lane. Gaining speed around the turn, the truck slammed directly into the blackened sedan, throwing some of its occupants into the roadway. The truck pinwheeled off the wreckage and spun to the right, folding the remaining biker under it as it careened into the ravine and came to pieces in a fireball against the dead trees.

Kane glanced for only a moment, holding his breath as he again turned his attention back to the road. Behind him, Molly was pinching her legs tight against the frame so she could use her hands to reload the Springfield. Instantly, the bike crested a small rise and left the ground. As it landed hard back on the road, Molly lost her grip monetarily as she grabbed at Kane in a spasm of fear. The Springfield and extra magazine bumped off her leg and hit the asphalt as they slid into the ravine. Molly moaned a desperately sad sound.

"*It's okay. Just let it go,*" Kane yelled over his shoulder. "Let it go." Molly was clutching at him again, leaning close and squinting her eyes as her short blonde hair whipped at her face. Kane retrieved two shotgun rounds, dropped them into the open shotgun under his leg, pulled it free, and snapped the weapon closed with a flick of his wrist.

The painted driver of the dune buggy began to slow around the corner of the wreckage, seeing the gang's injured men in the road. Ashteroth slapped him hard in the side of the head.

"*Go!*" he snarled. "Run those bastards down like the dogs they are!"

The driver pressed his foot to the floor, and the buggy whined as it increased its speed. The injured goons in the road were on their knees, waving their arms in desperation, when the buggy crushed into them, grinding them back into the road. Red life sprayed across the front of the buggy, and Ashteroth gave a whoop of psychotic pleasure as he wiped the blood spatter from his face.

The road began to level out, opening up into a long, straight stretch of highway. Gloomy, smoke-shrouded mountains rose up above them on either side as the highway entered the straightaway. The burnt, reddish dirt along the road gave the valley a desert like feel as a bitter, dusty wind bit at their faces and clawed at their eyes.

Kane could hear the wild yelling, jeering, and cheering from the vehicles behind them and gave a shudder. This stretch was where they were going to lose ground to the larger vehicles behind them. Sheer mass and horsepower would reign supreme in the straightaway. Flashes in his memory of the fight the day before echoed across the walls of his mind. If they were caught, he would be tortured and murdered, but Molly's fate would be unspeakable. Kane cranked the throttle wide open and watched the speedometer climb past 120 miles per hour. Life happened at a blur. Rusted vehicles, wreckage, and debris came at them at blistering speeds, allowing only microseconds to react as Kane rapidly leaned left and right, soaring across the burning highway. Behind him the other vehicles, led by the dune buggy, approached at an unnerving speed.

"*Get me up there!*" Ashteroth yelled. "I've got something for them!"

With a look of madness in his face, the tattooed man stooped and opened a case, removing several twelve-inch cylindrical metal pipe bombs with fuses. He drew his oversized combat knife and cut the fuses down to one-inch stubs.

"*Go off road, and get me up there!*"

The turbocharged dune buggy was approaching too fast on the right; another vehicle, the El Camino, on the left. Kane tucked the sawed-off shotgun behind his back and yelled to Molly.

"Take it, and keep them off us!"

Molly took the weapon from him. Suddenly something slapped and tumbled in the road next to them, followed by an excruciatingly loud explosion directly behind them. Molly cringed as the blast propelled them forward. The pursuing vehicles materializing through the smoke cloud as though jumping through a portal in time.

"Shoot, Molly, shoot!" Kane yelled.

Molly fired twice at the El Camino, the buckshot breaking the windows and deflecting off the body, causing minor damage. The El Camino dropped back and crossed over the road behind the dune buggy. Molly reached forward and into Kane's cargo pocket, retrieving two more shells, fumbling with them and dropping one. With her heart pounding in her chest, she broke the shotgun open, ejected the fired shells and inserted the one she had. She turned, pointing the gun at the dune buggy, and saw the crazy-looking tattooed man cocking his arm back to throw something at them. Trying her best to aim through her swollen eye, she pointed the shotgun center mass on the shirtless, tattooed figure and pulled the trigger. The gun recoiled upward, and the tattooed man flinched and grabbed his side, dropping the object in his hand. Molly watched as the silver object fell through the wheel well and bounced on the ground behind the buggy before disappearing under the El Camino.

Molly winced and closed her eyes at the flash of light and the deafening concussion as the El Camino turned into a rocketing ball of fire, skipping and thrashing its way across the ground as it launched flaming body parts into the air. The remaining passengers were fully engulfed in flames.

They screamed and thrashed about madly as they threw themselves from the bed of the vehicle. Kane was giving a triumphant yell and laughing crazily.

In a fractured instant, out of the corner of his eye, Kane noticed the tattooed man again. He was standing in the buggy with a terrible scowl of hatred on his face as his arm dropped to his side, the finishing of what looked like a baseball pitch. The force of the explosion pushed the bike sideways so forcefully that Kane felt as if he had made an involuntary ninety-degree left turn. They flew from the roadway, the bike skidding, jumping, and wobbling under them as it jumped and popped its way over the rough terrain. Kane held on for dear life but had the sensation that Molly was no longer with him. With a spine jarring conclusion, the bike was gone and all that remained was the ruddy turf sailing beneath him. His feet touched the ground first, and for a strange and surreal instant, he had the distinct feeling that he was going to be able to "jog it off." That was until the rest of him slammed into the dirt, and everything went black.

DAY 38

EMERGENCY FEDERAL FUEL RESERVE
SOUTH OF ATLANTA, GEORGIA

Jenna Gregory stood in silence, pressing her ear firmly to the door. She had been listening intently for the last five minutes to a conversation between her husband, Charlie, and Gavin, the director of the fuel reserve. They were talking about people that had recently arrived outside the main gate. She pressed her ear further and strained to hear the muffled words.

"Are you serious? We don't know those people," Charlie was saying.

"I am serious, Charlie. We are nearly out of food. What do you want me to do?"

"I want you to know who it is we're letting in here."

"They said they would trade us food and water for fuel. We need that food and water."

"Yes, Gavin we do, but these men look like pirates or bandits, not peaceable travelers. We've got to use a little common sense."

"Pirates? What century are you living in?"

The voices in the room became more muffled as Charlie and Gavin continued their argument. Jenna could no longer tell what the two were saying. What was it they were saying about pirates?

Jenna had moved with Charlie and their unborn child to the fuel reserve over ten months ago. Charlie had been assigned as the assistant director of this facility by American Oil Products, a company contracted by the government for emergency fuel storage. The walled-off compound initially seemed cold and alien when they had first transferred, but had soon enough become home. Only the unrelenting security measures upon entry and exit had been truly obnoxious. They had lived there about five months before everything had gone wrong and the world had fallen apart around them. She had been completely shocked when the attacks began in the early morning hours of that fateful day, but even more surprised that the underground reserve and the reserve's living quarters had remained largely undamaged. The place was built like a nuclear blast shelter.

Jenna pulled away from the door at the slight whine of her sleeping infant daughter, Lynn, but quickly resumed her position. Gavin was trying to talk calmly, but in the short time she had known the man, he had been an impulsive and sometimes hotheaded man who believed that his word was law. He didn't sound very calm.

"Because, I don't need your approval to do this, that's why!" he said raising his voice.

"Gavin, listen. I'm not arguing this just for the sake of arguing with you. We have ten families here on site. We need to make sure that whatever we do is the right thing for everybody. The world out there is different now, and those men don't look trustworthy to me," Charlie said.

"Okay, well, I think you're being a bit childish worrying about 'pirates.'" Gavin indicated quotations with his fingers. "We need to worry about real problems like food and water. Besides, our security contingent can handle any problems we might have. When you're ready to be realistic, let me know. I'll be downstairs speaking with the others."

She heard Gavin open the far door and shut it hard behind him. She was just pulling away from the door when it began to open.

"Oh....Were you?" Charley started, questioning.

"I was listening," Jenna said.

"Do you spy on all my conversations?" he said and kissed her.

"Not all of them," she said with a small smile. "What's the deal?"

"Gavin wants to barter with a couple of men outside the gate. They have an old truck filled with canned goods and water tanks, and they said they'll trade the food and water for fuel."

"So what's the problem?" Jenna asked.

"I dunno." Charley sighed heavily and ran his fingers through his short red hair. "Something just doesn't seem right."

"Phooey. You see nothing but conspiracy."

"And you pretend it doesn't exist," he said and kissed her again. "Jenna, I just want to make sure everyone is safe. I don't think the world out there is the one we remember."

She made a face. "Alright, but I still think you've seen too many science fiction movies. We should help those people out in any way we can. In fact, we should give them what they need and ask for nothing in return. That is what Christ would want us to do in times like these."

Charley smiled at his young wife.

"Yeah, I know," he said with another sigh. "I'll talk with Gavin and maybe we can work something out. Okay?"

Jenna smiled and nodded. She had been born an optimist, and would always be an optimist. There was something good to be found in everyone, and no one was beyond the grace and mercy of the Lord.

She smiled again. They would help these travelers, paying kindness to their fellow man, and do the Lord's will in the process.

✲ ✲ ✲

He was crawling. Through the red swirling dizziness, he was crawling and slithering like a snake on his belly. In an action controlled completely by his subconscious, his elbows and knees continued to writhe in the red fog. He gasped and sputtered as he tried to take in a breath devoid of the red thickness. His mind spun as his vision slowly returned to him. As though swooping in from a great distance, he began the descent back into his body, his senses reactivating. It was all coming back to him as he crawled—the highway chase, the crash, the bandits, and his separation from Molly. Kane continued to crawl toward his unknown destination, the corners of his vision revealing fire and smoke. He could hear the wild yelling of his pursuers. He hadn't been out for long.

Kane slowly dragged himself to his knees and then to his feet, testing the strength of his body as he stood. He could not tell if he was injured beyond some pretty decent road rash. His heart began to pick up speed at the realization that he had blacked out for only a moment and the pursuit was still underway.

The dune buggy and two rusted sedans slid to a stop in the red dirt. Kane looked left and right, steadily taking in the scene. These three vehicles were the only ones left, except for the ambulance, which had rolled on its side against a nearby hill, fire pouring from under its hood.

Kane directed his attention back to the vehicles and their occupants, who were now exiting and rushing toward him with psychotic screams. He still could not see Molly. As the thugs rushed in, Kane took a deep breath and exhaled it forcefully, his muscle memory gearing into action. In the blink of an eye, all the years of diligent training in hand-to-hand combat flashed through his mind. Kane, not being a large man, had devoted himself fully to understanding how to use what he had as a weapon. He had spent a considerable amount of time over the last fourteen years training in traditional Okinawan karate as well as police defensive tactics. His senses became ultrarefined as the adrenaline dump landed in his system. Amid the chaos, he had the perception that time slowed as his vision became ultrafocused. This would be the final fight of his life.

He took a defensive position and breathed deeply as the first crazy thug came in, howling at him with a crude short-bladed knife raised high. Kane sidestepped and deflected the knife with his left hand and came down hard with a brachial stun, slamming his forearm into the side of the thug's neck. The offender pinwheeled to the side with a grunt as Kane turned to his next opponent and stomped the heel of his boot into the man's pelvic bowl, knocking him off balance and backward.

Two wildly painted thugs came at him from either side with their barbaric weapons. Kane ducked, dodged, and spun as he evaded the attackers, eliciting screams and jeers from the small mob.

The ugly, angry thugs now surrounded him, and his muscles burned with fatigue. He ducked another swipe from a primitive club and came up inside the thug's guard, twisting his hips and slamming his fist swiftly up under the man's jaw. The thug's teeth crackled, exploding against each other inside the confines of his head as his knees gave and he collapsed to the ground. Spinning to his right and chambering his right leg to his chest, Kane threw a devastating back kick, slamming another attacker in the chest like a crazed mule.

The thug groaned and flew backward off his feet, striking the ground on his shoulder blades, toppling end over end and sliding across the dirt like a rag doll. Ducking to his left, Kane threw his body into another man, connecting with the force of a linebacker. He was moving faster than he knew possible, riding his flaming surge of adrenaline. He continued to punch and kick, dodging and evading his enemy's attacks, his only purpose to deliver blow after crushing blow to his opponents. But there were too many of them. Kane turned to his left just as a goon behind him drove a rusty blade through his left bicep. With a raging scream of pain, Kane jerked the blade from the muscle and slashed it backwards across the thug's neck, nearly removing the man's head from his body. He immediately lunged again, thrusting the blade into the chest of the nearest marauder, and tore it back out again, blood and dirt mixing under the stomping of furious feet. Kane spun to find his next target, but before he could, he was struck violently in the head from behind, and his legs gave way beneath him. Exhaustion taking over, Kane tried to stand, but his muscles quivered and shook as the mob closed in around him. His head was stomped against the ground by the angry thugs as what was left of his energy and resolve began to leave him. He was finished.

"*Stop!* Back up!" A voice came from above him. "Tie his arms and legs and draw him up," the tattooed leader commanded his soldiers. "We're not going to end this quite yet."

Kane's wrists and ankles were tied with chords, and a thin rope was looped around his neck in the fashion of a noose. Sharp and swift pressure on the noose brought him scrambling to his knees, gasping for air. Kane sat back on his heels as the thug behind him kept strong pressure on the rope. Kane slowed his breaths and tried to clear his mind of the fog and fear of battle. The thugs that were left numbered about seven, not including their leader, the tattooed man they had called Ashteroth. Those that remained stood in a semicircle facing him, nursing their wounds with hate in their eyes and evil smiles on their lips.

"Well!" the twisted voice said with enthusiasm. "I don't know who you are or where you've come from, but you've made the boss man very mad. And after this little demonstration here, I can't say I like you very much either. Pretty impressive, though, for one man to nearly take out my entire crew."

The tattooed man stepped forward, pulling a crying Molly by the hair. She had taken another beating. Kane winced and tried to swallow.

"I'm sorry, Molly. I...I...tried..." he croaked over the tightening noose.

"I'm sure you did," Ashteroth said. "But because you tried to move against the Coyotes, we're going to have to do some pretty strong lessons to you and your friend here. We have a reputation to uphold, after all," he added as he gave Molly's hair a significant jerk.

A small amount of blood streamed from a small wound, a 00 buckshot pellet wound, in his left side.

"The funny thing is, I'm a terrible person, and I admit that I do enjoy doing murderous things to people. You see, I'm really more animal than man, and I have learned over the years to obey my savage instincts." He smiled wickedly, the tattoos across his face contorting in animated gestures. "I'm going to enjoy helping you understand why you don't cross the Coyotes."

Kane remained stoic, silently observing his tormentor.

"Nothing to say? Neither does she, but she will. She's going to beg for us to stop." Ashteroth said as he licked his lips and gazed at Molly. "It's been a long time since I've put my hands on a clean woman. We're going to start with her, and you're going to watch," he said, a wickedly psychotic grin on his tattooed face

The engine compartment of the ambulance exploded in a hot shower of flame and burning electrical equipment, the force of which caused the side of the hill next to it to cave in. Though confined in such an intense moment of impending doom, Kane found himself curiously watching the side of the hill as it crumbled away under the blast. It was as if the hill was hollow altogether, crumbling and disintegrating inward, showing an odd honeycomb-like structure.

Apparently, what he was seeing was strange enough to distract the mob of sociopaths surrounding him—something black was now tumbling out of the gaping hole in the hillside. The forms rolled and spilled from the hillside, tumbling over each other like a sack of dried black beans turned on its side. As the objects flowed from the hillside, they began to animate, moving independently of each other. Their movements were swift and erratic, jerking this way and that. Kane's mouth was fully open now, and whatever had happened in the preceding moments was lost in the strangeness of this one. The rope around his neck hung loosely next to his arm. The goons that had surrounded him were scattering, fleeing in a wild hysteria.

What the hell?

He looked again at the hillside as the strange creatures continued to boil from it, moving quickly on their long black legs and swinging their anvil-shaped heads from side to side.

Kane was frozen in place, his limbs bound by more than just rope. He tried to yell in disbelief, but nothing came from his throat. It was not possible, not what he was seeing.

Ants.

Thousands of swarming ants, twice the size of men, were coming from the side of that hill.

DAY 38

EMERGENCY FEDERAL FUEL RESERVE
SOUTH OF ATLANTA, GEORGIA

Jenna held Lynn close, rocking her baby and humming a light, sweet tune. As she sat on the bench and rocked, the baby girl wiggled and grunted slightly.

"Shhhhhhh. It's okay, sweet girl. Shhhhhhhh," Jenna cooed.

She looked up from the edge of the courtyard as Charlie and Gavin walked together toward the main gate. She watched Charlie, noticing that his lanky stride was goofy and confident all at the same time. In his younger years, he had always been the one who stuck up for the other kid who was being picked on, only to receive a beating himself. He was a beautiful man, a balance of strength and weakness. She smiled and whispered a few more sweet words to Lynn. They had enjoyed a wonderful marriage, however short, and even through the horrific recent events they had grown stronger in their faith and in their relationship with each other.

She had persuaded Charlie to help the people outside the gate. Gavin had been pleased, because it had been his idea in the first place, of course. She, however, wanted to take every opportunity to create something purposeful from something terrible. Helping people in need was a wonderful way to witness to others of the love of Jesus, especially in the wake of such terrible events. If the United States was as ruined as she had heard, then all the people of this country had left were the fragile ties of brotherly love and the message of the gospel.

Slowly and methodically, the heavy steel doors began to crank open. She was able to gather her first glimpse of the two men and the truck outside the entrance. They slowly drove the truck in but stopped a little short, leaving the vehicle in between the two sliding doors. The men exited the truck and met with Gavin and Charlie. Looking to the left and right she noticed the small security contingent, handguns drawn, that had escorted Charlie and Gavin.

Definitely Charlie's idea.

As Jenna watched the silent exchange on the other side of the courtyard, she squinted her eyes at the entrance. Was that another person waiting outside the gate? She saw movement.

Jenna stood up abruptly, cradling her baby tight. Something wasn't right. Suddenly a volley of gunfire erupted with small clouds of dust in the courtyard, and the security detail collapsed to the ground.

Gavin was waving his arms wildly in front of him as the man across from him raised a handgun.

What?!

She watched and felt cold terror creep into her heart as Charlie stepped in front of Gavin. He was holding his arms up, palms out as if interceding. She heard a crack, and red mist blew from the back of Charlie's head as he dropped to his knees and slumped over.

An awful, unrecognizable sound forced itself from Jenna's throat.

They were storming through the gate. Ugly, savage raiders were entering one after another. Now the gunman was shooting Gavin over and over again as the man begged for his life. Someone triggered the emergency lockdown, and with a piercing alarm the heavy doors began rapidly sliding shut. Jenna looked left and right, unsure of what to do. She knew she needed to do something but was frozen in panic. The doors slammed shut on the truck and began slowly crushing it until they stopped completely, leaving an opening only big enough for a man to fit through. And fit through they did; man after man crawled over the crushed truck and into the compound.

Jenna couldn't think, couldn't breathe, couldn't act.

The sole words uttered from her lips, "Oh Jesus, Lord Jesus."

Forcing her right leg forward, she stepped into the courtyard. She had to get to Charlie. Thugs ransacked and raided all around her, kicking in doors and dragging innocent people out into the courtyard. A man on her left was screaming as two thugs held him down and sawed at his neck with a rusted machete. On her right, several half-naked goons were violently sodomizing a woman. They had been in the compound less than forty-five seconds. Jenna forced her left foot forward, dragging it from its place like a snagged anchor.

"Father God in Heaven...be my shield...be my shield," she said through the tears running down her cheeks.

She had largely gone unnoticed and had made it to within ten paces of her husband when a man stepped in front of her.

Jenna continued to look at the ground.

"Please, I need to see my husband."

The man waved his hand in the direction of Charlie and Gavin.

"Now, would that be the red head or the fat guy?"

"Please," she repeated as if in a trance. "I need to see my Charlie."

The tears in her eyes blurred the vision of her husband lying on his side with a long red trail leading from his head.

"Well," the man said casually. "Whichever one he is, they are both dead, so, look and see."

She looked up at the man for the first time, her gaze one of fear and confusion. She took in his dark hair and angular features and saw that his face displayed an emotionless mask.

"Why have you done this? Why are you doing this? We were trying to help you."

The man stared back, his face unreadable. "Why, why, why. *Why* does everyone ask that? Maybe it's fate, or karma...or maybe God hates you. Maybe that's it." The man smirked coldly. "Making sense of it doesn't change a thing."

Jenna stared in sorrow at the man's cold features as the tears rolled down her cheeks. With all the pillaging and death and rape happening all around them, the man spoke with a smoothness finer than silk.

"My name is Dagen. And you're going to help me."

Jenna bit her lip. "Jesus loves you, even though you do this," she said with a calmness that transcended her situation.

Dagen gave a smile that was sincere and evil all at once. "That's sweet, but Jesus doesn't love me, and he left the United States a long time ago."

He paused and glanced away and then back again, his face utterly serious.

"You're going to want me to hold your baby."

Jenna stuttered, "W-w-w-what?"

As he spoke, he slipped his hands in between hers and under the baby. "I said, you're going to want me to hold her," he said, cocking his head slightly to the left.

The butt of the rifle slammed into the side of her head and caused her to lose reception of reality, as though her head were an old antenna-equipped TV. She stumbled, or thought she stumbled, and became weightless, falling through the floor of her mind, her husband's words screaming in her ears: *Jenna, I just want to make sure everyone is safe.*

✡ ✡ ✡

Through the stampede of human panic, Molly crawled toward the dune buggy, her head throbbing and her heart slamming in her chest as she dug her fingers into the soil. She could not have seen what she saw. Not in a million lifetimes would she have ever expected to see that. Giant ants swarming from the hillside, their shrieking calls deafening in her ears. The men around her screamed and ran as the sounds of sporadic gunfire intermingled with the terrible shrieking of the creatures.

Gasping, she reached the dune buggy and crawled under it, positioning herself to try to get a better look. Straining and blinking through the red dust she looked for Kane, but she wasn't able to see him. The tattooed leader and some of his goons were making a stand against the creatures as they fired their weapons randomly into the swarm of approaching insects. Molly watched in amazement as the bullets pinged and zinged off the heads and backs of the marauding monsters, their exoskeletons defeating the projectiles like plate steel.

The only creatures that appeared to fall were the ones whose bulbous black eyes were pierced by stray projectiles. They shrieked and collapsed, sliding across the red earth in defeat as their comrades scurried over them without concern. The tattooed Ashteroth, who only moments before had held a fistful of her hair, was now screaming at his men and pulling his giant knife from its sheath. Molly watched, captivated, as the creatures descended upon the men with their jaws locked open, ready to strike. They moved quickly, swinging their broad anvil-shaped heads back and forth.

Molly put her hand over her mouth as the giant insects collided with the small squad of men. The men screamed and thrashed madly at the beasts as their bladed jaws slashed and tore them limb from limb, their blood spraying and splashing onto the dirt.

Ashteroth was yelling and swinging his large blade savagely, striking the creatures in their eyes. Down went one, then another, as he fought them off viciously, but the creatures were too great in number.

One of the large black beasts came at Ashteroth from his right, snapping its jaws closed around his midsection. He shrieked and flailed, dropping the knife and banging against the creature's head with his fist. The great beast shook him back and forth violently until his lower torso and legs separated and dropped free from the rest of him. The tattooed man continued to buck and thrash, wailing obscenities as the life flowed from him onto the earth. His movements slowed, and his posture began to sag. Without further concern, the uninterested creature dropped him and moved on to search the rest of the area.

Molly became painfully aware that Kane was most likely still out in the open somewhere. She scanned the area rapidly with her eyes and finally located his twisting form trying to free his hands about thirty yards from her. She croaked out loud as the creatures skittered swiftly toward him. Kane grabbed up a knife in the dirt and began quickly cutting away the restraints on his wrists as a giant black ant noticed him and redirected toward him, skittering, screeching, and alerting others around it.

Molly ground her teeth and moaned a desperate sound as she prepared to helplessly watch the death of her only friend. Kane snapped the restraints just as the monstrous insect came in, ready to attack. Kane ducked under the jaws, as they slammed shut, coming up and to the outside, as he drove the knife deep into its eye lens so that his arm disappeared to the elbow. Clear hemolymph exploded from the socket all over him as he grimaced and ground the blade in a scrambling motion around in the creature's head. The creature screeched and stumbled, collapsing over and on top of Kane, and driving him out of Molly's sight. More of them now converged on Kane and the downed creature, and Molly pinched her eyes closed. She couldn't bear the thought.

"Please. Please, God, protect him," she prayed silently.

She lay as still as a statue as a group of the ants approached the buggy, their strange, alien-looking forms jerking this way and that. Their screeching varied in pitch and tone and sometimes had variations of a trilling and clicking sound. They were communicating, systematically searching for every last enemy invader.

As Molly lay quietly in the dirt, she began to remember what she had learned about these strange creatures in a not-too-distant college biology class. The screeching sound was created either by the stridulation of the insect's gaster segments or by the mandibles themselves and was a form of communication. She knew that they would also be communicating by the use of pheromones, or chemical messages that were used to communicate with the colony. Though generally having poor vision, their eyes, which were composed of many tiny lenses—much like a housefly—were able to detect movement very well. Molly continued to lie still as the screeching and probing continued around the buggy.

If she was going to help Kane, or anyone else for that matter, she was going to have to know what she was dealing with and address the situation appropriately. Ants by nature were not extremely aggressive unless personally provoked or corporately defending the nest. That was assuming that these creatures had retained the same or similar instincts as their tiny brethren. She could not be sure, though. For one, as was obvious, their size had been altered by some chemical or radioactive interference, and their exoskeletons seemed to be hardened to the point that bullets did not penetrate them. This alone was most amazing, especially to have occurred in such a short time since the attacks. It would seem also that food shortages might have caused them to adapt from scavenging to a more predatory behavior. It would be reasonable to assume that other alterations could have also occurred, either physiologically or behaviorally.

The ants in the area were calming considerably, now mostly milling about in a busy sort of manner, as opposed to the attack frenzy that had just ensued. As some moved away from the buggy, they rejoined the group and began collecting their wounded and dead in twos and threes. Molly estimated them to range from eight to twelve feet in length, standing about a meter tall, with oversized scimitar-shaped mandibles that looked like double-bladed swords.

Molly lay under the dune buggy for hours, watching the large ants mill about and conduct business as usual. After they had cleaned up the battlefield, the large soldier ants retreated into the colony, leaving the slightly smaller worker drones to repair the damaged hillside. Molly knew better than to try to exit too early. Her reemergence could be considered a threat to the colony and start a second frenzy. No, she was staying under the dune buggy for now. In the warm oppression under the vehicle, Molly felt her weariness take over as the slow, methodical rebuilding of the colony wall took place in front of her. She dozed and nodded until sleep overtook her completely, her parasympathetic nervous system demanding control after the chaos of the day.

✵ ✵ ✵

Molly woke with a start, feeling as if she had missed her alarm. She looked around hurriedly and saw nothing but stillness in the fading light of the day. Peering through the dimness, she saw the fresh colony wall built around and partially covering the ambulance. She wiggled and began moving her stiffened body, wincing at the effort. Molly crawled from under the dune buggy and stood to survey the immediate area. She was shocked to see how much blood was soaked into the ground, and yet not a single body remained. She walked over to where she had last seen Kane. To her dismay, she found a large quantity of blood and the knife he had used to defend himself. She followed the blood trail with her eyes to the base of the colony and shook her head. They had policed him up along with the remains of the others to decompose and be used as a food source for the colony.

She clinched her eyes shut and wiped the tears from her face with a dirty palm. There was no use in trying to find him. He was dead like the others, and no effort on her part would help him now. But just as she meditated on this, a pang of guilt surged in her chest and a dusty wind kicked up and stung her cheek as if in response to her morbid judgments. She thought over the past few days and recalled how many times Kane had modeled Christ for her by saving her and placing himself in between her and certain doom. What kind of woman was she if she did not attempt a monumental effort to return the love and kindness her friend had displayed for her? Her favorite scripture verse stood out in her mind: "For God has not given us a spirit of fear and timidity, but one of power, love, and self-discipline."

Hang on, Kane, she thought, as that familiar look of determination set in across her dirty face. *I'm coming.*

✡ ✡ ✡

Jenna Gregory stirred on the cold metal floor, as she slowly began to come around. She had been dragged inside into some interior room.

"Where," she said out loud, "where's my baby?"

She squinted her eyes as the dark silhouettes of rough men slowly materialized from the walls of the pump control room like demons stepping through from another world, their shadowy forms drifting slightly in the dim artificial light. The smooth voice from the courtyard spoke to her from the far wall.

"I told you before, I need your help."

"My baby, where is she?" Jenna asked, as she raised herself from the floor.

The voice spoke again. "I need you to listen…"

"*Tell me where she is!*" Jenna yelled madly.

The room was completely silent, the men standing around her like stone pillars. It seemed that not a breath was taken for an eternity before Dagen spoke again.

"She is with one of my men, and in ten minutes he will suffocate her if you don't do exactly as I ask. Time is wasting, so listen."

Jenna mouth was open, gagging, choking, as an invisible vice of despair closed down upon her.

Dagen smiled mildly. "Don't mourn her yet. She still has almost ten minutes for you to save her."

"What, what do you want me to do?" Jenna asked desperately.

"One of your dead friends initiated a critical lockdown of the reserve. That means the fuel pumps are shut off. I need that fuel. Input your husband's codes for the fuel release valves."

"I don't know them! *Please!*" Jenna pleaded.

"Nine minutes, fifteen seconds."

"I'll do it, I'll do whatever. You don't need to hurt her. I'll give you what you want."

The steel resolve in Dagen's face shook her to her core. "Nine minutes."

"I think I can find them in his office!" she said, the panic like fire behind her eyes.

"Tick tock," he said, smiling.

She was up and stumbling out of the door and down the hallway, the thugs pacing behind her as she went. After making several turns and going up a flight of stairs to the second floor of the compound, she was in the administrative offices. She knew Charlie had kept all his most important and confidential information in the safe in his office. As Jenna clumsily navigated the cubicles toward Charlie's office, her head swam and pounded with injury, fear, and pressure. She burst into the office and dropped to her knees on the carpet.

"Oh, Charlie! What was it?" she said out loud as she fumbled with the combination lock.

32-17…something. He had been so concerned about forgetting it, he had made her memorize it, too. But now when she needed it, it wasn't there.

"Please! I…I…I don't…I can't remember," she stammered.

The thug's words from behind her were without emotion. "Then baby's gonna go nite-nite."

Jenna coughed and sputtered, hyperventilating as she grabbed hand-fuls of her hair.

"32-17…32-17…."

She cried, moaning and rocking back and forth on the carpet.

"Six! It's six!" Jenna yelled, as she input the last number, and the bolts released.

Her arms swept madly over the papers in the vault, raking them furiously out of the way as she looked for the red folder. She knew they were in the red folder. Seeing it, she snatched it up, stood, and ran back out the door past her dark guardians. Down the hall, down the stairs, and back to the pump room she streaked, her mind screaming. How much time had passed? She burst back into the pump room to find Dagen with his arms crossed, looking at his watch.

"I've got it...I...I...I've got it!" she said in breathless desperation, as she flung the folder open and dug the individual pump codes out. She moved to the first of three stations and pressed the numbers into the keypad. With a chime and a hiss, the red light turned green and she moved to the next pad. As Jenna typed the numbers into the pad, Dagen's watch began beeping rapidly.

"Wait...wait...I'm almost done. *Please!*" Jenna cried. Her hands shook violently as tears flooded her vision and terror began to cloud her heart. The watch continued to beep as she moved to the third station.

Her fingers twitched and convulsed in spasms, and the flood continued from her eyes as she punched in the final numbers, followed by a chime and a green light.

Jenna sniffled and clutched her hands to her chest, unable to speak.

In a most sincere voice, Dagen spoke. "Thank you so very much," he said, as he stopped the alarm on his watch.

"I did it. I did what you wanted," Jenna stammered.

Dagen winced and sucked his teeth, a practiced look of sorrow on his face. "Yes, you did, but you weren't quite fast enough. We had a deal, remember? Ten minutes."

"But, my Lynn!"

"If you really wanted to save her you, would have done it in the time I gave to you."

Jenna's body shook with the intensity of an earthquake. "Don't do it!" she sobbed. "She's just a baby!"

"Yes she *was*," Dagen said, stone-faced, as he moved from the room. He stopped and spoke to a thug at the door. "Is the fuel pumping?"

"Yes, boss."

"Good." He nodded toward Jenna. "When the men are done with her, tie her up and take her out to the rig with the other prisoners."

The world changed. Whatever it had been before, it was no longer the same for Jenna Gregory as she crumpled to the floor. Her husband and baby girl had been murdered because of her, and her own unknown fate was rapidly becoming clearer. The racking, pitiable bawl of a tortured soul filled the room and shook the very foundation of the reserve. And in the semidarkness of the pump room, the shadows of many lustful men converged upon the body of the woman who used to be Jenna Gregory.

☆ ☆ ☆

Molly stood silently, watching the exterior of the ant colony. Though darkness had descended, the smaller workers still occasionally emerged from one of many holes in the hillside and lazily moved across the face of the mound, only to disappear into another hole. The creatures moved slowly, carefully picking their way across the surface, strange sleepwalkers in the moonless night.

Molly ran a hand through her bloody, dirty, tangled blonde hair and winced as she touched her face lightly. She was banged up pretty badly.

Between several beatings and a motorcycle wreck, she was sure she looked like the walking dead. Her right ankle still hurt from days before, and her shoulder and left wrist made clicking sounds that caused her a lot of pain when she moved them.

She sighed deeply. She slowly moved and twisted her various muscles and joints trying to find points of weakness, but for all her small injuries combined, she did not seem to be very seriously injured.

She remembered something her dad used to say all the time when she was a little girl: if you're going to do something at all, do your very best, 'cause nothing else will do.

She was going to do her very best, but she was going to need some equipment if she was going into that hill. She looked around and decided to quietly comb the battlefield for weapons and then check the existing vehicles for other possible items of interest. She moved silently, checking her footing in the darkness. She moved to the area where Ashteroth and his soldiers had made their last stand. Probing each dark silhouette with her hands, she felt for anything that might be useful, often jerking her hand back when she found a severed limb or a pile of organs. She grasped a slim metal object and ran her hands over it. It was a revolver. She crouched and fumbled with it to release the cylinder. Dumping the shells onto the dirt she felt them over individually. Some of them had round noses, and some were empty brass cases. Molly kept the two good rounds and reloaded them into the cylinder, snapping it back into place and shoving it in her waistband. She also snagged Ashteroth's great blood-covered knife, and stepping gingerly, moved to the nearby vehicles.

A quick search of the first sedan revealed nothing of importance. She then checked the dune buggy and found a very large, heavy coil of rope and a metal carry case behind the driver's seat. Molly opened the case and revealed several pipelike fixtures with something protruding from their tops. She puzzled over them for a moment before suddenly realizing that they were pipe bombs. They had been what the tattooed bandit leader had thrown at them. She took the four that remained and cradled them in her right arm, thinking that they could come in handy. She shrugged the rope coil over her shoulder and also pulled a partially full plastic gas can from the floorboard of the buggy.

Molly walked toward the ambulance, which still remained half-buried in the hillside. She paused intermittently only when a worker ant nosed slowly from a hole in the hill, resuming her movement when it would reenter the colony. Reaching the back of the ambulance, she gently opened the double doors and exposed the interior.

Though all the good stuff had been looted long ago, with a little searching she found several usable items: a four-foot length of sturdy metal interior support pipe, a roll of heavy duty medical tape, an old used Bic lighter, and a dirty white sheet.

Stepping away from the ambulance, she worked quickly. She cut the sheet with the knife, making a small cloth satchel that she draped over her head and shoulder. Molly then took the length of pipe and, with the medical tape, began securing the large knife to the end of it, creating a short spear. She also threaded a wadded strip from the sheet into the nozzle of the gas can and tipped the can over to soak the cloth. Dumping the leftover materials in the makeshift satchel, she stood and stuck the lighter in her front pocket for easy access. She took one end of the rope and tied it to the rear axle of the ambulance. The other end she tied around her waist. With the necessary equipment loaded up, Molly picked up the spear and the gas can as she moved with purpose toward the closest opening in the hill to begin her descent into the unknown bowels of the earth.

✡ ✡ ✡

Deep inside the ant colony, Kane lay motionless, cocooned in something. His mind was a whirling, spinning prison of thought. In his mind's eye, everything was thick and clouded, and he had the perception that he was sinking, drowning as the waves of his memories lapped over his head. In the confines of his mind, he screamed and choked and tried to stay above the surface of the dark waters. His mind tried to grasp, tried to remember his situation. Was he dead? Or was this a dream, a product of his own insanity after the psychological and mental strain he had endured? As he lay alone and confused in the depths of his mind, a faint figure approached from the edge of his consciousness. A woman.

"Suz?" Kane said to the figure as she stopped, slightly concealed by a hazy light. "Susan, if that's you, I can't see you very well."

"Listen to me, Kane," she said.

"Susan! I found it, or it found me...my faith. God found me."

"I knew he would. But do you yet believe?"

"I'm trying to."

"The road ahead is still perilous, Kane, and God's plan for your life and his purpose are coming to fruition."

"What does he want me to do?"

"Listen, trust, and obey," she told him.

"Yes, but what does that mean?" he asked.

"It means that you have been chosen to stand against the rising tide of darkness."

"But I am just one man. How am I supposed to do that?" Kane protested.

"You will stand in the name of the King of Heaven, with his strength at your back. Nothing is impossible. But first you must give him everything and trust in him without reservation. Can you do this?"

"I don't know," Kane whispered.

"You must, or you will fail. This appointment is not one that you may commit to half-heartedly, for you must lead those who have been called. Some of them are aware of the call, and some are not. You will need their support, and they will need your commitment."

Kane struggled to comprehend what he was being told. "It's all so vague, Susan. I just need you to tell me that you and the kids are okay."

"Trust, Kane, and don't worry for us. Now you must follow the Spirit as it leads you."

"I didn't ask for this responsibility."

"You may not have asked for it, but it is your honor to bear it. The battle of eternity is at hand. Be strong, and become the man God created you to be."

"I...I'm..." Kane started.

"Seek the light, Kane. Seek with all your heart, and be made whole again," she said, as she began to fade.

Kane gasped as his head slipped beneath the murky waters and all went black again.

DAY 31

NORTHWEST-SOUTH CAROLINA

The young boy ran, dodging swiftly between the barren trees. He moved with a feline grace, unnatural to the step of man and at a pace that would tire the most seasoned runner. Each step calculated, each movement with uncanny precision, he ran, ducked and bounded through the forest, the animal skins about his shoulders and body moving only slightly. He was dirty, with long brown hair, and was no more than ten years of age. As he moved, he was shadowed by a strange, swift presence. Cresting the rise of the hill, he came to a stop and turned his head to the left, his chest rising and falling with measured breaths.

Up the hill behind him came the thud of heavy footfalls against the earth like the stomping of a titan. The boy made a slight whistling sound through his teeth and shook his head as a monstrous beast of an animal came into view. The creature was a great wild dog, or a wolf, or both, or neither. Its enormous form stepped up next to the boy and shook its great mane of hair, yawning and showing huge, white, daggerlike fangs that protruded from its gaping mouth. The animal was massive in appearance, standing four feet tall at the shoulder, with stacks of dense muscle that rippled across its shoulders and flanks under a flowing coat of black and grey hair. While closely resembling a wolf, this beast was much larger and thicker, like the great African cats with heavy, hairy, taloned paws at the base of its thick, muscular legs. Its appearance was such that it conjured up thoughts of myth and legend and shape-shifting fiends from times of old. Where it had first come from, to this day not even the boy knew, but by its strong, quiet gentleness, the beast showed that it was no fiend as it boldly stood next to him.

The boy stepped forward, grabbing a handful of the animal's mane, and placed his right hand on its snout. He turned its face toward him. For a long moment, the boy stared into the animal's silvery eyes, unspoken words conveying endless meaning.

The beast turned its face from the boy and licked its lips a few times. The boy pulled it back, staring again into its eyes.

"You let me win, didn't you, Az?" the boy said.

With an otherworldly look of intelligence in its eyes, the animal bowed its head and nuzzled its face against the boy's chest.

"I knew it," he said, as he grabbed handfuls of the creature's mane and pulled himself into a mount atop the animal's back. Rubbing its neck with both hands, he said, "Next time I'll win, you'll see."

With a swiftness that seemed to defy the very power of gravity, the beast was off, dashing through the charcoal woods, the boy riding him like a wild steed. The charred earth flowed like a swift black river beneath them as they moved as one toward their destination.

In a matter of moments, the two arrived at the ranch, and the boy slid off the animal's back to the ground. As they walked, there was a noticeable pattern of avoidance from the inhabitants of the ranch as they stared and spoke in murmurs about the odd couple, but neither of them batted an eye toward the visible shunning. They had both lived their entire lives on the fringe of society. The boy walked gingerly to the front entrance and turned to his ever-faithful companion.

"Would you wait here for me? I'll be just a few minutes."

The creature turned without a sound and moved to the edge of the entranceway to lie and rest. The boy entered the ranch house and quickly navigated the narrow hallways to his destination. He rapped three times on the door.

"Come in," came the reply.

The boy opened the door and stepped inside the small office.

"Ah, my wild Indian boy. How are you, Tynuk?" Vincent, said sitting up in his chair and pronouncing the boy's name "Tien-Nook."

"I'm fine."

"Still keeping company with that fearsome creature?" he said, as though scolding a wayward child.

"Yes," Tynuk replied evenly.

Vincent adjusted uncomfortably, showing visible disapproval of the boy's relationship with the animal. "Well, what can I do for you?"

"I have information from the outside for you."

"Excellent. And what would that be of?"

"To the Northwest there has been some kind of battle. Lots of fire and smoke, and I heard gunfire."

"So what of it? There is lawlessness everywhere."

"It was the Coyotes."

"What?" Vincent said, standing up out of his chair. "How do you know? Are you sure? How far away was this?"

"I'm sure it was them. I've seen their patrols before. I'm not sure how far. It took us a while to get back here," Tynuk said.

"What were they doing?"

"Fighting."

"I know that! I mean, with whom?" Vincent said, annoyed.

"I don't know, but it was just one man and one woman. It looked like a car chase that ended in a battle. The man fought bravely and defeated many of them, but I didn't see how it turned out."

"Did the Coyotes look like they were coming this way?"

"No. They looked like they were fighting, just like I said."

Vincent rolled his eyes.

"Keep your eyes peeled for their approach. I will need as much time as possible if we are to have to deal with them."

He paused, thinking deeply.

"That will be all Tynuk. Thank you," he said briskly.

Tynuk did not move.

"What is it?"

"We had an agreement."

"Of course," Vincent said, turning in frustration and opening a cabinet. He pulled out several canned goods and handed them to the boy as he ushered him toward the door. "Now, if you don't mind, I'm a very busy man."

Tynuk stepped into the hall as the door closed behind him. He tucked the cans into his satchel and was walking toward the exit, when a giant hand wrapped around his shoulder and turned him. Tynuk turned to see the giant form of Courtland, the only man that he and the beast called friend.

People naturally feared what they did not understand, and every single person that Tynuk and the beast encountered had either shunned them or fled in terror without first trying to understand the odd duo's intentions—everyone but Courtland. The giant black man had not shunned them nor fled in fear when they first encountered each other deep in the woods on a ragged, gloomy afternoon several weeks earlier. Courtland had smiled and warmly extended the hand of friendship, saying that he could see a likeness of purpose among them. They had sat and enjoyed a nice conversation over a few fire-heated cans of beans while Courtland had told them of what great things God was doing. Tynuk agreed and said that he had felt it too, that the Great Spirit was moving. Courtland had had been interested, but not nosey, as he spoke with an earnest conviction and a desire to better understand both Tynuk and his dark companion. With a mutual agreement and respect, they had resolved to be friends and to come to each other's aid should any of them need it.

The large man now had a sense of urgency in his face.

"Tynuk, tell me, did anyone survive that battle?"

Tynuk looked strangely at Courtland. "How did you hear?"

Courtland smiled. "Well?"

Tynuk shrugged his shoulders, "Maybe, I don't know."

"Is it possible the man the Coyotes were fighting survived?"

Tynuk grimaced and bit his lip. "No, I don't think so…we're talking about the Coyotes here."

"Did you see him die?"

"No, but there was much smoke."

"Thank you," Courtland said as he stood. "I'll see you later, Tynuk. Tell your companion hello for me."

"Why all the questions? Where are you going?" Tynuk asked.

"I've done enough waiting. I'm going to find the nameless warrior."

"He's dead."

"Not yet, he isn't."

✲ ✲ ✲

Inside the ant colony, darkness reigned supreme. Black mixed with black in unending, cloaking ink that felt as though it would suffocate all who entered and remained.

Molly stopped, set the unlit gas can down, and tested the rope around her waist once again. It was warmer here, as the intricate tunnels and chambers easily funneled the earth's natural heat toward the surface. In the darkness, Molly quietly listened to the colony as it spoke to her. The faint scratching, clicking, and trilling of its inhabitants deep in its core resonated through the tunnels and made the earthen walls themselves feel as though they carried life within them. A cold shiver ran down Molly's spine. She was an intruder, an enemy invader in someone else's home, and she knew she would be greeted as such. She pulled the lighter from her front pocket and crouched down next to the gas can.

How in the world was she going to find Kane? Small ant colonies could run very deep and extend for long distances under the surface. She could only hope for some indication of Kane's passing. She prepared to light the rag on the nozzle of the can and paused. This was it. Once she lit the can, she would start drawing attention to herself and would have to keep moving. She steadied her hand, lit the can, and began taking quick, well-placed steps down the tunnel, the granulated dirt under her feet crunching and sliding like scree on a lava slope.

The small flame flickered and showed the tunnel sloping steadily downward to a broader intersection of several tunnels. Molly continued forward, keeping her head on a swivel and tugging the safety rope for more slack every few steps. As she came to the end of the tunnel, she stopped and held the gas can up to get a better view of the intersection. She had yet to see any resistance to her intrusion.

From the tunnel there was a short five-foot drop to the floor of the intersecting tunnels. Molly peered at the strange, dark pattern that angled across the dirt floor and into another tunnel, leading further downward. She dropped down to the floor as quietly as possible and examined the pattern. Her heart picked up pace at the realization that the strange floor design was a trail of blood splatter.

Down the tunnel she moved, stepping on either side of the blood trail and holding the gas can forward to dispel the darkness. As she moved, she couldn't shake the sick, unnerving feeling that she was going so deep she would never return to the surface. Molly held the gas can high and squinted ahead as she approached another major intersection of tunnels. She squinted in the hazy, damp underground chamber, as lazy dust particles floated in the flickering light.

In the intersection the blood trail changed, growing larger and separating as it continued down three separate larger tunnels. Molly bit her lip and looked between the three choices. She had no way to know which way she needed to go. She decided to continue down the central tunnel. Molly took choppy steps around the blood, straining her eyes through the curling black smoke that poured upward against the ceiling of the tunnel. Something shuffled to her left, freezing Molly in place as she stifled a scream. She stood as a statue, frozen in time with the gas can and its burning nozzle outstretched in front of her. The shuffling sounded again to her left. Turning her head ever so slowly, she saw the large bladed jaws of a warrior ant protruding from a hole up and to the left of her. Molly swallowed hard and slowly lowered the gas can. Surely it had seen her; it couldn't be possible that it had not.

The creature shuffled again changing its position slightly. Molly took a half step back, monitoring its behavior. Nothing. She took another step backward, still not believing that she had gone undetected. The creature continued to peer at her with lifeless, bulbous black eyes that were neither awake nor asleep. She took another step back and then a third, as the giant ant remained in its hole, dormant.

Stepping backward quickly now, she re-entered the previous intersection, now taking the tunnel to her left. She moved as quickly and as silently as possible, turning the smothering blackness away with her small flame. As she moved, the tunnel became steeper, and Molly began to slide on her feet. She slipped and fell backward against the slope, sliding out of control as she dug her heels into the dirt. Then the tunnel became vertical, and Molly fell into the void. As hard as she tried to contain it, a muffled cry came from her lips as she tumbled into the blackness.

Molly struck the ground hard, landing on her side, the granulated dirt only slightly cushioning her fall. She covered her head as the dirt scattered all around her. The gas can bounced end over end across the dirt, effectively extinguishing the small flame.

Breathing heavily, Molly scrambled to her feet and fingered the revolver in her waistband and the satchel around her shoulder. They were still there. She then began sweeping her hands back and forth across the loose dirt in an attempt to find the gas can and spear. She quickly located the spear and pulled it over to her. She knew the gas can had fallen close by. She continued sweeping and shuffling until she bumped the can with her right hand. Snatching it up, she fumbled with the lighter as she pulled it from her pocket. She knew she would be in serious trouble if she dropped it. With no light and only the rope to guide her out, she would fall victim to the inhabitants of the colony. Molly flicked the lighter over and over, unable to get the now-dirty gas rag to catch. Molly clutched at the lighter, breathing hard, her fist shaking.

As her eyes began adjusting to the dark, she thought she saw a faint blue glow like a baby's nightlight from around the corner, down the dark descending tunnel. Setting the can down, she took one step toward the light and felt the rope around her waist tighten. She had reached the end of the line. Molly untied the rope and allowed it to hang where it was. She took the gas can up again and began shuffle-stepping through the semidarkness toward the light, feeling strangely drawn to it as though driven by both curiosity and fate.

As Molly shuffled, the tunnel became brighter with the strange glow. As she stepped around the bend in the tunnel, she found an opening in the tunnel wall with a bright, almost sparkling blue light coming from it. Molly entered to find a large, domed chamber supported by three large earthen columns down the center.

As her eyes adjusted, she began to see that the chamber was filled with many rows of strange ovular-shaped pods that glowed with a blue light. Stepping closer to one of the glowing pods, she instinctively reached out to touch its rubbery surface. As she made contact, something inside gyrated. Molly jerked her hand back. Stepping away, she scanned from right to left, taking in the depth of the room as her eyes settled on something she couldn't place off to her left. As she quietly moved closer, she began to realize what she was looking upon. Remains. Before her and against the wall, a large pile of human bodies was frozen in place by a shiny crystalline substance.

He was here. She knew it. She dropped the fuel and the spear and began desperately tearing at the upper layer of hardened mucus, pulling body after partial body from the pile and onto the floor. These men were the ones from the surface, the thugs who had tried to murder them. They were being stored here with the larvae. She paused and looked over her shoulder again at the large cavern filled with the glowing pods. They were ant larvae. These giant insects were reproducing.

As Molly turned back to the pile, she stopped. In front of her, almost in a sitting position, was the body of Kane Lorusso. Molly breathed in sharply and pushed her fingers against his neck, checking for a carotid pulse. The slow and systematic thump of his heart greeted her fingertips, and she watched as his chest rose and fell with each breath. Molly slowly put the back of her hand to her mouth. It seemed impossible that he was alive. The fluid he sat in appeared to act like a coagulant and had stopped the bleeding from his bicep. She wanted to do nothing more than hug his neck and whisper words of comfort and encouragement to him. She wanted to let her friend know that she had come for him, and for him alone. She couldn't tell him, though—she may never be able to tell him, but she would embrace him. She reached down to him and into the gooey mucus that surrounded his body. She pulled him forward toward her and wrapped her arms around his neck and held him tight. She wanted him to know, even if she couldn't speak it to him.

Kane's eyes fluttered, and he muttered under his breath.

"S-s-s-Su-Susan?"

Molly grunted and squeezed his neck again and pulled away to look him in the face.

"Molly," he said as he came to. "I didn't know what to say. She asked, but I couldn't answer right."

Molly looked curiously at Kane, as his face showed his visible confusion. She began to help him to his feet.

"Why?" he said, as he stood, the mucus clinging to him in long bandy strings. "We're inside that mountain, aren't we? Why did you come here?"

Molly helped him out of the pile while he struggled to keep his balance. As he stood, she pressed herself into him again and squeezed him tightly. The look in her face told him the answer to his question.

"It's good to see you too, friend," he whispered.

A worker ant, the size of a large dog, rounded the corner and came directly into contact with Kane and Molly standing in the egg chamber. Startled, it shrieked and backed away, but Molly wasted no time as she pulled away from Kane, grabbed up the spear, and pointed it at the creature. Grasping the pole, she drove the blade downward and through the top of the worker ant's head with little effort, destroying the nerve center. The creature gave a loud high pitched shriek that chortled and ended in a strange repetitive clicking sound as its smallish jaws opened and closed reflexively. She withdrew the spear, watching as the clear, syrupy hemolymph spilled onto the cavern floor. She looked at Kane as the creature collapsed, his shock and confusion morphing into a deeper understanding and remembrance of their situation.

Suddenly, in the surreal glow of the egg chamber, a strange, eerie chorus rose up from down in the depths of the lair. The sound rose and fell like the high-pitched, rapid screeching of a violin. The alien rhythm of it reminded Molly of a military base being put on high alert.

They were coming.

✣ ✣ ✣

Jenna sat perched in a slumped position, half kneeling sideways on a small ledge, her body tied to the left side of the fuel tanker as it rumbled down the debris-filled Interstate 75 into what was formerly the city of Atlanta. The throbbing of her body had been replaced by a dull, burning ache that seemed to push vertically upward and into her chest cavity. Her hands were bound behind her back with a coarse rope that bit into the flesh of her wrists and connected them to her ankles. The unusual position had caused her feet to go numb long ago.

She squinted her eyes, as the sand and dust kicked up by the large tanker stung her face. Licking her cracked and swollen lips, she turned her head and looked over her left shoulder toward the back of the rig. There were about six other prisoners that she could see on her side of the tanker, but she couldn't identify them, and none of them looked to be alive. Jenna turned her head back and tried to lick her lips again, but already her dry mouth was filling with more dust.

The gang rape and several beatings had wounded her, but all she could think of was how terribly she wanted her family back. She felt distant from her own self. She was a stranger, foreign and numb to her own thoughts and feelings. Her circumstances bored a hole into her soul and reminded her that there was no longer anyone she could trust. Not even herself. If only she had done more and tried harder to support her husband, rescue her child, and fight for her own body. If only she could weep. She desperately wanted to cry out for her murdered husband and child, but she found that no matter how deeply she mourned them, the tears failed to come. She had nothing left. Exhaustion and dehydration began to take their toll as the dust and sand lashed against her beaten face.

"Why has this happened to me, Lord?" she whispered. "What is it that you desire to accomplish through this? I am nearly ruined."

With a hiss, the vehicle slowed and rolled to a stop on I-75 right in the city's center, the gold of the capitol dome oddly scattered in pieces across the debris like an old treasure seeker's hallucination. The caravan of other fuel trucks and vehicles slowed and came to a stop behind them.

Jenna opened her eyes and took in the devastation around her. It was the first time she had seen any real destruction of a major city. Her eyes flitted back and forth. So it *was* true.

She sat in quiet awe of the fact that civilization as she had known it before no longer existed. She realized that her mouth was open as she stared at a scene that had to resemble Rome after its fall. Rubble, fire, ruined roadways and skeletal buildings mingled with twisted plumes of black smoke that rose from all over the city.

The driver's side door was opening, and Dagen was exiting and saying something to the passenger.

"Yeah, they're all going to be up ahead, guaranteed. There's always a big group of the bastards in town."

He slammed the door and began walking back to the tanker. "It's coming up!" he yelled to the next tanker back.

The thug nodded and exited the vehicle, yelling the same message back to the next vehicle. Dagen turned to Jenna and the other prisoners and laughed.

"You all look absolutely sorry! Are any of you still alive?"

He walked over to Stan Morrison who was tied against the tanker behind Jenna and shook him. The man flopped lifelessly. "This one looks dead," Dagen said, as he pulled his knife and drove it into the man's belly with a twist.

Jenna turned her head, wincing. Stan remained motionless.

"Yup," Dagen said, as he withdrew the knife and a watery, bloody mixture poured from the bloated wound onto the ground.

The living hostages began coughing, gagging, and crying.

"There we are! I knew some of you were still with me. I am so glad you are, too, because we have a real treat coming up. Especially you," he said pointing the bloody knife at Jenna. "I think you're going to enjoy this."

Jenna licked her lips and tried to force her swollen throat to swallow. Dagen turned with a sneer, moved back to the truck, and climbed in. She could hear the prisoners behind her crying and gasping as the truck rumbled to a start and began inching forward. As the large rig gained speed, Jenna thought she caught the faint smell of decay on the wind. She squinted her eyes, trying to see what it was he had been talking about.

As she blinked her eyes repeatedly against the stinging wind, a strange swaying mass appeared to be congregated in and around the highway up ahead. The mass moved and seethed like waves on the open ocean. Jenna tried fruitlessly to blink the hazy dust from her eyes as the gritty particles bit into the corners of her eyelids. She looked again as they grew closer. The mass was a gathering of people, a whole lot of people congregating in the road. The rig dropped into a lower gear and groaned ahead, gaining speed.

As the rig approached, the mass began to separate, and the people started running. Jenna's confusion quickly turned to horror as she watched the strange behavior. The people were running, screaming with fury as they charged toward the rig.

In a flash, the rig collided with the center of the group, and broken body and bone exploded across the front of the truck.

"*No!*" Jenna croaked.

Suddenly, there was a terrifying clamoring as scores of the mad people flooded against the rig and caused it to slow. Wild, wicked screams flew from their mouths as they scrambled and climbed over each other toward the truck. They were tearing the dead man behind her from the tanker in pieces and stuffing parts of him into their hungry mouths.

With a spasm of terror, Jenna howled and bucked against the ropes that confined her. These were not people. They had become something else. Jenna continued to scream and thrash violently as the monsters came at her, their disgusting, ruined skin drooping and hanging off their bones. The crazed wailing of the other prisoners filled the air behind her as they were pulled and torn from the side of the tanker by the insane mob.

Amid the insanity, Jenna shut her eyes and forced herself to be still as biblical verses from Psalm 69 and 70 filled her mind and poured from her mouth unconsciously.

"Save me, O God!" she shouted. "The flood waters are up to my neck! Deeper and deeper I sink into the mire, and the floods overwhelm me. I am exhausted from crying for help; and my throat is parched and dry. My eyes are swollen with weeping, waiting for my God to help me!"

Multitudes of hands were grasping and wrenching her limbs now and pulling out fistfuls of her hair, but she continued to pray amid the chaos.

"Those who hate me without cause are more numerous than the hairs on my head. Please, God, rescue me! Come quickly, Lord, and help me. You are my helper and my savior; *O Lord, do not delay!*"

They were beginning to pull her away from the tanker, their jagged nails digging into her flesh. She closed her eyes, shutting out the many ragged, moaning breaths, huffing and wheezing and smelling like spoiled flesh.

With a spine-jarring jolt, the tanker rocked and shook as it began to again gain speed. The monsters moaned and scrambled, falling away or under the large double tires as the tanker gained momentum. Jenna hung precariously away from the sidewall of the tanker and over the road as the last of the clinging monsters, a rotten, wretched female with a diamond-studded tennis bracelet, continued to grab and claw at her. With a desperate moan, the creature fell away against the receding pavement and under the rear tires as the vehicle stripped apart the remnants of her fragile body. The ropes still bound Jenna, but loosely now, as she watched the roadway speed along under her, the tanker groaning with the effort. She closed her eyes wearily.

"Thank you, Father. He who hears my cries and delivers me," she whispered.

Jenna looked over her shoulder toward the rear of the tanker and glimpsed only blood and torn rope dragging from the side of the rig where the other prisoners had been. She closed her eyes and lowered her head as the truck continued on.

Minutes later, the rig slowed again and came to a stop, long clear of the maddened horde. Exiting the cab and slamming the door forcefully, Dagen stormed back toward Jenna, the fury pouring from his features.

"*You!*" he growled. "How are *you* still here?"

"God is merciful," she said as boldly as she could muster.

"*Shut the fuck up!*" Dagen yelled as he spat at her. "Why do you persist with this? I've had enough of hearing about God from you! Renounce him!" Dagen pulled his knife and pushed it to her throat. "He has done nothing but ruin you, whore you, and murder the ones you loved! *Renounce! Renounce!*" He cursed, pushing the blade harder against her throat.

"No," Jenna wheezed in quiet defiance. "You can take everything from me but that. That you won't take, and I will not renounce."

"Yes, you will," Dagen said, regaining his composure slightly as he cut her body and legs free and threw her to the ground. "Yes, you will."

He took one of the ropes and tied it around her waist and attached the other end to the tanker. He then rebound her hands tightly in front of her as she lay on the ground gasping. Dagen lowered himself to Jenna's face and spoke in a forced whisper through his teeth.

"You will renounce, and I'll drag you all the way to the coast just to hear it spill from your swollen lips."

He sneered and stood, walking back to the cab, starting the tanker once again.

Jenna rocked her body to the right and twisted onto her knees using her forehead and bound hands to stabilize herself. As she raised herself, her feet and calves tingled and stung painfully as blood began to re-enter them. The engine roared to life, the exhaust pipes expelling long plumes of black smoke, as the great truck jostled and shook and began to move forward, taking the slack out of her rope.

"Praise be to God, who gives me strength," Jenna said out loud, as she began to jog.

✲ ✲ ✲

Molly ducked her head slightly and furrowed her brow at the over-poweringly loud screeching that now dominated the interior of the colony. Kane tore a section of cloth from his shirt and wrapped it tightly around the end of the spear. He poured some gasoline over the cloth.

"You got a light?"

Molly dug into her pocket and removed the lighter, handing it to him. As Kane lit the improvised torch, he was already shuffling toward the exit as he grabbed Molly's arm. Molly struggled against Kane's grip.

"Molly, come on, we've got to go!" Kane said. With a twist, she wrenched her arm free of his grasp.

Kane stood with a questioning look on his face.

"Molly!"

But Molly was not listening as she snatched up the gas can and ran with a slight limp to the far row of glowing pods. She tipped the gas can as she jogged down the long row. Fuel sprayed from the nozzle onto the larvae pods as Molly jogged. Suddenly Kane understood what she was doing. These abominations had to be destroyed.

"Hurry!" Kane yelled, as she reached the end of the third row.

He could feel the ground tremble as the monsters scrambled upward toward the pod chamber. Molly reached the end of the final row, ditched the gas can, and pulled three of the four pipe bombs from her satchel. While running back toward Kane, she tossed the explosives at the base of the three large columns that supported the ceiling. Just as she was reaching Kane, something moved in the darkness of the much larger opening on the far side of the cavern. Molly turned and looked with Kane as an immense pitch-black form with sweeping, gangly appendages pushed its way forward through the large hole. Kane and Molly stood in awe as the giant, bus-sized queen ant stopped just inside the cavern and tossed her head from left to right, sensing the gasoline fumes and the pheromones from the dead worker. She swung her head slowly back and forth, hissing as she focused upon the intruders and the threat to her young. From around either side of the giant queen came four massive horned warrior ants, the queen's guard. Each the size of a Kodiak grizzly, with cruel sharp horns protruding from their heads, backs, and legs, they were a vicious sight to behold. With furious shrieks, the four skittered forward rapidly, advancing madly upon the threat to their queen.

Reaching into Molly's satchel and removing the last pipe bomb, Kane tore the fuse short and lit it.

"We're outta here!" he said, as he stepped into the throw.

Heaving the pipe across the cavern with everything he had, it struck and tumbled under the queen just an instant before the explosion flashed and separated her at the midsection. The room burst forth into flames as the fire jumped from pod to pod and enveloped the approaching warriors. The wildly enraged queen emitted an ear-piercing shriek as she thrashed and flung herself against the walls before seizing and collapsing onto the flaming cavern floor.

The earth shook, and the walls began collapsing as Kane and Molly moved through the exit and up the darkened corridor toward the rope. Kane forged ahead, running up the gentle slope, severing the darkness with the torch as flame and smoke poured from the pod room. Arriving at the rope, Kane looked up and pulled Molly forward.

"Go. And when you hit the ledge, don't wait for me," he said, as he pushed her to the rope. As she passed him she took his hand and placed the revolver in it, giving him what looked like the peace sign with her fingers.

"Two shots," he said.

Molly nodded.

Grabbing the rope, she began climbing hand over hand, walking her feet up the wall as she went. Kane shuffled uneasily at the bottom of the rope as the undulating screeching continued to grow louder. After some struggle, Molly made to the ledge and pulled herself up onto it. Carefully balancing the torch and taking hold of the rope, Kane winced as he flexed his injured bicep. Behind him, shadowed, twisted, screeching forms rolled up the tunnel toward him.

"Come on, Kane," he said through bared teeth, as he began to hoist himself up the rope.

The newly healing wound in his bicep began to reopen with the pressure and strain of the climb. Looking up, he judged the climb to be not more than twenty feet. Molly leaned, perched over the edge of the ledge with her eyes fixed in fear and shock as she stared behind him. Halfway up the wall, Kane threw a quick glance over his shoulder and saw a violent, rolling mass of the giant bugs as they flooded the small room below him.

"Don't wait for me!" he screamed, as he put hand over hand as fast as his body would allow.

Molly paused.

"Goooooooooo!" Kane yelled again in desperation, as his muscles quivered with exhaustion and threatened to give way.

Molly ducked away into the darkness of the tunnel. He could hear them climbing, scratching, and clinging to the ceiling. It would be a matter of seconds before he was overwhelmed. The furious beasts surged up the wall below him, screeching and swinging their flat anvil-shaped heads. Kane kicked wildly at the savage creatures as they came for him, his boots glancing off their hardened skulls. Groaning and bleeding, Kane drew himself over the ledge and into the angled tunnel. Spinning and digging his heels into the earthen walls, he drew the revolver and firmly held the torch forward.

The first warrior came scurrying into the mouth of the tunnel, slashing madly with its bladed jaws. Kane steadied his arm and fired one round directly into the creature's right eye socket as it came at him. It had the desired effect—the beast crumpled and half rolled, sliding back into the darkness that had spawned it. The chamber below went wild with activity, fresh pheromones indicating the death of one of their own. The ants pushed and jockeyed for position over each other, their long, black, spindly legs reaching and stabbing into the dirt as they skittered into the tunnel with their jaws locked wide open.

"One more," he groaned. "Come on! Bring it on!"

Another creature forced itself through the narrow gap, and just as it began to crawl across its fallen brother, Kane fired the second round. The bullet struck the monster in the far right corner of its eye, punching through the side of its head. The ant went down, but was not dead as it screeched and continued to shake and drag itself forward. Kane dropped the gun and began rapidly shoving himself backward up the tunnel as the giant bugs pushed and yanked at their comrades' bodies that blocked the tunnel. Turning and standing, Kane began running up the tunnel, coughing and sputtering on the smoke from the fires below that floated and drifted and appeared lost in its journey to the surface. As he ran, the smoke enveloped and concealed him, wrapping around his body and stinging his lungs as he labored and coughed.

He blindly burst forth from the smoke-filled tunnel into a larger chamber, stumbling to a stop as hundreds of the maddened beasts swarmed into the chamber from all directions. He was trapped. Kane pivoted, searching for a way out—something, anything.

To his left he could see a small, raised tunnel that showed the rope and a very dim light coming from it, but it was too late. The creatures poured in and came in at him, their singing screams ringing in his ears. He sighed and closed his eyes as he raised the torch.

Hopefully Molly made it out.

The earth shook. With three successive concussions, the cavern shook and came apart as the ceiling rained down. The bombs in the pod room had detonated, and the blasts were bringing it all down. The floor in front of him caved in, taking a whole swath of the creatures as it went. Kane dropped the torch at his feet and with three steps jumped for the elevated tunnel, grabbing the rope as the entire room came crushing down on the giant bugs. Kane clawed and dug his way up the tunnel, choking and gasping in the dust and smoke. Blinded and terrified, he scrambled toward the dimly lit exit as the tunnel came apart around him. As he neared the exit, something disproportionately large moved in front of it.

"Please!" was all he could mutter, as he held his hands up to shield his face.

Kane flinched as the great form lunged in and snatched him by the arm, pulling and throwing him forcefully from the tunnel as it began to collapse. His body limp, he struck the ground and slid across the dirt, coming to a stop on his belly past the ruined ambulance.

Two of the queen's giant elite guards exited the mountainside just as the center of the hill depressed and sank in, folding and caving in on top of itself in a plume of fire, smoke, and dust.

Blinking rapidly Kane struggled to clear the dust and dirt from his eyes as he raised his head and coughed. The fearsome horned guardians screeched and began to circle him as he shook his head, trying to clear the red cloud around him. He had no defense. He would be their prey.

A large boot stepped over him, planting itself in the dirt in front of him, followed by a second, until Kane lay in the shadow of a massive dark form. Kane blinked again and sputtered, as his eyes began to focus upon the largest human man he had ever seen. It had been this dark giant who had yanked him from the hill.

The giant took two more steps forward and balled his fists, his enormous muscular forearms bulging. The guardians moved slowly, ducking their heads left and right and clicking their jaws as they circled the immense black man. Long strings of mucus dripped from their mandibles as the creatures clicked and swayed in the anticipation of claiming their next victim.

Kane sputtered again and began to crawl on his side away from what was about to take place.

With a guttural raging roar, the black man charged at the beasts. Dodging to the right, he avoided the bladed swipe of one of the creatures as he slammed his full weight into the beast on his right, crushing the left side of its exoskeleton. The creature toppled and fell to the ground as Courtland turned to face the second maddened creature. It shrieked as it came in at him, swinging its bladed jaws. Courtland ducked and then raised his arms to defend as it slashed back at him, sinking its sword-like mandible through the flesh and muscle of his forearm and imbedding in the bone. With a formidable shout of pain, Courtland raised himself up and swung his opposite fist down like a wrecking ball, obliterating the monstrous horned skull. As the creature dropped, clear hemolymph poured from its shattered skull. The giant man straddled the monster, grabbing its massive jaws and prying them apart with a primal scream. The ant's head cracked and splintered as the mandibles dislocated from their sockets, and the creature fell lifelessly to the earth. Breathing heavily, the enormous man stood to face his other opponent as he gripped a mandible in each hand like twin scimitars. The wounded, enraged beast skittered at him wildly, its cries echoing across the valley.

Kane continued to drag himself across the turf, glancing occasionally at the colossal war happening over his left shoulder. He winced, grabbing greedy handfuls of the red soil as he went. He needed distance, and he wasn't going to wait around to find out who prevailed.

Sweat beaded up on Courtland's broad dark forehead as he stepped back and forth, parrying the massive jaws of the beast with his own blades. It lunged again and again, swiping madly as its bloodlust grew. Courtland continued to move and parry as the great warrior ant came at him. Blocking the creature's bladed jaws with his left hand, he stooped low, swiping down and to the left, severing the monster's front legs from its body. The creature faltered, but lunged again on its four good legs, hurling itself into the huge black man. Courtland crossed his blades in front of him and deflected the creature's mandibles, shoving them down into the dirt at his feet. Pinning them there, he raised the blade in his right hand, high above his head. Striking down, he gnashed his teeth and delivered a crucial blow, partially severing the exoskeleton just behind the beast's head. The creature shuddered and shook, expelling its final scream of defiance. Courtland struck again and sheared the anvil-shaped head from the rest of the body. The beast's beheaded torso righted itself and mindlessly wandered a few steps away before crashing down onto the valley floor and spilling gobs of clear hemolymph onto the ruddy surface.

Kane rolled on his back, breathing heavily. As weariness began to consume him, he wondered if he would ever have the strength to move again. The lack of sufficient food, water, and rest had taken its toll not to mention what he had endured already.

As he lay there, the stern, breathless towering form of the immense black man stepped up next to him and looked down upon him. The man moved slowly, tearing a long section of cloth from the bottom of his shirt, and wrapping it tightly around his wounded forearm. His eyes remained locked with Kane's.

"Look," Kane said with breathless concern. "If you're here to kill me, then just do it, because I can't fight you."

"If I wanted you dead, I'd have left you to those monsters," Courtland said. "We should go. The rest will burrow out of that hillside soon."

"You don't seem surprised about them," Kane motioned toward the dead ants.

"Humph," Courtland retorted. "In this world, ruled by the Evil One—should I be?"

"Where's Molly?" Kane asked.

"The blonde girl?"

"Yeah."

"The Coyotes left with her, just before I arrived."

Kane exhaled and grimaced.

"You are the nameless warrior?" Courtland asked.

Kane made a helpless gesture with his hands. "I'm just Kane. Kane Lorusso."

"But you are God's warrior. The one he has called to fight the Darkness?"

"I don't think He wants to claim me anymore. I can't be much good to him."

"Don't falsely presume to know God's desires. He will always claim you, no matter the score," The giant smiled a big, toothy smile. "I'm Courtland, and he has sent me here to help you."

Kane closed his eyes and laid his head back on the barren turf as a dusty wind whipped moisture from the corners of his pinched eyes.

"Thank God for the help."

DAY 31

OUTSIDE OF COLUMBIA, SOUTH CAROLINA

Vincent stood, his arms hanging loosely at his sides, in the front courtyard of the ranch. As he stood, small tendrils of dust swirled at his feet, and the blackened sky glared down upon him threateningly from its shattered kingdom.

He looked at his hands, then at the ground, then back at his hands again. His hands looked so old and feeble, as if they lost control of everything they touched. How had his life passed him by so quickly?

"Did you get all that, old man?" the voice snapped.

"Um...uh...yeah, I got it," Vincent replied.

"You sure? You're pretty old; you might want to write it down."

Vincent continued to look at his hands.

"No, I'm sure I got it."

"Good, 'cause you know what will happen if you don't do what you're told. There are a lot of people here who are depending on you to get the job done. In fact, it might be said that their lives are in your hands."

Vincent gazed at his hands, the weathered, beaten hands of an old man. He was responsible for the lives of everyone at the ranch. They're lives *were* in his hands. He had no choice.

"I'll do it. I'll get the job done," he said, as he looked up at the rabid thugs.

"You'd better, 'cause we'll be back."

The thug took a step back and reached into the back of the station wagon.

"You see this?"

The thug pulled a young blonde female forward. She was bound and gagged.

"This little gem here is our trophy for the boss."

He jerked her by the hair, and she winced and groaned.

"She's ours, but they are going to come for her. Do you understand? If they get past you, everyone here will die. *Everyone.*" The thug pointed at a nearby mother and young child.

Vincent swallowed. The girl looked terrible. Who knew where they would take her, or what they would do? He could not make it his problem, though. He already had enough problems. He looked back down at his hands and nervously rubbed them together.

"I understand," he said quietly.

"Good. Now, where's our stuff?"

"Yeah," Vincent made a motion behind him and several men came forward with boxes filled with dry goods, canned goods, and jugs of water. The thugs snatched the items from the men and began devouring them in front of the small crowd that had assembled at the ranch. The stash would have fed the people of the ranch for a week. When they had had their fill, they put what was left in the rusted sedan they had arrived in.

"And the fuel for our trip?"

"Uh…we don't really have…."

"Oh, you don't? Oh, I'm so sorry to have asked. How rude of me," the thug mocked with false sincerity. "Guess we'll have to take something else then," he said, as he grabbed a hold of a nearby woman, who began screaming and thrashing.

"Ooh yeah, I like em' feisty," the thug oozed, as he slapped her hard.

"*No…no!*" The woman's husband was crying as he tried to hold onto her.

"*Back off,* you stupid piece of shit! She's mine now!" the thug screamed, as he pointed a large stainless steel revolver in the man's face.

Vincent held his hands high. "Wait…okay, wait, you can have it. Whatever we have, you can have it."

He looked at one of the men who had brought out the food and motioned him to get the fuel. The man's questioning gaze accused him of treason.

"*What?*" Vincent snapped at the man. "Just get it!"

The man hurried away and quickly returned with a full five-gallon fuel canister, which he handed it to one of the thugs.

"Now, please. Just let her go."

"What?"

"Please let her go," Vincent said with a tremor in his voice.

"I'm sorry? Are you giving the fuckin' orders now?" the thug snapped, still holding a handful of the woman's hair. He pointed the gun at Vincent, who instinctively raised his hands again.

"No…I mean…well…please, just let her go. You have what you wanted."

"Yeah? Well, we're keeping her," the thug said, as he shoved the two females into the back of the vehicle

"Keep up your end, Vinnie, or everyone pays—got it?"

The woman's husband had taken all he could take and flung himself in a wild, bawling hysteria on the thug. The angry thug cussed, kicked the flailing man to the ground, and fired one shot from the revolver, effectively blowing a gaping hole in the defenseless man's chest. The crowd fragmented, screaming people ran everywhere. Everyone ran—everyone but Vincent.

The thug swung the gun on him again.

"Remember what I said, old man!" he whooped, as he and the other thugs jumped in the vehicle and sped away in a cloud of dust.

Vincent stood there, shaking and rubbing his hands. The horror the last few minutes had produced was nothing short of catastrophic. It was terrible, and he mourned the decision that had been made, but there was nothing to be done. What could he do but comply with the directions given to him? How many would die if he did not? It was most unfortunate, most unfortunate indeed. Despite their differences, he had really liked Courtland. Now he would have to kill him.

DAY 37

EMRC STATION, SOUTH CAROLINA

The tanker truck's airbrakes hissed as it came to a stop inside the gate of the coastal emergency radio control station. Jenna coughed and blinked her eyes to try to clear them of the dust and fumes. As the last vehicle in the convoy pulled in, two armed thugs pushed the gate closed behind it. She wiggled slightly to the left and adjusted her footing. It would have been impossible to run alongside the vehicle for long, so she had jumped for the side of the tank and held on for dear life. Dragging and finally pulling herself up, she had looped her bonded hands over a peg that jutted from the base of the tank and wedged her feet in a crevasse in the underside of the rig. Though this had relieved the need to hold on, it also put a tremendous strain on the rope that bound her wrists. She had spent the entire journey alternating between hanging upside down from her wrists and holding onto the peg with her hands.

Her hands had turned purple, and small streams of blood ran toward her shoulders from the rope that cut into her wrists. She had lost count of the number of times she had lost consciousness during the trip. The overwhelming pain, the rocks and dirt that endlessly peppered her body under the truck, and the growing need for water had weakened her terribly.

The cab of the truck shut, and Jenna listened as Dagen spoke quietly to several others, of whom she could only see their boots on the other side of the truck. Jenna pulled her feet free and allowed them to flop to the ground. Unhooking her wrists from the peg, she fell to the ground with a grunt and rolled onto her back.

The relief was glorious, and she murmured a quiet praise to God for her small moment of respite. She lay there on the ground with her bound hands clutched to her chest and her eyes closed as the footsteps approached. Jenna took a deep breath and opened her eyes as she struggled to get into a seated position. Dagen and another much larger, bald man stood before her.

"Unbelievable," Dagen said. "You know, Malak, as much as I hate this woman's filthy rotten guts, I am starting to admire her perseverance. She's a hard nut to crack."

Dagen nodded at Malak, who stood motionless, staring at her.

"Maybe we should offer her a place on our crew? You know? She's been through a lot. At least she'd have a place to sleep, food, water, protection. We'd be her new family. That would be a lot better than this," Dagen said, as he looked at Malak. "What do you think, Boss?"

Malak continued to stare, standing emotionlessly. Dagen put his hand to his chin and scrunched his face up in mock contemplation.

"There's just this one thing, Boss. Just one thing she needs to say before we can do any of that."

Dagen crouched down closer to Jenna and looked her in the face. "So…have anything you want to say?"

Jenna blinked her eyes and swallowed hard, her lip quivering slightly. "Jesus is the—"

In a flash of white-hot rage, Dagen struck her violently in the face with his fist, knocking her back against the wheel well of the tanker. Jenna coughed and cried as the blood poured from her nose, across her face, and dripped onto the concrete.

"*Stupid bitch!* Not the answer I was looking for," Dagen said in disbelief, as he shook his aching hand. "See what I mean?"

Malak regarded her with empty, soulless eyes.

"Tie her up in the courtyard. We'll continue to make an example of her. She believes the God of the Bible is with her, but she'll swear his name in hatred before her time on this earth is through."

"Good enough," Dagen said, as he snatched a handful of her hair and began dragging her across the ground.

Jenna grabbed and tried feebly to hold on to his hand as he dragged her across the courtyard to a flagpole near the center. Cutting the rope from her wrists, he torqued her arms behind her back and retied her securely to the pole. Dagen then crouched and slowly cut her clothes free until she was completely naked. He tossed her clothes off to the side and grabbed a large, flat object.

"The boys made this for you. It seems fitting."

Dagen pulled forward a square sheet of tin roofing, which had large black letters painted on it that read, "The Lord's Whore." He propped it up next to her and took a knee, looking at her thoughtfully and speaking in hushed tones.

"It's about to go from bad to worse, baby. These guys..." he motioned over his shoulder at some onlookers. "Their leashes are off. Who knows what they'll do to you? Are you sure you don't have anything to say? Renouncing the God that you cling to so desperately will save your life and spare you so much pain."

He leaned in very close. "You can just whisper it to me; no one else has to know."

Dirty tears of sorrow ran down Jenna's face as she pressed her lips together and held her head high. She stared upward past Dagen, toward the sky, and sniffled slightly as the blood began to dry across her lips.

Dagen pulled away, stuffed an old rag soaked in salt water in her mouth, and followed it with a thin cloth that he used to gag her with.

"It's too bad, really, it is," he said as he tied the cloth behind her head. "If only your Charlie could see the disgusting, beaten, ugly whore you've become. He'd be so ashamed of you."

Dagen stood and half turned, giving her one final glance, and shook his head again. The line behind him was already forming.

✳ ✳ ✳

Kane shrugged into the worn-out long-sleeved t-shirt he had found in the bed of the beat-up pickup truck. It genuinely looked as though it had been used to mop up spills for the last twenty years. As the old rusted truck bumped over endless potholes, he tried to get comfortable in the front seat as he leaned against the window. It just wasn't happening. He sighed with weariness and frustration.

"What's the matter, brother?" Courtland asked, not taking his eyes off the destroyed road in front of him.

"I can't get comfortable."

Courtland nodded. "With the world in the shape that it's in, I guess we ought to get used to that." He looked again at Kane and gave a small smile.

Kane glanced sideways at Courtland with a slight look of irritation and continued fidgeting in the seat.

"You're worried about your friend."

"Molly," Kane said and nodded. "Yeah, I'm worried about her. Those freaks are capable of anything."

"She's a strong girl. Strong in spirit."

Kane shot back.

"How do you know? You don't even know her. What? Do you see the future or something?"

Kane's attitude fizzled as he saw the look on Courtland's face. He sighed again.

"Look, I'm really tired. I don't know you, and I...I didn't mean that. I really am grateful for your help and for what you did back there. I'm just really concerned about her. She's been my only friend out here."

They both sat in silence for a few moments.

"I understand your frustration," Courtland said softly. "But you must have faith in God and his plan, which unfolds as we speak. We only have to be open to our own purpose within it."

"Things haven't seemed to go according to plan," Kane said quietly.

"You say that because you doubt. You doubt the Lord, you doubt yourself, and you doubt his perfect will and purpose for every single thing that occurs. Like the disappearances that occurred when all this started."

"Disappearances?"

"Yes."

What, you mean people disappearing from their beds and moving vehicles? That sort of thing?"

"Maybe not just like that, but most of us Christians are gone. There's only a set number of us who have remained to form the resistance. At least that's what I've been told."

"Resistance."

"Yes, resistance, to the dark ones. The ones like you've already become acquainted with. You see, God has left us here because he has a plan for us. You have listened; now you must trust. Only when you trust will you find the strength to obey and allow God to use you for his glory.

They sat in a long silence while Kane wondered if his wife and babies might have been part of that disappearance. After a few moments, he looked over at Courtland.

"You are a wise man, Mr. Courtland."

"It's just Courtland," he said, and smiled again.

"Do you have a last name?"

"Thompson."

"I knew it! I knew something was familiar about you. The way you hammered those monsters back there. 'The Sledge,' right? You played with the United All-Stars and were a Pro-Crushball hall of famer!"

Courtland shrugged and smiled. "Those days are long gone."

"Not long gone. Not after what I just saw. I used to love watching you play as a kid. Nobody could stand up against 'The Sledge.' *Nobody*."

"Yeah, well a lot of years of that takes a toll on a man." Courtland said with a smile. "They were great years, though."

"When did you retire?"

"Oh, about twenty years ago."

"Did you have family? Did you…" Kane paused. "Lose anyone?"

Kane leaned his back against the door, facing Courtland.

"Yes, but not directly because of the attacks. My wife died giving birth to our daughter, but that was years ago, and..." he paused. "I lost my daughter in a car accident just before the attacks. What about you?"

Kane looked down. "Yeah, my wife and kids were in Miami when it was hit. There's no way they could have made it."

"Your wife was a believer?"

"Yeah, she was. She was a great example to me." Kane paused. "Do you think she and my kids may have been taken, like you said?"

"It's possible."

"So why us, then? Why me?" Kane shrugged his shoulders.

"Whether you are comfortable with it or not, God has touched us, so that we may bring glory to Him. It's that simple."

Kane smiled. "You make it sound that way."

Courtland had a warm way about him. Something wise and sagely in his personality stood out to Kane and welcomed him to confide in and trust his new friend. For a while they conversed like old friends, catching up as they both relayed the events that had occurred during and since the attacks. After a while they both grew tired of talking and became content to sit in a comfortable silence as Courtland drove and Kane rested, reading and taking comfort in Courtland's worn and tattered Bible.

They ventured deeper and deeper into the unknown future, neither of them knowing what exactly was in store for them in the coming hours. Courtland adjusted his position, his huge form taking up every inch of space on the driver's side of the cab. He peered ahead through the cracked windshield.

"It's just up here, the ranch I told you about. There we will get you some food and rest before we continue on to find your friend."

Kane leaned back in the seat and looked ahead as the vehicle slipped into the burnt woods on a lonely two-lane road. The black clouds boiled and rolled across the heavens, refusing to share its prime real estate with the sun, moon, and stars. Here a thick layer of that crunchy black substance covered the ground and trees, indicating a fairly recent rainfall. The black branchless trees stood still in the windless afternoon like spines down the back of an enormous porcupine.

Kane thought about Molly and hoped again that she was safe. She had come all the way into that ant colony for him and for no other reason. Why she had gone through with it still vexed him. She had only known him a matter of days. She could have easily ditched him and saved herself. He pondered on that thought and felt an amount of guilt for her obligation to him and for her capture by those fiends. Courtland had been right. There was no use in worrying about it, as the worry served no positive purpose. All he could do was trust that God was in control.

Courtland slammed on the brakes as the truck screeched to a stop in front of a downed tree in the road.

"Jeez!" Kane said putting his hands on the dash for support as several large dead trees crashed down across the road in front of them.

Courtland was grinding the gearshift into reverse as Kane shouted, "Get us out of here, Courtland! *Get us out!*"

The vehicle began moving backward just as several more trees crashed down behind the old truck, effectively trapping the vehicle where it sat.

In the stillness that followed, Kane squinted his eyes through the settling debris, trying to see whatever menace caused their current predicament. He glanced at Courtland and looked out the front windshield again. The two watched as shadows trickled down from the hillside and surrounded the truck, many of them carrying torches and weapons in the fading light.

"Here we go," Kane muttered furiously.

"Courtland, you and your passenger get out of the truck. If you produce weapons, we will be forced to kill you," a voice said from the crowd.

Kane balled his fists, but as he did Courtland stayed him with a hand on his shoulder.

"These are not our enemies," he said. "Misled, maybe, but not enemies. Go along with what they ask."

"They just tried to crush us!" Kane said, glaring at Courtland.

Courtland said nothing but returned Kane's steady gaze.

With a look of uneasiness, Kane relaxed his fists and shrugged his shoulders as the two stepped from the truck, each with their hands on the door.

"You want to harm us, Vincent?" Courtland said. "Why are you treating me like an enemy?"

"My reasons are my own. Now, both of you lie on the ground and put your hands behind your head."

"Has your mind been poisoned with lies against me? I don't understand this," Courtland said.

"My mind knows the truth, and I will do what I must to secure our safety from the Coyotes."

Kane broke in, "Whatever they've told you, they've got no intention of honoring any agreement. They will just as soon murder all of you as look at you."

"Shut your mouth, stranger! No one asked anything of you but to lie on the ground with your hands behind your head!" Vincent shot back.

Courtland and Kane hesitated.

"*Do it!*" Vincent yelled, as several rifle actions drew rounds into their chambers.

Kane looked at Courtland as he began to get down on his knees. "These are your friends?"

"I'm not sure anymore," Courtland said, as he lowered himself down onto the ground.

High on the craggy hillside above the road, a feral boy and a great black wolf watched with curiosity and caution as Courtland and Kane were tied up and loaded into the bed of a truck.

✡ ✡ ✡

Malak stood on the catwalk above the courtyard, as the evening began to set in, and surveyed the goings-on of his crew. The bitter, dead sea wind bit at his naked chest and shoulders as he unconsciously seized. Malak gripped the metal railing and refused to breathe as his massive muscular form tightened and clenched up. After a few moments, he rolled his shoulders and exhaled. It was time for another dose. Malak looked down upon the courtyard again. Now at 130 heads, his clan had grown quite sizeable. The new loads of prisoners that had been brought in had all been given the option to try out. Malak had been more than fair by granting them this option. In the end, though, only a modest handful had auditioned, and only half of that number had survived it. The rest of the men had been slain in a brutal fashion as a public example to the women and children of what happens to those who refuse to comply. Malak estimated that he currently held about forty women and children captive inside padlocked gates in the back of the station grounds.

With a snap and then a buzz, the darkening evening was pushed back as the generators kicked on, bathing the buildings and courtyard in yellow light. Malak breathed in deeply the cool, moist night air and rubbed his palm across the tattoo of a large coiled viper in the center of his chest. He had sought after and attacked the man named Kane as the voice had warned him to do, though he knew now that the man was not dead. Two survivors of Ashteroth's hunting party had returned and stated that there had been an attack upon the group by giant insects, and this kept them from completing their mission. They had sworn that the warrior had been killed in the slaughter, but they were all liars by nature, and it was an elaborate tale to excuse their failure. They had been rewarded with a public disembowelment in the courtyard. The voice had told him that Kane would come for the girl. Let him come. It would be no great feat to deal him a painful death.

It had been a great step forward that Malak had managed to take the fuel reserve by deception and force at no loss to him. The fuel had been a most precious and necessary commodity. He now owned a resource that everyone needed, and it was his alone to waste. Dagen had done a most effective job at the reserve, though Malak had begun to question his recent mental and emotional state. Dagen had become obsessed with the torture of the woman he had brought in earlier in the day. Not that Malak thought of it as excessive; quite the opposite, he fully endorsed the torture and death of the weak and pitiful followers of Christ, but he felt strongly that it should be conducted with an emotionless vigor, similar to stomping on a cockroach.

Dagen had developed too much of an emotional investment in the naked Christian woman in the courtyard to the point that it seemed to drive him. He had been out there constantly with her, shouting angrily, striking her, and stuffing saltwater-soaked rags in her mouth. He had stood by and waited patiently for her to break as the men had assaulted and raped her. Even after she had gone unconscious, Dagen had remained, watching eagerly, determined to witness her renouncement of God.

Christians were strange creatures, and they could prove difficult to break. Malak had found that if one proved particularly difficult, you had to just finish them and move on. It was much easier and less involved that way. He looked again down into the courtyard to see Dagen yelling and pointing his finger in the woman's face.

He is too involved.

Malak stepped back from the rail and reentered the concrete room off the elevated walkway that he was using as his place of command. The yellow light bulb in the ceiling flickered in the otherwise cold and somewhat empty room. All that occupied it was a wooden desk and a padded chair the men had brought up. At some point he would relocate to a more suitable setting for a man of his calling, but for now it would do.

He gazed at the young blonde woman that the survivors of Ashteroth's party had brought him. Arms bound behind her back, she lay on her side with her forehead touching the cold concrete floor. She was perfect. Though having been through a lot by the looks of it, she was young and attractive and pure. He had saved her for himself. She would be the sacrifice that the darkness demanded.

He had effectively stopped all threats to himself and, at the same time, provided for the needs at hand. He had done well, and he could feel that the darkness within him had been pleased. He now occupied the radio control station and had found that although slightly damaged, the radio equipment still appeared functional. He would use it to spread the comforting and irresistible message that the voice had given him. It was one of hope and life and renewal, and he knew that the survivors of this battered nation would flock willingly to it like moths to the warm glow of a lamp. They would never know that they would be journeying into the mouth of hell itself. It was beautiful. He moved to the chair and sat, rolling a Z-laced cigarette.

The voice had also told him of the great mutiny that was already in motion. It spoke of how he would be a god and that wealth and power and every indulgence would be his. He would command thousands as a guardian and keeper of the dark power, ruling and enslaving the hearts and minds of men. The voice had whispered easily as it poured its sweetened message into his ear. It had assured him that when he had grown sufficient in power and influence over this world, then it would give him what he truly desired: the defeated Lord of Heaven prostrate at his feet. It had promised that together they would tear him from his throne of self-righteousness and mock him as the Lord of weakness and mercy. There would no longer be room for him on the savage throne of the universe.

Courtland murmured the last few words of a silent prayer and opened his eyes. He rested his back squarely against the wall of the cool interior room. It was dark inside the room except for the faint glow of a torch outside the window. Courtland looked down at his bound wrists and ankles and shuffled his position slightly. He looked to his right to see Kane bound in the same manner, lying on his side. The man had been asleep for hours, ever since they had been loaded up into the truck. Courtland thought it strange that he was able to sleep while surrounded by such uncertainty, but he knew the man was unable to help it. His body was demanding a system shutdown after the rigors he and the girl had endured over the previous days.

Courtland leaned his head back against the wall. He still could not understand why Vincent had turned on him. They had not been dear friends, but they had been allies of sorts. All he could come up with was that somehow the Coyotes had bribed or forced him to go through with their capture. But to what end?

The guard outside moved past the window with the torch again. They were being guarded, which meant they were prisoners, but the why of it all continued to elude him as he sat in the dark.

Kane stirred and awoke in a confused state. "What the...?" he mumbled, as he tried to free his hands and feet. "Where...?"

"It's alright, brother; we are not in danger...at the moment."

"Courtland?"

"Yes."

"Oh, man, how long have I been out?"

"About five or six hours, but it's okay; you needed the rest. Here, have some water." Courtland pushed a bowl of water over, and Kane drank greedily from it. Wiping his arm across his mouth, he looked at Courtland.

"Do you know where we are?"

"We are at the ranch with The Family."

"They're the ones who took us from the road?"

"Yes."

Kane adjusted himself into a seated position against the wall and groaned.

"I feel broken."

"You should be grateful that you are not worse off than you are."

"I know it," Kane said as he tested the strength of his bindings. "They tie a good knot." Kane paused, testing it again, then went on, "Do you know why they are keeping us?"

"I don't. I was just trying to figure it out," Courtland replied.

The two men sat quietly in the confines of the small room thinking and wrestling with their own thoughts. Kane spoke first.

"Courtland?"

"Yes?"

"Tell me I'm not crazy. Seriously. The last month or so has had no semblance of reality. Am I going nuts?"

"Kane, if you're a little crazy, then I've gone completely mad."

They laughed in quiet wheezes for a moment in the stillness of the room. Then Courtland spoke again quietly, his positive attitude beaming. "It does seem crazy—but what an amazing journey, and it's just beginning. What a truly magnificent calling and a perfectly noble purpose. Neither of us could have ever dreamed of a greater or more valuable mission for our lives. And if our lives are forfeited on this mission, what better cause is there to die for?"

Kane nodded slowly and leaned his head against the wall of the dark room. "I'm so tired, Courtland. I'm so tired, and we have yet to confront the darkness."

"My friend, you've been fighting the darkness this whole time in the physical world, in the spiritual world, and in the confines of your own heart. Through your weariness you fight it still."

Courtland cleared his throat and allowed his deep voice to resonate within the walls of the small room. He wanted the guard to hear.

"With this news," he began, "strengthen those who have tired hands and encourage those who have weak knees. Say to those who are afraid, 'Be strong, and do not fear, for your God is coming to destroy your enemies. He is coming to save you.' And when he comes, he will open the eyes of the blind and unstop the ears of the deaf. The lame will leap like a deer, and those who cannot speak will shout and sing! Springs will gush forth in the wilderness…and they will satisfy the thirsty land."

A hurried shuffling sound began outside the door, as the torch flickered and went out. Courtland and Kane sat completely still, listening. After a minute of silence, they could hear a faint dragging sound that slowly disappeared. Kane and Courtland looked at each other quizzically, and when they looked up again, a longhaired boy wearing animal skins was crouched in the window to the room.

"Tynuk! What are you doing?" Courtland exclaimed in a whisper.

"We're getting you out," Tynuk whispered.

"Don't trust Vincent…."

"I know. His plans do not involve releasing you…either of you. You both are to be held for the Coyotes," Tynuk said, looking at Kane.

"What?" Courtland said.

"He's not motivated by anything that does not serve him, that man. He has always been that way. He will kill you to try to save himself and his pride," the boy said, as he hopped down into the room and moved like a wraith to the door, rapping lightly. He opened the previously bolted door slightly as a giant wolf like creature pushed its head through the crack in the door.

Kane stiffened and forced air through his lips, seeing the great beast.

"Look at that…*monster*."

The boy stood proudly with his hand over his heart.

"I am Tynuk, the last warrior of the great Shoonai people." He moved his hand to the beast's neck. "This is my companion, Azolja. Though he is fearsome, he is *no* monster."

Courtland, seeing a man's legs behind the door, asked, "Did you kill that man?"

Tynuk scrunched his face, puzzled, and looked over his shoulder. "He'll be fine."

Courtland sat forward and popped the restraints on his wrists and ankles like old rotten rubber bands. Kane sat, staring, and tried again to loosen his bindings. Courtland was standing and stretching. "It is time to go."

"You could have done that this whole time?" Kane asked in shock.

Courtland shrugged. "It wasn't necessary until now."

"Hey," Kane was saying as he held his wrists upward to Courtland. "A little help here, big man. I think they tied mine."

Courtland reached down with one hand and twisted as the ropes disintegrated under the force of his fingers. He did the same to the ropes on Kane's ankles, then offered Kane his hand.

"Maybe I am losing my mind," Kane said, as he took Courtland's hand and stood.

"The truck is out front—still has the keys in it," Tynuk said, as he tossed a tin can to each of them. "Both of them are plain, canned black beans. It's not much, but you both look like you need to eat, especially him," Tynuk motioned at Kane.

"Thank you, Tynuk. You and Azolja are good friends, and we will pray for you," Courtland said as he laid his hand on the boy's shoulder.

"Yeah, thanks a lot," Kane said. "For everything." He motioned with the can.

"We are going with you," Tynuk said.

Courtland paused giving the boy a stern look. "Tynuk, I don't think you understand. We are preparing to enter the maw of the beast, the place where evil reigns."

"I understand what you say. I may be a boy, but I am also of the great Shoonai warrior tribe. I am not afraid....Besides, Azolja will be with me."

"Tynuk..." Courtland began.

"Mr. Courtland, we too have been called to serve the Great Spirit alongside you. It is not a matter for you to choose whether we are involved or not. The choice was made by the Spirit long before this planet was formed with dust and water. To obey the call, it is what we all must do."

Courtland looked at Kane, who shrugged and opened his arms. "Welcome then, we can use your help. But we need to go, like right now."

They nodded in silent agreement and, sneaking quietly from the room, the four glided together down the hallway and out across the courtyard, mere shadows in the moonless night.

They arrived at the truck, and Kane slowly and quietly lowered the tailgate as the great beast crept silently into the bed. Tynuk opened the front gate to the compound with slight creaks and pushed it until it stuck open before jumping with stunning grace through the passenger side window of the truck. Courtland quickly searched a nearby shed and found a full fuel can, which he placed in the bed of the truck before climbing in.

Kane cranked the truck and mashed down on the gas. The truck took off, its tires spinning in the dirt. Shouting was heard all over the ranch as torches were ignited and began moving, but the Family was too late. The truck cruised away speedily through the silent woods, carrying the four unlikely heroes ever closer to the destiny that they had each been created for.

DAY 40

Molly awoke with a start, realizing immediately that she was still among the enemy. She kept her eyes closed and relaxed her body, wanting to continue giving the impression that she was still asleep. Her arms were tightly tied behind her back and her feet bound together at the ankles. Her ears felt ultrasensitive, picking up every little sound within the complex: the laughter and jeering of the creeps inside and outside the building; the faint humming and vibration of what sounded like generators; and the consistent, desperate sobbing of a woman somewhere down in the courtyard. The night air was cool and smelled of rust, decay, and incense, or what smelled like incense. The smell was heavy in the room, like something had been or was being burned. It was a fragrant, pungent smell, strong like a bitter musk. She cocked her head ever so slightly to hear further what was going on around her.

She dared not open her eyes. The false sense of safety and security of the action gave her immense comfort and helped her to half convince herself that none of this was happening at all. But it was; it was happening.

Something moved slightly behind her left shoulder. It scraped along the ground with a sweeping motion. With a jarring sound, something slammed down behind her, causing her to jump involuntarily and almost cry out.

Molly squinted ever so slightly, trying to see the nature of the disturbance. She tilted her head to the left. There was a wooden desk behind
her. A scream shattered the air, followed by more slamming and shaking
of the desk.

The air near the ceiling was thick with smoke, and a dim yellow bulb
flickered intermittently through the haze. Out of the corner of her eye
Molly could barely see a large, massively muscular bald white male sitting at the desk. He had his eyes pinched shut and was grimacing and
clawing as he slammed the desktop with his bare fists. He did not appear
to breathe for what seemed like an eternity, as his body shook and his
muscles bulged and pulsed in a wretched, alien manner. The man exhaled
a smoky breath and opened his eyes very wide, looking around as he
appeared to survey the room slowly and with great interest.

The man began speaking in low tones, conversing with himself. As he
spoke in a low growl, the strange mumbled incantations spilled out in
words that she didn't understand. Sounding almost inhuman, the unusual
language snapped and clicked off the man's tongue with a strange and
ancient sharpness.

Molly's eyes were completely open now; she could no longer hide the
curiosity and fear she felt toward her captor. She watched as he continued
the wild and rapid sounds with repetitive upward flicks of his head and
was completely overcome with the most dreadful sensation.

He was summoning something.

☆ ☆ ☆

Kane had seen the glow of the station on the horizon long before he
had gotten close to it—the small lights like dying stars in a sea of black-

ness. He cut the truck lights off and slowly rolled the last half-mile to the edge of the slope that overlooked the radio control station. Easing the truck to a stop, he put it in park and stopped the engine. The low hum of the distant generators vibrated in the restless night. Kane stepped from the car and allowed the door to shut lightly as Courtland, Tynuk, and Azolja moved to meet him around the front of the vehicle. Kane silently observed the structure for a moment, noting the ocean on its rear side and a rubble-filled frontage road at the bottom of the hill.

"Well, it doesn't seem very fortified, other than the chain-link fence," he said, as the rest of them crouched down in front of the truck. "For sure, they've got some small arms, rifles and handguns, but limited ammo."

Kane pointed at a large central area in the middle of the station with two tanker trucks parked in the center of it. "As soon as it starts, a lot of them will most likely hit that large courtyard there in a boil of mass confusion. These guys, they've got crazy going for them, but not order or cooperation, so expect chaos."

Kane paused and rubbed at his stubbled chin. "Do we have any weapons?" he asked, looking at Courtland.

"Yeah, hang on a sec," Courtland said, rising and silently opening the passenger side door and moving to the bed of the truck.

Kane looked at the boy and his monstrous shaggy companion. "Tynuk, you will have to fight, maybe even kill people. Are you up to this?"

Tynuk nodded seriously. "They will not be the first," he said boldly.

As strange as the words seemed coming from a boy, something in the way the boy spoke led Kane to believe in his competence.

"Right on, then," Kane said, as Courtland rejoined them. "Whaddaya got?"

"Here," Courtland said handing the sawed-off shotgun over to Kane. "I found this near where you wrecked your motorcycle, but there's no shells."

Kane felt inside his left cargo pocket and produced a single 00 buck-shot shell, holding it up like his prized possession.

"We got one shot. I'll have to make it count," he said, taking the shotgun from Courtland.

Courtland held up the large, black, sword-like ant mandibles. "I believe I can make good use of these."

Kane nodded and looked to Tynuk.

The boy, sensing the question, touched at the pouches lashed to the cord around his waist. "I have what I need."

"Good deal. Alright, I'll keep this simple. We're relatively unarmed and badly outnumbered, which means our greatest assets are surprise and violence of action. We're going to hit 'em and hit 'em hard. We'll start by sending the unmanned truck through the gate to breach it and draw their gunfire. There will be no stopping once that gate is compromised."

Courtland and Tynuk nodded.

"Tynuk, you and Azolja are responsible for the taking out the perimeter guards and the men with the long rifles on that building there. Can you see them?"

Tynuk nodded.

"They have to be down before we send the truck, which means you two will have to be stealthy to get the jump on them. I'm depending on you."

Kane looked at the wolfish beast as it shifted in its prone position and licked its lips, its silvery eyes regarding him with unknown thoughts. It was a bold and predatory creature like nothing he had ever seen on earth.

He realized for the first time that it had not struck him as strange that a giant beast was being treated as a conscious and intellectual presence, expected to follow a plan and execute a mission. He wanted to ask Tynuk about the reliability of his primal companion, but hesitated.

Regarding the great and fearsome animal for a moment, Kane took note of its demeanor and presence as it seemed to watch over them like a noble guardian. The creature returned his gaze unflinchingly, and Kane was overcome with the strangest of realizations: it understood its purpose. Whatever their meager group's greater purpose was, it already understood completely, maybe more than Kane himself did.

Kane broke away from the animal's stare and turned to Courtland.

"My friend, you will be the primary distraction. Do whatever you can, but get their attention. Beyond that, defend yourselves and free any innocents that you come across, and if at all possible try to preserve those fuel tankers."

"And you?" Courtland said.

"I'm going after Molly."

"That will take you to Malak. I'm sure of it," Courtland said.

"Their leader?"

"Yes. Be cautious of him, Kane. He is a desperately evil man, and I believe he can channel the dark ones."

"Well, I think if we can down him, the rest may scatter. Just keep them off me until I can find him. I know it's not much of a plan, but it's all we've got."

The four sat silently for a few moments as the bitter ocean breeze whipped at their faces and clung to their skin. Kane looked out past the station compound and could see the slightest brightening on the horizon beyond the toxic ocean as day threatened to push back the night.

Courtland put his arms around all of them. "May we find our strength in the Lord alone, may we show mercy where mercy is needed, and may we have the wisdom to overcome the adversaries of the Lord. 'For even when you are chased by those who seek your life, you are safe in the care of the Lord your God, secure in his treasure pouch. But the lives of your enemies will disappear like stones shot from a sling!'"

Raising his head, Kane looked up at his companions with the deepest sincerity.

"Whatever happens, I want you all to know how grateful I am for each of you. May we never back down, in Jesus's name and for His sake."

✶ ✶ ✶

Tynuk and his relentlessly shadowy friend crept with a patient slowness toward the edge of the fence, moving as one presence. They paused, short of the fence, and scanned for enemy activity. Seeing one patrol group down the fence to the left a short way, they moved with an urgent quickness to the fence and crouched. With a lightning fast movement, Azolja swiped at the fence with his paw, and the steel mesh came apart easily under the razor-sharp talons. The beast pushed first through the gap and began running away to the left as Tynuk stepped through the gap behind him.

The two sentries stopped and turned. A bearded man with long greasy hair spoke first. "Did you hear that?"

"Hear what?"

"Something moving. Behind us," he said as he ground his rotten teeth and pulled at his goatee.

"You can't handle your Z, man."

"Look, you idiot, right there!" He pointed into the darkness.

The two stared with great effort into the pitch black as a great inky shadow moved forward, silvery eyes above the whitest of fangs. A chilling guttural growl came rolling in from the phantom presence as the thugs went for their weapons, but they were too late. Azolja leapt through the air, slashing the first thug's chest with a swipe of his taloned paw and sinking his fangs into the throat of the second. Gore sprayed across his dark mane as he shook the dying man by the neck. Dropping the lifeless body, he moved quickly to the other man, who was shaking and trying to cry out as he clutched at his flayed chest. He never had a chance to scream.

Tynuk approached from the shadows as Azolja finished off the second of the two sentries. Tynuk patted the beast twice hard on his flank to signal that he was going ahead. The great beast tossed his head at the boy, a sign that he understood, his jowls foaming and dripping with fresh blood.

The boy moved noiselessly to the fire escape and ascended rapidly, jumping and grabbing as he swung his legs up to the next point of purchase. In a matter of seconds, he had climbed to the top of the four-story building. Crouching low, he looked over the rim to survey the rooftop. Three men, all with assault rifles, stood and watched over the station. They would clearly be able to put fire on anyone seen as a threat down below them. Tynuk crouched at the rim silently for a few minutes, watching their behavior and patrol patterns.

Reaching into the leather pouch he kept at his waist, he removed a rounded stone, blackened by fire and about the size of a golf ball. He rotated it slowly between the fingers of his right hand and pulled a thin cord from his belt with his left.

"May the Great Spirit guide my hand, and lend me his strength," Tynuk murmured to himself.

In an instant, he hurdled over the rim with a fluid grace and tucked his body into a forward roll. Utilizing his spinning forward momentum, Tynuk fired the stone from his hand and was instantly up and running. The stone struck the far right sentry in the head, just behind his left ear, buckling his knees as his body dropped and folded against the ground. The thug on the left was on to the boy, spinning and unleashing a burst of automatic gunfire from his AK-47. Tynuk dashed to the right and back to the left, avoiding the spray with blinding movements and launching himself at the center goon, who was turning. Kicking hard with his right foot, he struck the sentry in the abdomen and pushed off in the direction of the shooter, planting both feet in the center of his chest. The man screamed wildly and let loose another burst of fire as he crashed through the fire escape and fell four stories to his death.

Jumping up, Tynuk dodged to his right as the last remaining shooter steadied his balance and began firing wildly. Rising inside the man's guard, the sound of automatic gunfire deafened his left ear as he vaulted upward off the bandit's thigh and drove his knee under the man's chin with a crack. The dazed man faltered and dropped the rifle as the boy landed with planned precision. He circled and readjusted his angle on the man, hands raised, palms open in a defensive position and with a focused look of intent on his painted face.

Swearing, the unsuspecting thug was turning back into him as the boy leapt, stepping on his hip and up his back. Stretching the hidden cord between his hands, he lashed it fiercely around the thug's neck, just as his grandfather had taught him. Tucking his knees down onto the man's shoulders and into either side of his head, the fiercely feral boy pulled his elbows into his body and straightened his back. The thug scrambled and gagged, clawing at the invisibly thin cord that sliced into his neck. Exhaling, the boy leaned back further as the man gurgled and dropped to his knees, digging the nails of his fingers into the flesh of his own neck. Tynuk rode the thug to the ground and released, rolling forward and into a crouched position. He watched intently as the disabled sentry convulsed soundlessly for a long moment before the boy stood and made a fist that he pumped multiple times in the air.

The jig was up. The gunfire had alerted the whole camp. Tynuk rubbed his left ear, which was still ringing, and hissed through tightened lips. His execution of the three should have been much smoother. He was better than that, but it made no difference now. As he stood on the roof, he could hear the echo of gunfire and screams of confusion as the truck made its rapid descent down the hillside toward the control station.

It had begun.

✫ ✫ ✫

Dagen ran with a cool, steely determination across the courtyard, his military bearing showing in his command presence as the full-sized truck crashed through the main gate in a shower of sparks. Drawing a Sig P229 handgun from the back of his pants, he steadied himself and fired five rounds through the driver's side front windshield. Gunfire erupted from all around him as the mass of armed thugs unleashed a hail of bullets upon the truck as it barreled forward. The windows and lights exploded, and the vehicle body became riddled with holes as the truck crashed into the side of the main structure.

Dagen stopped firing and stared intently.

"Stop! Cease-fire! Cease-fire!" he yelled at the crazed mass of armed bandits. "Save your ammo! It's empty"

The gunfire slowed as Dagen continued to chant. "Stop! There's no one inside! It's a diversion!" He yelled with authority, pointing at the broken gate caused by the truck. "We're under attack! Fill that gap and maintain security. I need men in that hole, now!"

As the men began to move toward the battered gate, screams of terror broke out on the front most fringe of the group. The entire mass of seething people churned and changed directions, moving back toward him like a frightened school of fish. Dagen shouted angrily at them to continue onward, but they did not. The mass of deranged thugs was separating, dissolving, and fleeing something.

Fleeing from what?

"Fight! We are under attack! Defend the station, you bastards!" he was yelling as he stormed toward the disturbance. Dagen had survived war, prison, and countless other atrocities in his life. He wasn't afraid of any man. He grabbed hold of a blabbering goon as the man tried to push past him in a frenzy.

"*What?* What is it?" he yelled, shaking the man, but the thug twisted free and continued to run in the opposite direction. Dagen pivoted and fired two rounds into the center of the man's back, causing him to drop and slide across the ground.

"All fucking cowards will be shot!"

More gunfire tore from all directions at unknown threats as his men continued to be cut down by their own comrades. In a fit of panic, they were killing each other. It was madness, pure and simple. Cursing as he stomped forward, Dagen gritted his teeth and shoved his way through the center mass of confusion and panic. Suddenly, a primal roar stopped him midstep. Through a gap in the crowd, Dagen watched in disbelief as a fearsome black monster leapt from the shadows of a nearby building and tore a bandit's head from his shoulders with a swipe of its massive paw. A fountain of gore sprayed from the man as he fell, clutching the trigger on his assault rifle, which rapidly mowed down a swath of his comrades from the maddened crowd.

Dagen ducked low, his instinct to become a smaller target taking over. He tried to open his mouth, to organize his people and address the threat.

What the fuck was that?

"*Hey! Get! Find!*" he squawked. His brain flailed as he and tried to find the words that would bring order to the chaos. Screams filled the air, followed by more geysers of blood as sporadic gunfire punctuated the madness. All around him men writhed in pools of their own blood, guts, and feces.

Something massive slammed into the chaotic group of bandits like a wrecking ball, swinging its massive bladed arms left and right and tossing their severed bodies through the air like so many torn rag dolls. Dagen took a step back as a dark giant waded through the seething masses toward him, slashing apart its foes and bellowing. Dagen took another step back, his legs refusing to move fluidly. The dark giant was repeating something to the crowd, over and over. Dagen's face went slack as the realization hit him.

Scripture. The giant was destroying the men in his path and spewing verse after verse of Biblical scripture.

For the first time, true fear climbed up Dagen's spine and swarmed into his mind as his body froze in panic. After all the years of violent persecution, torture, and hateful murder of God's people, God had come for him. Dagen tried to move, tried to call out, but the violent mass of hysterical thugs blocked his vision and impeded his movement. Everyone was dying.

Now it was Dagen's turn to run. He had to get away, as far away as possible. He would run to the ends of the earth to avoid God's judgment. Dagen broke from the crowd and crossed the courtyard at a sprint, dropping the Sig from his hand as he ran. Past the tankers he ran, past the dead bodies that had been left to rot, and past the infernal Christian woman to the metal stairs. He took them three at a time to the third story and began running across the length of the catwalk toward Malak's chamber.

Dagen soared up the catwalk and into Malak's quarters without knocking.

"*Malak!*"

The large bald man stood undisturbed as he pulled the wide-eyed blonde from the floor and stood her up.

"*Malak!* What are you doing? Leave the girl! We have to *go*! They are here! God is here!"

Malak calmly looked the girl over, inspecting her with a strange faraway look in his eyes. The girl's knees quivered slightly as he stared at her.

"God is dead," Malak said calmly.

In a giant fireball, one of the tanker trucks exploded with an ear-shattering blast. Dagen ducked instinctively and glanced over his shoulder, squinting, to see the dark giant silhouetted in front of the burning tanker. He turned back to Malak.

"*Fuck you,* then! I'm getting out!" he screamed, snatching an H&K G3 fully automatic assault rifle and two twenty-round magazines from the wall next to him.

"I'll be taking this!" Dagen yelled in a paranoid panic as he ran from the room with the rifle.

Jogging quickly down the walkway, Dagen stopped and surveyed the courtyard again. Dropping a magazine in one of his cargo pockets, he slapped the other hard into the magazine well of the rifle and slapped the charging handle of the weapon with a downward motion. Flicking the safety off, he braced himself against the railing and pulled the trigger. In a blaze of raw power, the rifle recoiled as Dagen held the trigger and sprayed the crowd with a long burst of fully automatic fire. He dropped the magazine from the weapon, inserted the second, and chambered its first round

"If God wants me, he can come and claim me himself!" he yelled, laughing crazily as he took aim at the dark giant.

Something whistled slightly behind him, and he released the pressure on the trigger. Straightening, he turned, but before he could adjust his feet, a man lunged in from the shadows behind him. The man collided with Dagen, slamming his elbow into his chest, snapping him backward. Dagen grunted and dropped the rifle as he flipped backward over the railing. He scrambled for a moment at the railing, believing he could grab it. With a ragged scream, he twisted end over end, plummeting toward his inevitable encounter with the cruel, hard earth.

✳ ✳ ✳

The tanker truck billowed and surged as the flaming liquid poured en masse from its fiery shell, pushing the shadows of the night back alongside the dawn as it began to break. The majority of the bandits had either fled or met their doom, and Courtland relaxed slightly, as the immediate threat appeared to have subsided. Blood poured in rivulets down his arms and from the massive ant blades he held in each hand. He moved past the burning tanker, laboring to catch his breath, and wiped his blood-soaked hands across his trousers. Tynuk and Azolja met him on the far side of the tanker.

"Is everyone alright?" Courtland asked.

"We are fine. The Great Spirit has granted us victory," Tynuk said and looked at the beast, who appeared even more fearsome covered in blood.

"Yes, he has, but we are not finished yet," Courtland said. "We must find and release any innocents that are here, just as Kane said. You two must scour the compound for any prisoners of these fiends," Courtland went on, waving his hands over the area.

"And what will you do?" Tynuk questioned.

"There is something else that I must see to."

Tynuk nodded, and the three separated as Courtland began moving toward the main control tower.

As he moved, a thin form began to materialize through the smoke and darkness. He approached slowly, straining, taking small steps and squinting his eyes to make out what it was. As he neared and clearly saw the young woman who was naked and lashed to a pole, Courtland's face became full of sorrow. He could see from the look on her dirty face that she had been through hell itself as he stepped close and pushed over the vulgar sign that stood next to her.

"Oh, child," he said as he cut her free with a small knife. "You who suffer in the name of Jesus are most blessed." Courtland helped her to her feet and pulled the gag from her mouth. "This will not do," he said as he took her to the side and rummaged around before pulling a blanket from the second and still intact tanker truck. Wrapping the blanket tightly around her, he held her shoulders and looked her in the face.

She slowly returned his gaze, the dirt, grime, and tears like a permanent fixture upon her swollen and battered features. Courtland pulled a small flask of water from his pocket and handed it to her.

"Praise Jesus for you, young one," Courtland said as his eyes filled with tears. "May your endurance be an example to us all."

Jenna slowly drank the cool water from the flask and wiped her mouth with her wrist.

"Thank you for your kindness, sir," she said with a raspy croak.

"Courtland."

"Thank you, Courtland," she said as she continued to drink quietly.

After a few moments, Jenna looked up at Courtland, her eyes nearly swollen shut from the beatings.

"May I keep this water?"

"Absolutely," he said with a sad smile.

"And may I borrow your knife?" she questioned most seriously as she motioned to the lock blade.

"Dear, you need not fight; we will take care of you."

"Please, I must have it," she insisted.

Courtland questioned her with inquisitively silent eyes as he handed the small knife to her.

"God bless you, Courtland," she said as she turned and began to walk away.

"We will be here for you when you are ready, child," Courtland whispered as she disappeared into the smoke.

✲ ✲ ✲

Taking small steps, Jenna walked through the smoke and debris across the courtyard. As she walked, she hummed a light tune like the ones she used to hum for her sweet Lynn. The men who wounded and assaulted her were all around, some dead and some dying. She stepped past them and toward the main radio control station building. As she neared the building, cries of anguish greeted her ears, and her eyes came to rest upon the form of Dagen, lying broken on the ground. He gnashed his teeth and rocked his body, clutching at his ruined legs where the bones had pushed through the skin. He looked up to see her approaching with an unfolded lock blade knife in her right hand.

"*Get away from me!*" he yelled in a high-pitched tone as he ground his teeth. "*Get back!* Don't come any closer, you crazy bitch!"

Jenna continued forward, holding the knife firmly in her right hand, her face unreadable.

"I know why you've come! I know! You will have your vengeance in the name of God!" Dagen stiffened. "*Do it, then!* Give me what I deserve!"

Jenna knelt next to Dagen and slowly began cutting up the leg of his pants. She worked slowly, carefully avoiding the protruding bone as she cut up toward his thigh.

"Get away from me! What are you doing?" Dagen faltered, his voice quivering.

Jenna did not answer as she cut three-inch-wide strips from the large blanket that shielded her nakedness. She held up the flask and unscrewed the top, moving to pour it over his wounded legs. Dagen snatched her wrist forcefully, restraining her from pouring.

"Why are you helping me?" he demanded, his body shaking.

Jenna looked him in the face. "I forgive you, Dagen," she said as tears ran from the corners of her swollen eyes and off her chin.

"You can't! You should hate me!" he clamored.

"I don't."

"After all I've done to you! After I murdered your family!" he said, his voice cracking.

More tears ran from Jenna's eyes as she rinsed the trauma points and wrapped his legs tightly with the cut strips.

"Tell me why! Tell me!"

Jenna looked up into his face again. "Because Jesus first loved me, and the things I've done are no worse in His sight."

Dagen seized up and rolled back on the turf, clawing at his eyes and crying. Violent tremors shook his body as he helplessly pinned his arms to his chest and moaned. "I'm so sorry. I'm so...I'm so...ruined," he wept as he writhed on the ground.

Jenna shuffled closer and pulled Dagen up and into her. He continued to cry and moan sadly as she wrapped her arms around him.

"Jesus died for you, Dagen, and He would still have died if it were for you alone," she said as the tears poured down her face. "He wanted me to tell you that."

DAY 40

EMRC STATION, SOUTH CAROLINA

Kane stepped into the dimly lit room from the darkness of the cat-walk. A hugely muscular bald man stood in the center of the room, staring coldly at him. With Molly in front of him, he stood with his left arm around her, his hand on her throat, and his right arm concealed behind her. She breathed in sharply at the sight of Kane. The small yellow bulb in the center of the room flickered slightly. The door to the catwalk slammed shut and bolted behind Kane, pulled shut by some invisible force.

"You must be Malak."

"I have many names. Why have you come here, warrior?"

"To find my friend."

"Liar. You come to take—to destroy what I have earned. What I have *created.*"

"Just let her go, Malak. We're all tired. The world is dead. It's over," Kane said, watching Malak with cold determination in his eyes.

Malak laughed, a throaty and menacing sound. "So, God's warrior comes to make demands. But, O holy warrior, are you prepared to sacrifice?"

"I'll do what's necessary."

"Yes? How important is God's mission to you? Are you willing to sacrifice your friend?" Malak turned ever so slightly to show his right hand, holding a large knife pointed in Molly's back.

Kane worked his jaw back and forth and thought of the sawed-off shotgun tucked in the back of his waistband. He had one shot.

"So, hero, what's it going to be?" Malak demanded.

"It's not going to be anything. Let her go."

Malak shook his head. "No, you still don't understand. There is always sacrifice. You should have learned this from your savior. Sacrifices must be made. So...the friend or the mission?"

Kane balled his fists tightly and shifted his weight. "Whatever you're trying to do, it won't work. God has sent me here to destroy you. You're finished regardless."

"I knew he would choose that," Malak said, turning Molly's face toward him. "You see? You don't matter to him."

"Don't listen to him, Molly. It's going to be alright."

Malak shook his head with mock sadness. "No, it's not," he said as he thrust the knife into Molly's back. Molly's eyes grew wide and she groaned as the tip of the blade protruded from her chest.

"*Yessss*...bleed!" Malak hissed as he looked up from the girl, but Kane was already moving.

In three lunging steps, Kane crossed the room and launched himself into the bald man, landing a devastating knee strike to the solar plexus and knocking Malak and the knife from Molly. The two men crashed across the top of the wooden desk and onto the floor as the shotgun skittered into the corner of the room. Molly's knees buckled, and she fell to the floor, the blood gushing from her chest and back.

Malak and Kane slid to a stop on the floor, wrestling in silent groans with each other before Malak centered himself over Kane, pinning him to the ground. Kane struggled feebly under the weight of a man more than twice as heavy as him. Kane bared his teeth, spitting, "*Youuuuuu!*"

"That's right!" Malak cursed. "She's dying, and there's nothing you can do about it. *Hate God!* Hate him for taking her from you!"

Kane shouted, delivering blow after blow to Malak's ribs and midsection, the bones cracking under the force. Malak remained unfazed, entranced.

"Hate your precious God! *Hate him!*" Malak closed his fingers around Kane's neck and began to squeeze.

Molly rocked across the floor, gasping, pressing her back as hard as she could to the floor, hoping to stop the bleeding.

Kane gasped, and his head began to swim in a black mist that slowly swallowed him. Sputtering, Kane braced Malak's left arm against his throat and, swinging his right forearm to the outside, began striking the outside of Malak's left elbow. On the third blow, the elbow broke as Malak's arm hyperextended, releasing some of the pressure. Malak did not blink as he continued to grunt.

"*Die!* Die, worm! You are no champion of God!"

Kane slammed his fist into the big man's square jaw and then upward under his chin, causing the jawbone to splinter. He gasped for air, the blackness consuming him, changing him, turning him from the light, as Malak slammed his head against the floor again and again with an animalistic savagery.

"*No!* Not by my power!" Kane sputtered.

"Shut up and die!" Malak's words rang in his ears.

"Not by my own! But by the power of Christ!" Kane felt himself falling away as the darkness enveloped him.

With a thunderous sound, Courtland erupted violently through the concrete block wall behind them as though it were made of wet cardboard. The giant had a fire in his eyes and a luminous aura about him as he strode forward and collided with the demonic man, pulling him from Kane and hurling him into the opposite wall.

As the thin haze of dust began to clear, Malak raised himself up off the floor with his good arm and stood to face the righteously imposing Courtland. As he stood, he seemed to swell and grow, his muscles bulging and twisting as his skin began to split.

Something inside was trying to get out.

"Soooo, there is more than one champion. Maybe this one will give us a challenge," Malak said as his voice changed with a strange twittering sound.

His body continued to contort, his lower jaw elongating and cleaving in half, his forehead bulging, his human form slowly changing into something far more grotesque. As his torso mutated, black, oily tentacles emerged from his back, twisting and coiling as they pulled from his flesh. Talons sprouted from his fingers and fangs from his jaws as he began to laugh gleefully.

"*In the name of Jesus, I command you to release this man!*" Courtland shouted evenly, concern vivid in his face.

"Jeeeesus does not rule here, and we will not release what is ours!" the unearthly voice growled in inhuman tones.

"Release him in the name of Jesus the Christ!" Courtland commanded.

The demon lashed out with its tentacles, striking at Courtland as the two titans collided once again. Back and forth they slammed from one wall to the other, each trying to get the upper hand on the other.

Kane rolled on the floor as his vision returned and he came to his senses. Molly was not moving. Kane pushed himself to his knees, coughing and trying to steady himself. Courtland and the great demon continued to fight it out with devastating blows on the other side of the room.

Courtland pinned the disgusting creature up the wall with his arm against its throat as its tentacles swarmed and lashed all about him. The black man began belting scripture at the top of his lungs as the demon dug its foul claws into his chest.

"God remains the strength of my heart. He is mine forever, but those who desert him will perish!"

The vile creature bucked and thrashed and sounded out with an awful, ear-piercing shriek that made the hair stand up on Kane's neck and arms.

"Arise, O God, and defend your cause!" Courtland yelled. "Unleash your powerful fist and deliver a deathblow!"

The demon screamed that most heinous of sounds again, its eyes and tongues bulging and twisting as it shoved Courtland back to the center of the room, where its tentacles struck at his legs. Courtland cried out and dropped to his knees.

"Kneel before your new god!" the monstrosity gurgled as it loomed over him, its filthy tentacles wrapping and coiling around his neck. Courtland bellowed and raised his arms as the creature lashed out with its fangs, sinking them into the top of his shoulders and back.

Still gasping for breath, lungs laboring and knees shaking, Kane stood and seized a three-and-a-half-foot length of lead pipe from the floor as he moved to the brawl. Stepping into the hardest homerun swing he could muster, Kane swung at the demon, fiercely slamming the pipe into the base of its skull to the sound of distorting bone and tissue. The monster faltered, groaned, and gurgled as a pressurized jet of blood peppered the ceiling and a nearby wall.

In a burst of raging, whirling energy, the demon slammed the unsteady Courtland off his feet and into the far wall, where he slumped to the floor. Spinning back, it lunged at Kane, striking him and sending him flying across the room into the cinder block wall, where he fell to the floor.

Spitting, Kane raised himself up on his hands and knees, trying to regain his breath. There was nothing he could do as the vile creature shuffled in toward him, laughing.

"May God forgive your betrayal," Kane said in breathless defiance from all fours.

"*God only loves himself!*" the demon screamed, slashing down at him from the left as Kane ducked into a forward roll to his right and into the corner of the room, where he grabbed the sawed-off shotgun. He pivoted quickly on his knee and pressed his back into the wall as the shotgun roared and recoiled in his hand. With a bloody shriek, the demon clutched at its ruined face and raised a taloned claw to finish him. Kane had nowhere left to retreat as he stared upward at the towering, bloody beast.

Glowing with blinding movement and righteous anger, Courtland crashed into the monster with an incredible force and a deafening clap of thunder. Crushing through the far wall, oily black tentacles tied them together in an awful embrace as the two warring titans fell in a screaming shower of debris into the courtyard below.

"*Courtland!*" Kane gasped, his hands up in a feeble attempt to shield himself as he knelt in the corner.

An eternity passed. Nothing moved in the silence that followed as Kane continued to hold his hands up, heart still racing in the dimness of the early morning.

"Kane," came the whispered voice next to the table. He turned to see Molly looking at him.

"Molly," Kane whispered back. "You're going to be just fine." He moved to her and scooped her up. Moving to the door, he unbolted it and stepped onto the catwalk of the structure. Kane hurried down the catwalk to the stairs, taking them as fast as he could muster. He looked into the courtyard below for his friend, but could not see anything through the thick smoke as he went. In all the hurry and confusion, he never thought about the fact that Molly had spoken his name.

Hitting the courtyard in stride, he moved quickly, carrying her in his arms. To his right, a stooping Courtland limped slowly from the smoke. Kane saw him.

"Are you okay?" Kane yelled across the courtyard.

"It's...it's gone," Courtland said, sounding bewildered.

"Is it dead?"

"No. It's just gone...Malak is dead."

"Are you okay?"

"I'll be alright," Courtland said, supporting his left knee and covering the puncture wounds in his shoulder.

Kane looked at Molly as he moved. She was fading.

"You're going to be fine, Molly. We're going to get you some help, okay?" he said as her blood poured over his arms and onto his clothes.

"Kane," she whispered.

"Yeah, you're going to be just fine, 'cause we're going to get you some help."

"Kane, stop."

Kane slowed and really looked at her for the first time. "What did you say?"

"Stop."

"Molly, you're speaking," he said and smiled sadly.

"Kane, listen to me. God told me something I have to tell you."

"We've got to get you help, Molly."

"Where? There's no one here who can help me now. I need you to listen to me. Let's sit down, okay?"

Kane reluctantly lowered Molly to the ground and knelt next to her as he supported her body.

"Okay, Molly, I'm listening to you," he said as he looked at her. She was ghostly pale and only whispering.

"Will you do it?"

"Will I do what?" he asked as he put pressure on the massive wound through her midsection.

"Let me go, Kane. My time has come. You don't have to save me; that was done a long time ago by a man on a cross," she whispered. "I need to hear you say you will do it."

"Do *what,* Molly?"

"Answer God's calling for your life. It's the most important decision you will ever make." She gasped and clutched her arms to her body.

"And what *is* that calling, Molly?"

"You know it; you're just afraid come to terms with it. You must listen, trust, and obey, and take His light into the darkness, wherever it is. That thing inside Malak isn't dead...and there will be more of them. You have been chosen to resist them."

"But why? To what end?"

"There are still others, Kane—your family is among them. They all must hear the call and rally for our cause before this can be over. It will get much worse before it gets better. The darkness will seek you as its mortal enemy, if you choose this path."

"My family is…"

"Alive, Kane. They're alive."

Kane looked intently at his friend as she continued to fade. "Even if I have to do it alone, abandoned in this dead world, I'll do it, Molly," he said as tears ran without restraint down his face and dripped onto her shirt. "Don't you worry, I'll do it."

A large, bloodstained hand rested on Kane's shoulder.

"Not alone," Courtland's deep voice resonated from behind him. "Never alone, brother," he said, and nodded at Tynuk and Azolja as a small crowd began to develop around them.

Kane hung his head and looked at Molly. "I'm sorry, Molly," he whispered as the weary tears dripped from his chin.

"I'm not, Kane. You're the best friend I've ever had. I can see why God chose you." She blinked and swallowed hard. "Praise the Lord, who faithfully delivers us from our foes!" She smiled that brilliant smile as she quietly stiffened and then relaxed, the last sparks of life slipping away.

Kane leaned his head back and cried out in anguish, holding tightly to Molly's lifeless body.

"I'll do whatever my God commands of me!"

As he uttered these words, several rogue beams of morning sunlight tore through the clouds and shimmered across the courtyard. The small crowd remarked in whispered awe, and everyone raised their hands in response. Kane sat, tears streaming from closed eyes as he let the beautiful rays of light soak into him and warm him down into his soul. And for the first time, for as long as he could remember, he knew who he was and what it was that he was meant to do.